FOR *the* FIRST TIME, *Again*

TAKE THEM TO THE STARS, BOOK 3

ALSO BY SYLVAIN NEUVEL

The Test

TAKE THEM TO THE STARS

A History of What Comes Next
Until the Last of Me

THE THEMIS FILES

Sleeping Giants
Waking Gods
Only Human

FOR *the* FIRST TIME, *Again*

TAKE THEM TO THE STARS, BOOK 3

SYLVAIN NEUVEL

TOR PUBLISHING GROUP
NEW YORK

This is a work of fiction. All of the characters, organizations, and events portrayed in this novel are either products of the author's imagination or are used fictitiously.

FOR THE FIRST TIME, AGAIN

A Tordotcom Book
Published by Tom Doherty Associates/Tor Publishing Group
120 Broadway
New York, NY 10271

www.tor.com

Tor® is a registered trademark of
Macmillan Publishing Group, LLC.

Library of Congress Cataloging-in-Publication Data

Names: Neuvel, Sylvain, 1973– author.
Title: For the first time, again / Sylvain Neuvel.
Description: First Edition. | New York : Tor Publishing Group, 2023. |
Series: Take them to the stars; book 3
Identifiers: LCCN 2022056774 (print) | LCCN 2022056775 (ebook) |
ISBN 9781250262578 (hardcover) | ISBN 9781250262585 (ebook)
Classification: LCC PR9199.4.N476 F67 2023 (print) |
LCC PR9199.4.N476 (ebook) | DDC 813/.6—dc23
LC record available at https://lccn.loc.gov/2022056774
LC ebook record available at https://lccn.loc.gov/2022056775

Our books may be purchased in bulk for promotional, educational, or business use. Please contact your local bookseller or the Macmillan Corporate and Premium Sales Department at 1-800-221-7945, extension 5442, or by email at MacmillanSpecialMarkets@macmillan.com.

First Edition: 2023

Printed in the United States of America

0 9 8 7 6 5 4 3 2 1

The visions we offer our children shape the future. It *matters* what those visions are. Often they become self-fulfilling prophecies. Dreams are maps.

CARL SAGAN, *PALE BLUE DOT: A VISION OF THE HUMAN FUTURE IN SPACE*

Please note that all chapter titles are song titles from the years the story takes place in. You can listen to each song as you read or enjoy the playlist on its own. You'll find the playlist on Apple Music by searching for "Take Them to the Stars" or at tinyurl.com/TakeThemToTheStars3. Spotify users will find it at tinyurl.com/neuvel3. You can also re-create the playlist yourself using the song list at the end of this book.

FOR *the* FIRST TIME, *Again*

TAKE THEM TO THE STARS, BOOK 3

INTRODUCTION

The Slow March of Light

CYCLE 7543 (APPROX. 1220 B.C.)

Light is slow. Like an old couple walking by the shore, photons amble without a care as I lie alone in this flying coffin, unable to outpace their leisurely stroll. The darkness stays still while I inch my way to a place I may never reach. Light is cruel. There's purpose behind its sloth, deliberateness. It *wants* me to suffer. I can hear it sometimes, snickering, while I beg death to come for me. I beg, and threaten, and scream, but I'm too far from anything for her to hear. I *need* to die. I need this to stop, but I'm not strong enough. WHY CAN'T I WILL MYSELF TO DIE? I can't move. I can't DO ANYTHING. This pain. Constant, relentless torment. It's everywhere, in the air I breathe, the water I drink. I try to sleep, but it keeps me awake until I can't tell if I am. I thank the stars when I lose consciousness, but it never lasts. I wake up to the SAME. *SHEKRET.* PAIN! It's been two cycles. I can't take another seven.

I want to die. I want it more than anything because there *is* nothing else. There is no mission. There's no duty. There's only pain. I'd kill myself without hesitation, but I can't move my arms anymore. I can't reach the controls and vent all the air into space. I can't overdose on pain meds. I can't alter course and drive myself into a star. I found thirty-seven different ways to end my life, but every single one of them is out of my reach.

"You are a hero to your people," he said. "Remember that

when you think it's too much to bear." I didn't know what he meant. I imagined. Apparently, I lack a proper imagination. I smiled at him. "Thank you, sir. It's an honor to serve." Lies. I didn't do this for *my people.* I did it for everyone who doesn't fit the definition. We have plenty of time to find a suitable home before ours turns into a fiery hell, but it'll take centuries to move everyone. And they won't really move *everyone,* of course. They'll start with the fertile. Then the citizens. Miners next, I guess—gotta have someone to dig—but they'll find every excuse to leave the rest of them behind. My son's half *Xo.* They'll move cattle before they get to people like him. The sooner we find a place, the better their odds. These scout ships are all we've got. It's a one-way ticket, but it's also the best I could do for my son's children, or their children. I volunteered. I . . . *chose* this.

Somewhere out there is a man who didn't choose. Another ship headed to the same world. Another being suffering endlessly. He attacked a superior officer, broke his neck from what I heard. Nothing they couldn't fix, but the boss wasn't pleased. This was punishment. I don't care if he slaughtered his entire unit and ate them. No one deserves this. There is no crime, no horror or savagery, that merits *this.* I never met the man, but I wish him dead. I wish him dead with all my heart.

I wonder if he knew, if he clenched his teeth the moment he climbed aboard his ship. He must not have. If I'd known. If I'd had even the slightest indication, I'd have grabbed my service weapon and blown my brains out on the spot while I could.

The ship's drive was still warming up. I felt the needle plunge into my neck. I started warming up myself when the flight plan popped up on my monitor. *Aneba 3.* I'd never heard of it. I figured it'd be a barely habitable shithole. Toxic air, giant bugs, that sort of thing. Nope.

INHABITED. POSSIBLE CONTACT WITH HOSTILE SPECIES.

There's no way we can ever relocate to that place if an enemy's there. This was pointless. I'd abandoned my son for absolutely nothing. I was . . . upset. So much so I didn't see the bio-warning blinking at the bottom of my screen.

SIGNIFICANT MORPHODIVERGENCE WITH NATIVE POPULATION. BIOMODIFICATION ADVISED.

Advised? The *shekret* needle was already in my neck. Whatever backwards oafs lived on that rock, I was going to look like one.

The virus spread like wildfire. I could feel it take over, tickling every corner of me. The little buggers are fast. They rewrote my DNA in less than a day. A letter here, a letter there, until the words weren't the same and my body told a discordant story. I had to be retold, reborn to fit the narrative.

Targeted apoptosis. Every cell in my second heart committed suicide in a matter of weeks. My entire secondary cardiovascular system dissolved itself. It was scary to watch on the monitor, but that part was painless. So painless I didn't notice when my one good heart stopped beating. I bit part of my tongue off when the ship zapped me with a thousand volts to restart it. That was the easy part. The real carnage was about to begin. Hundreds of genetic switches turned on to make me something else, like a *yershak* digesting itself inside its cocoon. My body merged white blood cells to make osteoclasts, legions of them, to eat at my bones. Like a growth spurt in reverse. Only worse, and endless, and everywhere. I live in agony while my body dissolves and rebuilds every bone, every joint. It will go on and on for nine cycles until my entire skeleton is replaced and I'm as tall as a *SHEKRET* CHILD!

My muscles atrophied all on their own. Lying immobile in a flying coffin will do that pretty quick. I'll lose a third of my body mass before this is over. A *third of me* will kill itself. Trillions of cells. That's a lot of corpses to deal with. My marrow's working overtime making white blood cells to mop up the dead. Unfortunately, it's not making any red ones while it's doing that. Every organ I have left is oxygen deprived. Kidney failure. Severe anemia. I watch the yellow liquid that was once my blood circulating in tubes above my head and I know the ship is the only thing keeping me alive. I despise it for it.

Even with dialysis and a machine oxygenating my blood, I might not make it. It's my bones. Too much calcium running through my veins. The medicine helps, but I pass kidney stones almost every day. I'm sure it hurts like hell, but I don't know which pain is which anymore.

The only bright spot is that these aliens have big heads. Can't shrink brain cells, so I would have had to lose some. I get to keep this part of who I am. Some of it, at least. My entire DNA thinks I'm something different. I know my brain is adjusting as well. New connections are made; old ones are erased. I don't know if I'm really me anymore, or how much will be left when this is over. I *can't* know. This is how I think. There's no way to tell if this is how I *thought*. When I'm not finding new ways to kill myself, I try to remember things. My son's face, childhood memories, the good and the bad. That trip we took to see the last ocean creatures. The day my mother dropped me at the academy. "I'm doing this for you, Sereh." I think that's what she said. I remember clear as day, but maybe that's not how it happened at all. I can't know what I forgot if I already forgot. I can't know what's real. Maybe I don't have a son and that face I see never even existed.

I don't know what I am now, what I'm turning into. Something else. Something small, and weak. Had I been born like it, my parents would have killed me. I'll know, eventually. I get to watch all of it. I can't go into stasis until the carnage is over. Seven more cycles of this. Just pain, and silence because I'm too weak to scream. I get to sleep for the back half of the trip, but I'll go mad long before. I'm already broken. Whoever lands on that rock, I know it won't be me.

ACT I

1

Just a Girl

DECEMBER 17, 1999

Gawd, I'm starving. I been watching feet go by under the tablecloth for over an hour. Scuffed loafers with tassels. I seen his shoes before. Whoever he is, he better not eat all the chocolate mousse. Oh no! He dropped a shrimp on the floor. He's gonna step on it!

Oh, so close! He missed it by a frog's hair. All right, I need *new* feet if I'm gonna get dessert. I need tipsy feet. Folks don't eat much when they're drunk. What's that? Wobbly high heels. Two pairs of them! Jackpot. Time to stick my head out.

—AH! You startled me, Aster. Why are you hiding under the table?

—Oh, hi, Mrs. Sparks. Just playing. The floor over there's all sticky.

—There's not much to do here for a twelve-year-old, is there?

—It's okay. I brought my Game Boy.

Mrs. Sparks is nice, but she smells like an ashtray. Everyone here smells like booze and cigarettes. Even Pa. I seen him smoke on the gallery not five minutes ago.

—Can I get you something, Aster? There's four kinds of Coke.

—No, thank you. But . . .

—But what? Don't be shy!

—Are you going to eat your chocolate mousse, Mrs. Sparks?

—My—Oh, you can have it, Aster.

[*You can have* mine *too. Love the dress, by the way. You make a nice princess.*]

I think she's a sailor, Linda, not a princess.

—It's . . . It's from a TV show.

[*Aye aye, sailor! Eat your spinach!*]

It's not Pop— Never mind. Thank you for dessert!

Back under the table. Score me mousse number four! I shouldn't have worn that costume, though. Dad was all gussied up. I wanted to wear something special, not the same old dress I put on for church every week. He was *sooo* excited for this. "You'll love it, Aster. There'll be a buffet." He's extra proud right now. Smoking cigars with the engineers. Calls everyone by their first name and all. He said there'd be other kids. No kids. He also said there'd be cake. This buffet's all fishy, mushy stuff. It's like none of these folks have teeth. There's *tons* of mousse. There's shrimp mousse, salmon mousse. The white, smoky, something mousse no one's touched. There's chocolate mousse. I *love* chocolate mousse, but they're supertiny and there's a big paper sign on them. "ONE PER PERSON." I'm starving.

I—Why'd the music stop? Crud! Another speech. Come on! Y'all done like fifteen already.

[**Tap* *tap* Can you hear me? Last speech of the night, I promise. It's been a big year for us at Stennis Space Center and I want to make sure we celebrate everyone's work 'cause we're not all working on the Space Shuttle main engine. There's lots of space plane stuff going on right now. Jim's team—Where's Jim? There you are—spent pretty much the whole year testing the Fastrac engine for the X-34. And we just started full testing of the engine for the X-33 on the A1 stand. What else? I don't want to forget anyone.*]

[THE RELIC!]

[*Shit! Sorry. I forgot the relic. For all of you wondering why*

Bernie's hair is going gray all of a sudden, his team is doing propellant tests on the—How old is that thing? Thirty . . . some years old?—on the AR2-3 engine for, you guessed it, another space plane. X- . . . Thirty-seven! All right, I think that's it. Thank you all again for a great year. Enjoy yourselves. Have another drink. Bernie, you can have two. I wish us all . . . What's happening? Ma'am? Ma'am! This is a private party; you can't—]

Who crashes an office party? Especially this one. I think I heard a dozen math jokes already. An infinite number of mathematicians walk into a bar. Two random variables walk into a bar. . . . Oh my god, they're screaming now. *Big* ruckus. I'm curious, but I'm not *that* curious. Headphones on. Me and Link are gonna explore that weird-ass island while the grown-ups throw a tantrum. A couple more instruments and I get to wake up the Wind Fish. Whoa! I think a chair just flew by. This ain't some squabble over free booze, more like an all-out brawl from the looks of it. I wonder what got them so riled up. Maybe someone's ex doesn't like the new boyfriend. I blame Christmas. The holidays make people do weird things. Still, folks here ain't exactly the fighting type. Math whizzes and science nerds getting physical, it's gotta be pretty bad. Whatever, I don't wanna know. Plus I might get more chocolate mousse if a ton of people leave.

Pa's gotta be trying to talk them down by now. He does that. He doesn't like conflict. It doesn't have to be serious, even. Star Trek versus Star Wars. Boxers or briefs. He can't stand people arguing about anything, so he plays arbiter all the time. He can't help it. No way he'll sit still when folks are throwing chairs around. You think that lady would take a hint and leav—

Gunshots! I think those were gunshots! Okay, crud. What do I do? Nothing. I'll stay right here under my table. Crud. Crud. Crud. I'm burning up again. This really isn't the time for one of my episodes. Stay calm. Stay. Calm. How do I stay calm? I'll do the stupid flower thing Mrs. Abney taught me. Breathe . . . in. Breathe out. Breathe . . . in. . . .

AAAAAHHH! Someone fell face-first right in front of me. It's . . . It's Mrs. Sparks. Her glasses are all bent up. She's staring, but I don't think she's really looking at anything. Is she dead? I think she's dead. Oh yeah, she's dead! There's blood pooling around her now. Lots of blood slowly creeping under the table. I need to move. I'll lean back against the wall and roll into a ball. Breathe . . . in. Breathe out.

I'm sweating up a storm. I'm going to black out again. What do I do? What do I do? I got nothing to defend myself, ain't nothing but plastic knives on that buffet table. I don't even know who to defend *from*. Maybe I can short the power outlet next to me. If the lights are on the same circuit, I can make it out in the dark. What the hell is wrong with me? I'm not going out there. Close your eyes, Aster. Close 'em tight. Crud, the blood's at my feet now. Breathe in. I could . . . Break a bottle of wine and use it as a—No no no! Mrs. Sparks's shoes. Those high heels are basically hammer knives. SHUT UP, ASTER! You're staying right here. Breathe in. Breathe out. Too many things going through my head, I can't turn it off. TURN IT OFF! TURN IT OFF!

The room's spinning now. That's it. I'm gonna pass out.

2

Why Does My Heart Feel So Bad?

I don't feel sad. I don't feel much of anything, really. I ain't crying. I ain't cried since they told me. I *should* be, I know—but I ain't.

I woke up to the smell of bleach. Bleach and something lemony. Clean, in a scratches-at-your-throat sort of way. I opened my eyes and there was more clean. White walls. White bedsheets. White cabinets. I figured out where I was when I saw the heart monitor next to the bed. The white door opened to let a nurse in. She stared at my clothes for a second. "I'm so sorry," she said. Sorry? Sorry for what? I asked where my dad was and that's when she told me. Well, not at first. She said she'd call someone, but I asked again where my dad was. *Then* she told me. Pa had a heart attack. They did all they could, but he was already gone when he got to the hospital. This hospital, I guess. Then, more sorry. *Terribly* sorry. Then she left.

And I just . . . lay there in my stupid costume. No more Pa. No more anyone. I lay there until the white door opened again and another woman came in. Gray suit. Supershort hair and Drew Carey glasses. "I have something to tell you, Aster." It sounded more real that time. Pa had a heart attack. They did all they could, but he was already gone when he got to the hospital. This hospital, for sure. More sorry. Terribly sorry. I could tell she'd done this before. I figured she was Child Services. People say bad things about Child Services, but they said they'd find me a good family when my mom got rid of me, and they did. They found Pa. He was a good family. I thought maybe she could find me another. I asked her when we'd be leaving. I got a "soon" and a big fake smile. I ain't leaving soon. I seen people hide things and she was *definitely* hiding things.

I feel bad for not crying, like I didn't love Pa, or not enough or something, but I ain't crying here. Not in a bleach-and-lemon-smelling white room. I want to cry in my room, or in *his* room. I want to cry where it smells like him. Gray lady asked if I wanted to see him. I liketa said yes, but Pa was always so happy. I don't want to remember him all sad and all dead.

The door. She's ba— Oh no. It's a man this time, a soldier. No, a general or something. Lots of bling on the uniform. Tiny flags. Shaved head. He looks like Bruce Willis. Like, for real.

—Hello, Aster. How are you feeling this morning?

— . . .

—Aster?

—I'm sorry, sir. It's just . . . You look exactly like—

—I know. I know. My name is Benjamin Veilleux. I came to see you.

Me? What does he want with me? I don't think Pa was ever in the Army.

—Are you a doctor?

—I am, actually. I'm a colonel in the U.S. Army, *and* a doctor. I work at the Walter Reed Army Medical Center.

— . . .

—It's in Washington.

—I—Wait, we're in D.C.?

—No, Aster. You're still in Mississippi, in Picayune. But the doctors here did a blood test last night—you were unconscious when you came in—and they didn't know what to make of it.

The results, I mean. They didn't know what to make of the results, and they made some calls, and, well, here I am. I came a long way just to see you.

—No one said anything about a test. Is there something wrong with me?

—No, Aster. There's nothing wrong with you. At least, that's what they tell me, but that makes your test results all the more peculiar. That's why I came. I work for an agency called the Armed Forces Medical Intelligence Center and we have very smart people who are trained just for this sort of thing.

—I'm sorry, sir. What sort of thing?

—They're . . . detectives, like the ones on *Law & Order,* but for medical things. I'd like you to meet them. Will you do that for me, Aster?

—They're here?

—No, they're in Washington. There's a helicopter waiting for us on the roof. It will take us to Biloxi; then we'll get on a plane. Have you ever been on a helicopter, Aster?

—No, sir, but I—I don't want to go to Washington. I just want to go home.

— . . . Did someone explain what happened to your father?

— . . .

—Then, you see, Aster, there *is* no home for you to go back to. I'm terribly sorry. When we get to the hospital, we'll—

—How'd he die?

—He had a heart attack. I thought you knew.

—No, I mean why? What happened last night?

—What do you remember?

—There were people screaming. I heard gunshots. Mrs. Sparks, she worked with my father, she . . . she was shot, I think. I don't remember anything after that.

—You're right. Someone walked into the reception at Stennis

Space Center uninvited. The . . . individual opened fire with a high-caliber rifle when security stepped in.

—Who?

—We don't know. But several people were killed. A dozen or so were injured; one is in critical care. Your father, well . . . I know this is a lot to take in. There must be a million things running through your mind. It's perfectly normal for you to be scared.

Scared. I wasn't until he said it just now. I was all kinds of things—worried, sad, confused—but not scared. Now I'm scared. He wants me to get on a helicopter with him and go to Washington so I can talk to some people. That doesn't make sense. He came here. Why didn't they? He said they're like detectives on *Law & Order.* They put people in *jail* on *Law & Order.*

—There was a woman from Child Services. She said we'd be leaving soon.

—Is that what she said?

—Yes, she—

She said soon. She did. I asked when we'd be leaving and . . . Crud. "When do I leave?" That's what I said. I asked when *I*'d be leaving and she said soon. I guess she meant with him, not her.

—I already spoke to Child Services and informed them we'd be taking over your case. We'll take good care of you, Aster. I promise.

My case? I don't believe a word coming out of his mouth. Take care of me. How is the Army going to take care of me? I want to go home. I *need* to go home. I just need a reason.

—We . . . I have a cat.

—Don't worry. I'll send someone for your cat and your personal effects. We'll make sure you're comfortable. You'll feel at home with us in no time; you'll see. . . . May I ask a personal question?

—What?

—What are you wearing?

—It's—

—Excuse me for one moment.

What's going on? He looks worried. Oh, I hear it now. There's screaming down the hall, lots of screaming. And running, I see heads flying by through the door window. AH! Loud bang. It's—This can't be happening again.

—Was that a gunshot?

—Don't worry, Aster. I'm sure it's nothing. I'll be right back. Stay right here, okay?

—Yes, sir.

. . .

Stay right here. Yeah, right. Like hell I am.

3

Run

My bed's covered with broken glass. It's pretty, like the sun reflecting off a lake, or when they find the diamonds in those heist movies. It's making my head spin a little. I never been drunk, but I bet this is what it feels like. My heart's racing, even if I'm supersleepy. Everything's . . . not real, like I'm in a dreamworld or some magical realm. Like *Labyrinth.* "It's only forever, not long at all. . . ." Crud, I stepped on my Cabbage Patch Kid crawling in through the window. I must have had a shard on my shoe, 'cause there's a cut above the eye now. I think I like it. She looks badass. Desirae Chandelle, the destroyer.

I don't know what happened at the hospital. There were people running in the parking lot. This woman said: "You can't stay here, kid!" I got into her car and we drove off. She drove me all the way to Gulfport. I told her my dad couldn't pick me up till later. It didn't take them long to start looking for me. There were two cop cars parked out front when I got here. The regular kind. I guess they think I'll see a cop and think: Yes! Take me back to Bruce Willis so I can live in D.C. with the Army *Law & Order.* Fat chance. I let Mrs. Bloom's dog loose to distract them—sorry, Mrs. Bloom. Damn dog likes to scratch at our lawn and Mrs. Bloom sounds like a fire alarm when she's upset. The cops were still chasing the dog when I jumped the fence and climbed to my window. Anything to turn Mrs. Bloom off.

—Oh, there you are. Come here, Londo. The house is empty, I know. Don't worry. I'm taking you with me. We'll pack you some kibble for the road.

I told myself I came back for the cat, but I had to see the house again. I wonder what they'll do with it. Pa had no family that I know of and I doubt houses go to adopted children, at least not to the fugitive kind. That's what I am now. This is so messed up. Like, what do they want with me? I'm not the one shooting at people everywhere. They should just— Where are you going, you crazy cat? Food's down in the kitchen.

Oh, Pa's room . . . It's so tidy. It's always just me and him—I don't remember the last time someone came over—but he keeps his room spick-and-span like the Queen's spending the night. He used to travel before . . . before me. He said he liked sleeping in hotels. I thought he just missed traveling, but what he really liked was climbing into a well-made bed. Three pillows, not two, and bedsheets so tight you have to put your feet sideways. It seemed like a lot of work for ten seconds getting into bed, but he always liked the little things. Fancy bowls for breakfast, silverware for grits. I think those were a wedding gift. I wish I'd known his wife. I wish he were here. . . .

—What'd you find there, Londo? Oh, the box. We're not allowed to look in the box.

I suppose he won't mind if we take a peek. Still feels wrong, though. That box was for private, precious things. He scolded me just for being *near* that thing. What's this? Perfume. A woman's, must have been his wife's. What does it sm— Ew, gawd. I think it's gone bad. A bunch of Greyhound tickets. He really *did* miss traveling. There's nothing but paper in here. Crud. That's my last school report. Really, Pa? That's *all* my school reports. I knew he was proud, but . . . See what you did, Pa? I'm crying now, on your supertidy bed. I can't stop. I want to; it hurts, like someone tickling me for too long. It hurts everywhere inside, but I can't . . . I'm shaking like a shitting dog now, making a big wet mess of things.

I miss you, Pa. And I *hate* you! You're not allowed to leave me like this. . . . "Me and you, Aster. Me and you." That's what you said. You said it all the time. It didn't matter if I had a bad day at school, or if it rained for three days, or . . . whatever. None of it mattered because we had each other. That's what you said. You lied! Now say it's not real! Say it! I'm gonna close my eyes and sleep till you shake me awake and tell me it's not real, all right? . . . Just come back, Pa . . . please.

Just for one day. We'll go to Blockbuster like before. Three movies for the price of two. We'll do the crossword puzzle over breakfast. God, I miss that. Remember how you used to cut my toast in the shape of things? Always something different. Toast in the shape of a turtle, a sailboat. Cat toast. Car toast. None of them really looked like anything—oh, Yoda! Yoda looked like a Siamese cat. I loved guessing what it was, though. First thing I did when I got out of bed was think about the day's toast. Why'd you stop, Pa? I grew up, I know, but why that day? One morning you looked at me and thought: Aster's grown-up. No more fancy toast. I wish I could be in your head for a minute. Was it something I did? Something I said? Maybe it's just . . . I ain't never said thank you, have I? I meant to. Thank you. Thank you for the toast, Pa. Thank you for everything.

I should get up and go, but I can't move a muscle. I can't keep my eyes—

☆

Where— Oh. I'm still here, lying on his bed. He's still gone and I'm . . . nowhere close to knowing what to do. The cops didn't go anywhere either. I can't stay here. One of them will need to use the bathroom sooner or later. It feels wrong to leave everything. Those were his things; now they'll throw them away, or give them to someone. I should take a picture with me at least. This one, maybe. No, I want one of the both of us. There's a good one in the living room.

—Here, Londo. Let's go downstairs and pack you some kibble.

There it is. I always liked that picture. I have no idea where we took it, though. This ain't our yard; it's— I don't have time for this. Cat food, cat food. There it is. I should eat something too. I haven't since . . . then, but I don't think I can. My stomach's all *gwaaargh*. Cheez-It. That'll have to do. I can eat on the way there, wherever "there" is. I don't have any money. I don't *know* anyone. Where am I supposed to sleep? I'm pretty sure shelters will call the cops if a minor shows up at the door. Kids run away from home all the time. Where do they go? I don't know any movie that can help either. Well, there's *Wizard of Oz; she* runs away. Oh, and *E.T.*, but they get caught. I need—

Knock* *Knock

Someone's at the door. Cat, backpack, and out the back. I know, Londo. I don't want to go either. Crud, I didn't even change. . . .

4

Bitter Sweet Symphony

They look happy. They're kind of funny looking, but they look happy. Father and son, sharing a meal in a crummy truck stop. They don't care about the hundred-year-old wood paneling, or all the holes in the red leatherette—my seat looks like it's been chewed on by a horse. Maybe they're on a road trip. Driving coast to coast and stopping everywhere. The Brain Museum. The world's largest pistachio! Or maybe the son's going to a new school and Dad is driving him there. A good school. Like, his parents were superproud when he got the letter, but he's worried 'cause he won't know anyone there. Pa said I could probably go to a school like that if I really wanted to. Maybe they're going to buy a dog! A Dalmatian. No, one of those really big ones that save people after an avalanche, and they have to go where there's snow to get one. Colorado . . . Maybe they live right next door and Dad didn't feel like cooking. Well, whatever they're doing, they're having a good time doing it. They're a family, with food. I should really stop staring, but that sweaty glass of iced tea looks darn yummy right now. So's the—I'm not sure if it's chicken or what, but I'd kill for those mashed potatoes, and gravy. God, gravy. I'm starving. Londo peed on the Cheez-Its. *Bad* cat.

I feel like I ain't slept in a *month*. I did sleep, though. I slept at the park, at the bus stop, in that woman's car when I was hitch-hiking. I slept the whole time. It was supernice of her not to talk.

I'm still plumb sleepy all the time. Everything's slow, and hard, like walking through snow or molasses or something. I think I just need food.

No food. No father. No home. No money, no clothes. Clothes would be nice. I ain't got friends I can call, an aunt I could stay with. I don't know where I'm going. I don't know where I'm gonna sleep tonight. I don't know how I'm gonna eat. I ain't got a plan. I really need a plan.

What do I got? I got cops chasing me, and Bruce Willis. He's out there, somewhere. And I got . . . I got folks shooting other folks like it's turkey season, at a Christmas party no less, *and* a hospital. What kind of person shoots up a hospital? That's horrible! Even for a mass murderer. Oh, I got a cat in a stinky backpack and nowhere to let him loose. At least he stopped crying. He's either too tired or he's come to terms with life's suckiness. Poor thing. He just wants to sit on Pa's lap and watch TV. He can't anymore, but there has to be something between that and living in a bag.

Crud, I got something else now. I got a waitress coming my way again and still no clue how I'm supposed to get myself a free meal. Has "I found a hair" even worked in a place like this? I mean, it's got lots of things going for it, but cleanliness ain't one of them. I been in the bathroom. Also, the waitress looks nice, even with a black eye. I wish I knew what happened to her. Maybe not. Anyway, I'll feel bad if she ends up footing the bill. What do they do in movies? I seen *Down and Out in Beverly Hills*, but I ain't digging through this place's trash. Ewww. No way. I need to eat, though.

Maybe I should just tell her everything. "Hi! I'm a wanted fugitive running from the police, *and* the Army." Plenty of folks hiding from the cops, but I got the *Army* on my tail. I'm a special kind of fugitive. Anyway, I'd really like to eat something before I walk back to the highway and hope to God I don't get picked up by Jack the Ripper. Also, I can't pay. . . . Yeah, right. I'm better off finding a hair. What if I find a whole strand of hair? She's here. Make up your mind, Aster!

—You going to eat something, dear?

—I . . . I was waiting for my dad. He . . .

—You said that twenty minutes ago. You all right, honey?

Ha! No. I'm not all right. I'm broke, and starving and scared. I just want someone to say: "Everything is going to be fine," and hug me, hug me so tight I can't breathe. I want a hot shower. I want clean socks. I want someone to take me home and give me a bed. Will you do that for me, lady? Will you take me home with you? Right. I didn't think so.

—I . . .

—You don't have any money, do you?

— . . .

—Tell you what. It's on the house.

—Really?

—Free meal on your birthday! It's your birthday, right?

—I—

—Oh, for Christ's sake! Just say yes. Nod or something.

—Yes?

—HEY, Y'ALL! BIRTHDAY GIRL HERE! WHOO! What can I get you, hon? Anything you want.

—Can I have what they're having?

—Good call. CARL! ONE CHICKEN-FRIED STEAK! Anything to drink?

—Iced tea?

—Coming right up.

—Excuse me, ma'am? Why are you doing this?

—Only two kinds of people coming through here. Those going someplace, and those running from someplace. I figure if you catch a break now, maybe next time I see you, you'll be the kind going someplace.

—Thank you, ma'am.

—You're welcome. Just help someone else when they're down, okay? And a bit of advice: See that big man over there shining the gum machine? That's my boss. Don't let him see the cat.

—Yes, ma'am! You hear that, Londo? You have to stay in the bag. I'll let you out in the parking lot, I promise.

—Be right back with your iced tea. Nice costume, by the way. I love Sailor Moon!

—Thanks!

Finally! Still, I really need new clothes.

5

Criminal

I been on a downward spiral the past couple days. Very downward, more like a straight line to the ground. I didn't think I had it in me. I was ready to give up, surrender to the cops, or Bruce Willis. I *would* have without that chicken-fried steak. I'm glad I didn't 'cause now? Now I think I got it. I went to Sears.

I made it all the way to Houston yesterday. I hitchhike at night now. I figured that out last night, hitchhiking. I got on I-10 and this old man picked me up right away. He said he fixed copy machines for a living, which sounded interesting, but I was so tired I asked if he minded me sleeping. The passenger seat reclines almost all the way. It's free, and you only have one person to worry about, not like everyone when I slept in the park. I got four hours of rest and I crossed two state lines. I don't think the cops will look for me here. I ran out of a hospital; that shouldn't put me on *America's Most Wanted*, right? *Right.*

The old man dropped me at the mall, like I asked. First time I ever went without Pa. He used to give me money and a list of things. He'd drop me off and wait in the car. Hours if need be, he didn't care. Anything *not* to go in. Pa hated shopping, like *hated* hated. He went *on* and *on* about how dumb Sears was for stopping their catalog. . . . It was weird not having him there. I might have cried a little. I was hungry like a big dog afterwards, so I walked all around the food court looking for free samples. It was breakfast, though. They never give samples for breakfast. I shopped for clothes instead. I had no money, but the shopping part was fun. I felt normal for an hour or two. I found an STP shirt at the record store, a *nice* one. I found good jeans, tried them on and all. Oh, and a bag, to put money in if I ever got more money than it cost to buy the bag. Shopping took longer than I thought. It was past noon by the time I made it back to the food court. I took my sweet time. I walked *slooooow,* read all the menus, smiled at everyone. All I got was a piece of chicken the size of a grape and an iced coffee I didn't want, but it looked like it had chocolate in it so I took it anyway. I thought I might faint I was so hungry. I sat down at a table for two and I noticed the butt end of a burrito sitting in a tray at the table next to me. It was full of lipstick. Supergross. Then I saw another tray with food in it, and another. I don't know what's wrong with people. I always bring back the tray. I got dizzy looking at all the half-eaten food everywhere and that's when I saw it. Nachos. A plateful of them. Like, whoever sat there got a phone call or had a heart attack. Oh, and two wings, but the nachos! It's the perfect food! You don't *touch* a nacho chip unless you're going to eat it. It's because of the cheese. No one wants to touch cheese if they don't have to, not when all you get is this one napkin. Wings are sort of the same, I guess. It's a weekday, so there wasn't anyone my age at the food court, but I talked to an old couple—they were nice—and the lady who cleans tables after I brought back all the trays.

Then I went to Sears. Well, first, I found an old newspaper lying on a bench. I went to the Sears entrance and I threw the newspaper in the trash. I said some cuss words out loud and I dove into the bin looking for receipts. I found a butt load of them. Cheap stuff, mostly. A lipstick here, a bra there. And boom! Next to a McDonald's cup, jackpot. I walked in, went straight to the sporting goods section, and asked for the Fila Jr. golf set. They were all out. They *did* have the Pierre Cardin 4 Piece Luggage Set at $99.99—that thing is *humongous*!—and the Sixteen Minute Digital Voice Recorder for $49.99. I stopped to look at the telescopes for a minute—I want one so bad—but you can't really look at anything in the store. I ripped off the suitcase tags in the bathroom, dragged my butt straight to Customer Service, and asked for a refund. I was so nervous I liketa peed myself. The lady asked if my mother was with me. I told her she was buying me something for my birthday and I couldn't be there because it was a surprise so I was taking care of this for her. I wasn't sure if I made any sense. Must have; she said it was sweet of me to help my mother out, how she wished her daughter did things like that, but she doesn't even call 'cause she's too busy taking care of that lazy no-good boyfriend of hers. "Here's your money, dear. Have yourself a nice day."

I did! I had a *great* day. I went to the movies. *Galaxy Quest* just came out. I got butter on my popcorn, the real deal. It was awesome. I *love* Sigourney Weaver, and the guy who only plays villains was in it, but he wasn't a villain. He was supposed to be supersmart but wasn't, but then he was. And I thought: me too!

I'm a genius. I'm a brand-new-jeans-and-STP-T-shirt-wearing genius. I threw my Sailor Moon costume in the trash. I liked it a lot, but it smelled funny. I have forty-six dollars and thirty-three cents in my shiny new bag. Also, I ate. The best part is I have a plan, sort of. I can go from Sears to Sears all the way to California. I never seen the ocean. I *lived* by the ocean, but it was called gulf, not ocean. This'll be my first *ocean* ocean. Everyone on TV says they moved to L.A. when they were superyoung, so maybe I can find work there, if I lie about my age. If not, at least it'll be warmer. I can sleep outside like I did at home when the house got too hot. It's all because of that waitress and that chicken-fried steak. I think she was right. If I ever see her again, I'll be going places. I *got* this.

6

Interstate Love Song

Where am I? Right. I'm in a car, with . . . young lady gripping the wheel like someone's trying to take it from her. We're not moving. Wait, why aren't we moving? She's talking to herself, but I can't make out most of it. I think she mumbled "roadblock." I guess that's what it is. I can't see a thing; it's raining cats and dogs outside. It's pretty, though. Water streaks breaking the blinding light ahead. I wonder what state we're in. Texas, probably. We're always in Texas. There's a silhouette approaching. Blue raincoat. Headlights behind us light up the three yellow letters on his chest. He knocks at my window. Smile, Aster. He's talking to someone. Did he just say: "It's her"? Crud! Crud! Crud! Lock the doo—Too late. Two big men dragging me out of the car.

—Let me . . . GO!

I'm kicking, screaming. I'm squirming, facedown, federal agents gripping my every end. This ain't about Sears, not for a Pierre Cardin luggage set. This is Bruce Willis, has to be. How could they find me? *I* don't even know where I am. And *why*? Peculiar blood test. It's got to be more than that if they're putting up roadblocks all over. Do they think I killed those people at the Christmas party? Do they think I killed Pa? Crud, I'm burning up again. I'm so hot it feels like the rain is steaming off my skin. Bad thoughts going through my mind. Grab a gun. Shoot from behind that truck's headlights. There are dead people everywhere.

I did that. There's a horror movie playing in my head. Wake up, Aster. It ain't real. This is, though: four grown men holding me in midair. I can't fight them off. There's too many of them, and nowhere to go even if I broke free. This is it. Game over.

I stop fighting them. They stop fighting me. Tit for tat. We can get out of the rain, now. I don't know where they'll take me. Jail, maybe, if they think I killed Pa and Mrs. Sparks. If they don't then I'll end up in Washington. He said they'll take good care of me. Plenty of folks want to join the Army; living with them can't be *that* bad. And there's things to do in D.C., I think. I might not be there long. I mean, how "peculiar" can my blood test be? Low blood sugar? Anemia? It'll take them a week tops to figure it out; then I'll be boring again. They'll grow tired of me and send me back to Child Services. Whatever, there's no point thinking about it now, not while I'm flying a couple feet aboveground. Why won't they put me down? They're not paying attention to me at all. What are they— I can't see what they're looking at. My eyes hurt too much from all the rain and tears.

—YOU THERE! GET BACK IN YOUR CAR!

Whoa. Vertigo. I hit the ground chin first. The feds dropped me like a sack of spuds. I'm dizzy now. The road tastes metallic; I must have bit my tongue. I feel the cold water spreading through my shirt, my jeans clinging tighter to my legs. It doesn't matter. I ain't getting up. There's nothing for me up there, except a jail cell or a hospital room. I'd rather lie here and watch raindrops hit the ground. Life's simpler when you stare at something small. A ladybug, a penny, a bit of oil making rainbow swirls on the pavement in front of me.

Bang. The pavement goes bright all around my shadow. I recognize the sound, like I knew it was Pa from hearing his footsteps. More flashes, more bangs. A mob of paparazzi heckling a movie star. A box of fireworks going off all at once. This can't be real. It's make-believe, has to be. I want it to stop. If I want it hard enough, maybe someone'll yell, "Cut!" and it'll go back to normal. This normal, I don't care. I'll go to jail. I'll go happily if they make it stop. My heart's pounding against the sidewalk like a jackhammer. Please, anyone.

UGH. Something fell on my back, something heavy enough to knock the wind out of me. I turn to look. It's a person. Blue raincoat. "FBI" on the shoulder. There's this blank look on his face. It's Mrs. Sparks all over again. He doesn't know he's dead any more than she did. Another head hits the ground. Another. They're dropping like the rain now. I can't watch. I won't close my eyes either; that just means a different nightmare. I cover my ears and hide my face against the road.

Silence, almost. I hear the rain again, and the sound of idling cars. I turn to see. PUSH. THE. DEAD. MAN. OFF. OF. ME. . . . Whoa! There's a woman with a rifle standing above me. From down here she looks like she's eight foot tall. Did she kill all these people? She's not FBI, that's for sure. She's wearing coveralls, like a boilersuit. Square jaw. Wet hair in her face. She looks like Demi Moore in *G.I. Jane* after they put her through hell. I crawl backwards and sit against a car. I'm really scared, but I'm also awed. It wasn't perspective. She's André the Giant. She's . . . I never seen anyone this big. She's a *demigod*.

—*Shyesecht het?*

She's a Russian demigod?

— . . .

—*SHYESECHT* HET?

I don't underst— Oh my god. She's reloading. Did she kill all those people just so she could kill me? I don't wanna die like this.

—Please, ma'am! Please don't kill me!

Silence. The rain stopped in an instant. She gives me her

hand. I take it and she helps me stand. "You can let go now. Or not." I think she wants me to go with her. Where, though? We can't just w—

Whoa! The rain is louder than ever. I'm on the ground. She's still standing above me. I guess none of that was real. I think I'm slowly losing my mind.

Aaaahh! She's raising her gun now! I DON'T WANNA DIE! I DON'T WANNA DIE!

I— Am I dead? It sounded like thunder this time. Deeper, louder than before. I don't think I'm dead. I can move my hands. They're covered in . . . something. AAAAH! She— Her face is gone! Her whole face! Ewwwww, that's what it is. That's her face on my hands. It's everywhere! There's bits of brains and bones and . . . *eyes* on the car headlights, on my shirt. Oh crud, it's in my hair. There's eyes in my hair. There's a tiny bit of bone. I can't get it off. I CAN'T GET IT OFF!

She's still standing there, even without a face. How could she be st—Now she's falling, slow, just like a tree. There's someone behind her holding a shotgun. It's not a cop. They're on a motorcycle. Black leather, black helmet. Whoever it is, is raising their visor. I can't make out a face. I—

—Come with me if— Just come with me, Aster.

He knows my name.

—Who are you?

—My name is Samael. I'm a friend of your mother's.

ENTR'ACTE

Fire from the Heavens

Kaas-ma woke up in complete darkness to the sound of his damaged ship counting down to self-destruction. When the hatch opened, he was hit in the face with four thousand pounds of water. Salty liquid filled his mouth and nose before he could hold his breath. He managed to extricate himself from the ship, but his muscles hadn't worked in years and refused to comply when he tried to swim towards what he thought was up. Panic had already turned to resignation when he felt something brush against his back—the air-filled pillow his head rested on for eighteen cycles. Kaas-ma extended his arm to stop it, brought the pillow to his chest, and held on. He was convulsing, taking in more water with each cough, but he never let go. Giving up was not an option now, just as it wasn't then.

Growing up, Kaas-ma could never stomach the affectation and obtuseness of his family's entourage and spent as much time as possible away from home. Though he could easily sneak out of the family estate, it proved impossible to escape his last name. He would always be "Son of Waari" no matter where he went. His path to citizenship was a ritual of weekly beatings from fellow recruits hell-bent on teaching the rich kid about the "real" world. And though he rose rather quickly through the ranks after graduation, his superiors never missed an opportunity to remind him that he didn't deserve it. It was during one of those reminders that he'd grabbed the head of his ranking officer and spun it a hundred and eighty degrees. When he was demoted from Kih to *Tereshiin* Kih, he thought that he'd gotten off easy. He thought wrong.

The punishment was as cruel as it was unusual, but the only thing bigger than the pain he would endure on his long voyage was the chip on Kaas-ma's shoulder. Every aching moment spent in his flying coffin made him more determined to succeed. When the ship informed him it was time to sleep for the latter half of the trip, his last thought was of waking up on the bright world his people would resettle on because of him.

When he woke again, Kaas-ma was lying on a rocky shore. The small pebbles digging into his hands were the first familiar thing he'd felt for ages and his genetically altered face sketched a first, clumsy smile. Sharp pain rushed to his brain when his eyes opened. The world he lived on spun much farther from its star. *This* sun also burned brighter than the slowly dimming ball of fire he watched set every night.

Kaas-ma felt a hand squeezing his right arm, more hands. His every instinct screamed to defend himself, sequences of deadly blows flashing through his mind. His body couldn't have cared less and offered no resistance when the two men helped him to his feet. Kaas-ma was scared, lost, but something else felt wrong, or if not wrong at least odd or out of place. He could not put his finger on it until they sat him up on a chariot and everything looked right again. Kaas-ma was still much taller than the men aiding him, but his head was a couple feet lower than it used to be. He'd never seen the world from that angle, except when crouching or sitting.

The men repeated the same thing several times, bringing

their hands to their chests. Kaas-ma deduced they were speaking their names and introduced himself formally, last name first, first name, followed by his rank and unit.

—Hah-Waari Kaas-ma Tereshiin Kih Traahen

For whatever reason, the men started referring to him as Tereshiin. On his world, that would have been an insult, but he did not object, out of respect and an utter lack of linguistic knowledge. The landscape was more "normal" than he expected, recognizable even. An endless field of dirt and rocks with resilient patches of green breaking the beige monotony. Kaas-ma had often imagined what the land he grew on looked like before it was defaced by mining rigs, and this was surprisingly close. He was taken to the men's dwelling in a town called Ḥalpa, where he was presented with a fresh set of clothes and a bowl of something presumably edible.

The substance rolled in his mouth and he gagged a few times before swallowing, but he did not feel sick that day or that night. He had noticed people carrying oversized metal knives upon entering town, had seen other metal objects. Kaas-ma did his best to contain his excitement, but the evidence at hand led to only one conclusion: His people could live here. The air was breathable. This world could provide sustenance and minerals. The people were small and frail, making for an easy conquest. The only question left to answer was whether enemy forces were also present. There was another small problem that dampened Kaas-ma's enthusiasm. Whatever he found out about this world, he had no way to tell anyone. The beacon he carried was at the bottom of the great Salt Lake and likely exploded with the ship. His only hope now was that the other ship had made it and landed intact. He had to find his only ally. How hard could it be to find one person on a whole planet?

It took several weeks for Kaas-ma to regain his strength and gain a basic understanding of his surroundings. Learning the Hittite language, the "language of Neša," as people called it, proved harder than he thought. He picked up the grammar easily but did not know what most of the words referred to. He understood enough, however, to know the men who came to his rescue had been drawn by a streak in the night sky—no doubt his ship entering the atmosphere—and had come to collect "fire from the heavens." He had asked if another of these streaks had been spotted around that time but received only headshakes as answer. One night, he heard his host yell, "Tereshiin!" from across the wall and ran outside. He arrived just in time to see a bright streak of light disappearing into the eastern horizon. Kaas-ma had a goal, and now he had a destination.

He stole a horse and chariot the next day and headed east towards the Mala River. He had hoped to get supplies in Emar, but he found the city in ruins. An entire city destroyed, presumably quite fast, or those he spoke to in Halpa would have known about it. Kaas-ma realized this new world was not a peaceful one. Its inhabitants, it would seem, had at least one thing in common with his kind.

The people on the other side of the river spoke a different tongue, something that really puzzled Kaas-ma. The river itself had different names depending on which side one stood on. Everything he'd learned was now useless, dangerous even. If the two sides of the river were at war, using the wrong word for bread could get him killed. Madness, he thought. He wondered how far the next river was, and if this new language was even worth learning.

Despite his reservations, Kaas-ma learned Akkadû very quickly, but while he knew the names of things, he still lacked knowledge of the things themselves. He didn't know the kings and gods who ruled over these lands. He knew only what he had experienced, and had no time to form a concept for most of the words he learned. That ignorance, paired with the fairness of his skin, made him seem out of place no matter where he went. The words "Sea People" were often whispered behind his back, and the sword he'd picked from his victim after his first fight saw almost daily use during his travels.

His reputation soon preceded him wherever he went and most stayed clear of the ghostly man searching for paths in the sky. They called him Rādi kibsi.

ACT II

7

Stupid Girl

The woman at the cash register keeps staring at me. You don't know me, lady. Yes, this T-shirt is too big for me—mine was covered with *eyes*. We stopped in this *tiny tiny* town. I might have hallucinated the sign, but I think it said Strawberry. Maybe this is the real Berry Bitty City. Whatever this place is called, I didn't mind stopping. I ordered soup and a biscuit. *Really* good soup. I needed it. My brain turned to mush after last night. I think I'm in shock. I should be crying, screaming, but I'm supercalm. My hands are a bit shaky, but I'm pretty sure that's the cold. I'm a walking Popsicle. That man, Samael, gave me a jacket, but it's freezing out there. Literally. Still, I never been on a motorcycle before. I like it. Him, I don't know. We didn't talk much. You can't hear anything on the bike.

I didn't see his whole face until we stopped just now. He's white as hell. And old, like forty. He looks . . . I don't know what he looks like. A cop, maybe. A detective. A vampire detective! He does look like Angel on *Buffy* now that I think about it. He seems . . . niceish, but he's *super*serious. He did save my life, so . . . I asked why he was helping me. He said he owed my mother. Whatever, I don't wanna know. I want nothing to do with her. I wish we could talk about something else, though. Anything. We just been sitting here, eating our soup. Oh no, Londo's getting restless again. I better let him out before he throws a fit.

—If you don't mind, sir, I'll go outside and feed my cat before we leave.

—I strongly suggest we leave the cat behind.

—What? No! I'm not leaving him!

Poor Londo traveled halfway across the country in a bag. He was in a firefight with the FBI, and at Sears, and on a motorcycle at like thirty degrees. I'm not leaving him to freeze in Berry Bitty City after all that. He's earned a couch and a bowl, at least.

—You must understand, Aster. We will be on the road a lot. We need to keep moving, unless you want people to keep dying everywhere you go.

—But why? You killed that woman. I saw you do it. You shot her in the *face*! Behind her face. Anyway, she's superdead.

—More will come. You need to be prepared.

—More of who? What the hell is going on?

—It is difficult to explain. Let's just say something very bad is about to happen.

—Worse than this? That woman killed like ten people! My dad's dead!

I don't have a home. Everything I own is covered in eyes and brains. I don't know about him, but things look pretty bad to me already.

—I meant that bad things are about to happen on a much larger scale.

—Like what? Y2K?

—Now is not the time, Aster. We need to put some distance between us and last night's carnage. The police and the FBI will be looking for you.

—There was an army colonel at the hospital before. I think it's because of him.

—Yes, he is the one giving orders. I set the hospital lab on fire, so he no longer has a sample of your blood, but he still has your initial test results.

—You torched the hospital? Wait, how did you know I was there?

—I was tracking you. And I did not "torch" the hospital. I set a small fire in a refrigerated storage room.

—Whoa.

—It will not stop the colonel from coming after you. He'll want more blood, more tests. You can be certain of it.

—Okay. Couldn't I just . . . give him more blood and get this over with? I don't mind giving blood. I done it before.

—He will not be satisfied with blood. He'll want to look at your every cell under a microscope. You will spend your entire life being poked and probed like a lab rat and he will dissect you when he's done.

—What? Why? I didn't do anything.

—As I said, now is not the—

—So he's just going to keep chasing us forever?

—You. He is going to keep chasing *you*. He has no idea I exist; neither does the police. I would prefer to keep it that way. That said, the woman from last night tried to kill me shortly before she found you. I can only assume her associates also want us dead.

—Is she the one who—

—Yes. She was at the hospital, and at your father's office reception. She was looking for you.

—For me?! I don't understand. What does she want with me? What does *everyone* want with me?

—She . . .

—WHAT? WHAT? JUST SAY IT! What's happening to me?

—This is going to be hard for you to accept.

—Like any of this isn't?

—How can I put this? You *do* know that you are physically stronger than most people.

—I am?

—I was asking if you knew.

—How would I know?

—Never mind. Do you know that you are more *intelligent* than most people?

—Yes, sir! I have really good grades too. Pa— My father said I could be an engineer.

—That's great. . . . Do you sometimes have . . . violent urges, difficulty controlling your temper?

—Who told you that? Who've you been talking to? Y'all think it's my fault. It's a condition. Like, it has a name and everything: asynchronous development. I'm a twice-exceptional gifted child with hypersensitivity and anxiety issues. So yes, I have a hard time controlling my emotions sometimes. I see a social worker at school, and a psychologist, Mrs. Abney. She says I'm making progress.

—This is going to be more difficult than I thought.

—I take Ritalin. . . . Well, I did. I forgot them at home.

—I seriously doubt medication would have any effect on your condition.

—That's what I keep telling them, but the school wouldn't take me back without it and Mrs. Abney said it could help even if I don't feel anything. . . . Am I going to go back to school? I'm not, am I?

—You can never go back, to your school, or your home.

I can never go back. I suppose I knew that already, but it's weird to hear someone say it. I ain't going back home, ever.

— . . . So where are you taking me?

—To Las Vegas. I left some things in storage before I came

looking for you. Once we get there, we'll get ourselves a car and supplies. You are in dire need of new clothes.

—Those *were* my new clothes. I bought them yesterday.

—We'll get you more. I will also look for a small transport cage if you insist on keeping the cat.

—His name's Londo.

—As I said, you should seriously consider leav—

—Please, sir! He's all I got now. I just lost my father, my home.

—I know this may be of little comfort, but you and your father were not genetically related.

—I know. I'm adopted. That doesn't mean—

—My apologies. I was not implying that you didn't love your father, or vice versa. I—I suppose there's no other way than to just come out and say it.

—Say what?

—You, Aster, are . . .

8

Common People

What a *fruitcake*! "I realize this is difficult to accept, Aster." Huh huh . . . Like, please don't hack me to pieces, mister tin-foil-hat serial killer! I guess he could be pulling my leg, but he shot that woman for real, so I think he really believes it. What am I supposed to do now? When we left the restaurant, I thought: let's just get to Vegas and then I'll bail. Now I don't know anymore.

We have a suite! An actual suite like in the movies when they ask for a room and the guy with a French accent says, "We have a suite available." It even says "Suite" on the sign by the elevator. I keep walking in circles 'cause the carpet is supersoft and mushy. I was a bit bummed out when Samael told me I had to sleep on the couch, but there's a special couch that's made to lie down. I sleep on *le chaise longue. Merci beaucoup.* There's a view, of course, 'cause it's a *suite*! I get dizzy just looking. So many lights, and cars, and people. This place is awesome, and weird. There's a pyramid. The Eiffel Tower is right across the street! Venice is . . . somewhere over there, and New York is just down the block. None of it's real, but I'm fine with fake Paris. I never been to the real one. I never been anywhere until now. I wish I were home with Pa, but this is . . . exciting, in a messed-up Bonnie and Clyde sort of way.

Back to normal isn't really an option, so it's either a suite with him, or food courts and Sears. I don't know if I can do that anymore. I lasted all of two days on my own. Truth is I don't want to be alone again. Besides, he might be out of his mind, but I don't think he means to hurt me. All he had to do was *not* save me if that's what he wanted. That's . . . pretty easy. Everyone else that night chose to *not* do anything. Also, he let me keep my cat.

Speak of the devil. He's back.

—I got you some clothes. I hope they fit. They're not the latest fashion, but you'll have something to wear when we go shopping for more.

—Thank you, sir. It's fine. . . .

—I presume you're still skeptical of what I told you.

That's one way to put it. I don't know what I'm supposed to say. Sir, I think you're in serious need of medication? You're really nice, but I'm worried you brought back fava beans and a nice Chianti? "Your ancestors were not of this world, Aster." Yeah, I'm skeptical all right.

—Sir, I'm really, *really* grateful for everything you done, for what you're doing now.

—Maybe this will help. This is a picture of your mother when she was your age, perhaps a bit older. It's not dated, so I can only guess.

I'm not sure I want to look. I never seen my mother bef— Whoa. I'll admit, it's eerie. It's . . . me. This could *totally* be a picture of me. Same face, same hair even. And I really like that jacket. She seems . . . semihappy, like she's having a good time right there and then, but there's something eating at her at the same time.

—She looks a lot like me. I look like her, I guess. That's true, but it doesn't mean anything. Our neighbor, Mrs. Bloom, she has a nephew who visits twice a year and he's a spitting image of his dad, except with braces, and shorter, but it doesn't make him, you know . . .

—This one is a picture of your grandmother when she was pregnant with your mother. It was taken in 1961 if I'm not mistaken. And this is three generations of your ancestors in one picture: your great-great-grandmother shortly before her death, along with your great-grandmother and your grandmother when she was just a child. It's from 1931.

—Where did you get these?

—From your mother.

This is just creepy. They're all the same. They're exactly the same. Maybe they *are* the same. Maybe someone took a bunch of pictures of the same woman and mixed them together. That doesn't explain why they all look like me, but still. Even if they're not fake— Say those pictures are real, then what? His story still doesn't make any sense. If he'd shown me those and said we were time travelers instead, I might could have bought it.

—Okay, sir, it's weird, but it's not impossible, is it? It could be a genetic thing.

—It is *entirely* a "genetic thing." I didn't say you were an apparition, or a fae. *Your* genetics just happen to be different from everyone else's, for reasons I already explained.

—Well, it's the reasons I'm having problems with. I'm not . . . different! Maybe a little. There's the gifted thing. I'm a bit awkward and I have a hard time fitting in, but that's everyone, right? I'm "different," but I'm not *different* different.

—So says the twelve-year-old with an eight-foot-tall hunter on her tail. Not to mention a U.S. Army colonel, one who is so adamant about finding her after seeing the results of a simple blood test that he has enlisted the police, the FBI, and God knows how many other government agencies to help. Strange as it may seem to you, you are likely the most wanted person on the planet at this very moment. Why do you think that is, Aster? Is it because you have "a hard time fitting in"?

— . . .

Fine. I don't have all the answers. That's no reason to make fun of me. How weird can my blood test be? Weird enough, obviously, or the colonel wouldn't be so hung up about it. But "not of this world"? There has to be about a billion explanations to consider before you get to that one. Maybe they screwed up the test and this is one big mistake. People screw up all the time. They gave a woman the wrong baby at the hospital. Did I read that or did someone tell me? I don't know. Maybe they used the wrong blood. Maybe someone dropped a chocolate milkshake in my sample. Oh my god! She has chocolate for blood! Call Bruce Willis! That still leaves the giant woman with a gun, but, clearly, that woman had her own issues to deal with. The really weird part is that for like a second, it felt like she was there to help me.

—While you ponder on the nature of your existence, it might be time for you to learn something about your family. We can stay here for a few days; that will give you plenty of time to read.

—Read what, sir? What's all this?

I shouldn't have asked. Two brown banker's boxes. You don't put anything fun in a banker's box. They look heavy too. He moaned a little when he picked them up.

—These are journals. Only a handful are in English. The one on the very top is your mother's. You can start there.

Why does he have my mother's journal? Whatever. It doesn't matter.

—I don't want to read it.

—Why not?

—Because!

—That's not a rea—

—BECAUSE SHE DIDN'T WANT ME, OKAY?

9

Karma Police

I watched my prey die in my arms. Lifetime after lifetime spent hunting a woman I knew nothing about. I drew closer to her near the end, both literally and figuratively, but I could not, *did not* save her. I hated my brother for ending her life. Now I realize it was my actions that killed her. Like a freight train speeding down a hill, I started a chain of events that inexorably led to a death. Hers or mine. She drew the short stick. As much as I like to remind myself how deeply I cared about her, I know it was the thrill of the hunt that I truly mourned. I missed my prey. She was my purpose.

I thought she was selfish, evil. I thought she was a traitor. I had no inkling of her motivations until I saw my own hands wrapped around my mother's throat. Mother was my reason to live; she was *everything*. I did . . . horrendous things to keep her safe. I killed my brothers for her. I killed my father for her. I thought she was finally out of harm's way, but I was wrong.

I could see my hands around her neck, but I couldn't *feel* myself hurting her. All I felt was resentment, a deep-seated anger towards the person whose hands I was looking at. I would call it an out-of-body experience, but it was quite the opposite. It was *definitely* my body, my true self taking control of a weak mind. I never much cared for fables, but I could not help but think of the scorpion and the frog. The scorpion, unable to cross the river, asks the frog to climb on his back. The frog tells the scorpion she's afraid he'll sting her, to which the scorpion responds: "Of course not; if I do we'll *both* drown." The frog reluctantly accepts, and midway across the river the scorpion stings her. While both animals begin to sink, the frog cries out: "Why?" and the scorpion replies: "I couldn't help it. It is in my nature." The story, I recognize, is overly simplistic. Surely, the scorpion could suppress his murderous tendencies for however long it takes to cross a river. But the moral remains, and both creatures' odds of survival significantly decline should the scorpion be required to cross the river morning and night every day. Being aware of my basest instincts, I can, or at the very least I choose to believe that I can, control myself somewhat reliably. But that belief does not make constant awareness and effort any less required, nor does it completely remove the threat. More to the point, whether this particular scorpion and frog survive their journey is quite irrelevant. If not one but a billion scorpions are introduced into the ecosystem, then frogs as a species are likely bound for extinction.

I suffer no delusions of grandeur. I am but one scorpion and my life is, to everyone but myself, rather inconsequential. So are the lives of the handful of people I could kill if I let my instincts get the better of me. Put enough of me together, however, and we would turn this world to dust. As I have seen firsthand the ease with which that woman killed a dozen armed men, it is obvious now that even my darkest self pales in comparison to the rest of our kind. I dare not imagine five hundred thousand, five hundred million, of like mind and body. Despite my relative insignificance, I bear responsibility for what happens next. It was me who invited them. I did it to save a world I've never seen, or so I thought. In hindsight, I did it because that's what I was supposed to do. For a hundred generations, we only dreamed of activating that beacon. I was . . . like a dog, a Labrador jumping in water, a golden retriever fetching a thrown stick. I did what had been ingrained in my every cell for three thousand years. It never occurred to me to think of the consequences, not until it was too late. I turned the sphere off a week later, but the damage had already been done.

I tracked the home of my dead prey not long after I left my mother's home. I do not know if it was mere curiosity or a false sense of closeness that drove me to it. I think I entered that house searching for myself. I was filled with an unhealthy mixture of pride and guilt, doubt and confidence. My pr—Lola—was going through the same. I tore through her journal as if it were a mystery novel. She was everything but what I imagined her to be. She clung to her sense of self, as her mother did, but unlike her mother, she never came to terms with the woman she was bred to be. Unable to envision herself the savior of many, she tried to save the one who mattered most. She faced me to protect her daughter, from me, and to free her from her cursed bloodline. A selfless, if foolish, act. She was insecure, impulsive, irresponsible, and without doubt the bravest person I'd ever met. I was . . . enthralled, ashamed.

It could have been temporary. Guilt is something one learns to live with, a load, I knew from experience, that would get lighter every day. I was nonetheless faced with a choice. Embrace the mission that was my heritage and let the chips fall where they may. Or attempt, however vainly, to right some of the wrongs I committed. Perhaps it was a twist of irony that I would look to our prey for answers. Whatever ill will they bore towards my kin, however misguided their struggle might have been, they always strived to do good and they suffered immensely for it. They could have been queens and empresses, ruled this entire Earth had they wanted to. They could have indulged in all manner of vice with impunity, but instead they chose to help, even if it cost them their lives time and time again. They were born scorpions, but they chose to live as frogs. I found the idea fascinating.

I looked for ways to honor the life of my prey, to repay the imaginary debt I had burdened myself with. She . . . *They* had built their entire existence around one goal: to save humanity, or part of it, from our kind by sending them away. "Take them to the stars," they repeated over millennia. I, of course, lack such inclination, nor do I possess the skills to contribute in any meaningful way. That said, I thought it appropriate to enlist the help of others. I offered $10 million of Lola's money to the first private venture to successfully fly to space. As far as I can tell, my prey had always relied on governments to advance their goals, inserting themselves into existing projects. That placed most of the responsibility in the hands of the same people for nearly half a century. While these people may have been ahead of their time in the forties, they are old men by now most likely out of groundbreaking ideas. Nothing has come of my project yet. Nothing may, I realize, but it helped relieve some of the discomfort I was experiencing after watching Lola die. That relief was only temporary. One cannot erase a lifetime of evil simply by writing a check with other people's money. My redemption, if it were to be, would require more commitment.

I could have spent years weighing the pros and cons—that is how one rationalizes procrastination—but various powers in the universe conspired to force my hand. Habit brought me to Union Square for my morning walk. The kid on his skateboard scared a pigeon away. The bird flew straight at my head and made me turn to the newsstand. The tabloid editor penned yet another outlandish title. "Giant Aliens Land on Earth." I laughed, of course. Elvis was also on the cover, live and well. As I walked away, I felt a shadow pulling at me. The farther I walked, the harder it pulled, like a rubber band tied around my waist. What if? I had, after all, just activated a device whose sole purpose was to bring aliens to Earth. I had summoned my kind. It was at least conceivable that they'd answered the call. There was nothing enlightening in the tabloid piece, of course, but I could not stop looking. I was one of those people now, chasing ghosts, Bigfoot, the Loch Ness Monster. Like most conspiracy theorists, I found nothing tangible, only rumors, hints, clues, in just the right amount to keep the doubt alive. Then, one morning, I heard a knock at the door. I looked through the peephole and there she was, my Loch Ness monster, standing in the hallway, rifle in hand.

I could, in hindsight, have answered the door. I could have fought her there and then. I could have talked to her, bargained for my life. There were a thousand things I could have done. I chose to run. It's not every day one realizes they've brought on the apocalypse. I was . . . unprepared. When she did not pursue, I surmised she had found another target and what had been little more than a philosophical exercise was now very real. I had to decide what kind of animal I wanted to be.

I chose to save the last of our prey. I think it was a selfless act, but I know that part of me wanted to feel "heroic" again. I killed my entire family to save my mother, and while it came with a fair amount of pain and regret, the feeling of righteousness that came with it was very real, and quite addictive. The line between frog and scorpion isn't always obvious.

I must also admit to a certain shortsightedness. I never once considered that this one act would turn into a long-term obligation. I thought knowing Lola meant I also knew her daughter. I was wrong, as I was about having enough patience to care for a clueless child. Perhaps I was never meant to be a parent. We shall see. One thing is certain: if Aster has to die, she should die peacefully, in her sleep, perhaps, and not in a senseless bout of violence. I owe her mother that much.

10

Exactly like Me

I wasn't sure yesterday, but I had a good night's sleep and I think I made the right choice staying with Samael. For one thing, I had a good night's sleep. I don't remember the last time I slept on something horizontal, with a blanket and a pillow. I didn't know how good I had it before, but a good place to sleep is worth a lot, like *a lot* a lot. I just need to remember to close the curtains so I don't wake up this early. The windows here are as big as a football field. I don't know how Samael pays for things. He doesn't seem to have a job, unless he took a vacation to help me. We're in Las Vegas, so it would make sense. I wanted to ask—I *almost* did—but I'm afraid he'll say God gave him the money or something.

—Eat your breakfast, Aster. We'll start your training when you're done.

He's a morning person, though, so he must have had a job at some point. I don't deal with morning people really well. They're all peppy, and we-have-to-start-your-training intense. Also, I have no idea what he's talking about. Should I ask? I don't really want to, but I have to say something. He'll just stare if I don't.

—What exactly are we training for?

—*We* are not training for anything. *You* are. You have to learn to defend yourself.

—Defend myself *from*?

—As I said, there are two more hunters looking for you.

—Yes, you said that. . . . Are you sure? I mean, how do you know?

—I know.

—But *how* do you know?

—Are you always this annoying?

—I—

—That was a rhetorical question. On June 20 of last year, one of the largest meteorites ever observed hit near the small town of Kunya-Urgench in Turkmenistan. A giant ball of fire brightened the sky. Residents in nearby villages heard a deafening whistling sound, followed by a loud crash. The impact left behind a relatively small crater—about six meters wide—in a cotton field, yet not a single fragment was found. Cotton farmers who were working the field at the time swear they saw three *devs*—mythical giants, sometimes called *daevas*—walking out of the crater moments after the impact.

—I'm sorry, sir, what? It sounded like you said these people came here on a meteorite. Maybe I heard wrong, but that's what it sounded like.

Not that anything he said before made him sound particularly sane, but this . . . It reminds me of that cult up north who drugged their kids and set themselves on fire because they thought they'd travel to a star. The kids part is what got me. Like, you're sure enough of that travel thing to pour gasoline over yourself and light a match, but not sure enough to take your kids with you. Mythical giants traveling on a meteorite. I'll admit, those pictures he showed me shook me a little. That and the blood test and—I don't really know *what* to believe anymore, but I'm pretty sure this ain't it.

—To the contrary, Aster. I believe it wasn't a meteorite at all. I think they came on some type of spacecraft. They would most likely destroy it to hide their presence, but judging by the look on your face, I'd say you're not particularly interested in what I believe.

Actually, that makes more sense. I mean, it doesn't make *a lot* of sense, but it's *way* better than a meteorite.

—I don't mean to be rude, sir. I'm just . . . You said yourself this was a lot to take in. You can't expect me to believe all of it right away, can you?

—It would certainly make things easier if you did. I take it you haven't read your mother's journal either.

—I told you, I don't want to read it.

—Then read your grandmother's journal! Your great-grandmother's! Or are you mad at them too for ruining your life? Poor little Aster was abandoned as a child. You can wallow in self-pity all you want, but do not waste my time doing it. You had a home and a loving father. You actually *had* a childhood. As for what you should or should not believe, let us start with this: Do you think the person I shot on the highway was a figment of my imagination?

—I— No! Of course not! But—

—Then trust me when I say there are more. It doesn't matter who they are, where they're from, what mode of transportation they used, or whether you accept the fact that they are not human. They are very real. They *will* find you, and they *will* kill you.

—Do you know where they are?

—I believe one of them was involved in a shooting in Rome three days ago. I don't know where the other one is.

—Okay. How do we stop them?

—I don't know that we can. The best we can do is make sure you're ready when they come.

—Ready how?

—You already know how to fight, but you've spent your entire life repressing those instincts. I can help you reconnect with them. That's the easy part. You must learn to control them as well. There are other things I can teach you, things your instincts aren't honed for. Stealth, for example, does not come naturally to us. We prefer open combat to surreptitiousness. Given their size and strength, you would likely fare better in a furtive attack than you would face-to-face.

—Face-to-face?! I don't know what you're talking about, sir. I don't know how to fight! Like, *at. All.* I never been in a fight, except that one time with Nicole at school. That lasted a whole two seconds. I pushed her. That's it. She broke her wrist, but it ain't my fault she doesn't know how to fall. I got suspended for a week. You wouldn't believe how much trouble I was in at home. What I mean, sir, is I can't do what you think I can do.

—You can fight, believe me.

—I can fight *Nicole*! You never seen Nicole, but she's, like, shorter than me, ninety pounds if she just ate. That lady on the highway? She's the Terminator. No way.

—Then you will die.

—*You* can fight them, right? You shot that lady, in the face! I was there. One minute she was standing above me then *BAM!* Dead. *Really* dead! You did that. You did it without breaking a sweat.

—She left her back exposed. I doubt the others will be so careless. Even if I killed them all, others will follow. More to the point, I won't always be there, Aster. You must learn to fend for yourself.

—You're going to leave me too?

— . . .

—Figures.

—You seem surprised. Did you think we'd spend our whole

lives together? Go fishing? Did you think I'd help you with your homework before we watch your favorite movie together?

—I don't need help with my homework.

—Good. I'm not your father, Aster. I'm not your friend either.

—Then what are you?

—I'm the only chance you have.

11

Army of Me

He just keeps staring. I can't eat with someone staring at me. Now my cereal's all mushy, but I have to keep eating or he'll want me to do things. I don't want to do things. I don't want to "train." I *really* don't want to train at 8:00 A.M. Please go away! What I want right now is to lie down and think about nothing. I like nothing in the morning. Another bite. This is . . . kind of disgusting.

—That's enough, Aster. Please move your bowl and put your left hand flat on the table.

—What? Why?

—Just do as I say.

What are the odds he'll leave me alone if I do? I'm guessing not good, but still worth a shot.

—Like that?

—Yes. Thank you. Now imagine I were to pull out a knife and pin your hand to the table with it. What would you do?

—What?

—Stop saying "what." You heard me. How would you defend yourself?

—I wouldn't. I'd pass out is what I'd do. Dial nine-one-one. "Please send help: there's a knife in my hand!"

—That is not the answer I'm looking for. Think again.

—Can I finish my cereal first? I'm not even awake yet.

—Those are no longer cereal. I saw you gag on the last bite you took. Now answer the question.

—Okay, I . . . Why would you pin my hand to the table?

—It doesn't matter why. What would you do?

— . . . Because if you were trying to kill me, then I don't think stabbing my hand makes a lot of sense. Also, are we talking about *you* you or is this someone else? If it's you, then I think it kind of matters why. Like, maybe it's just a misunderstanding. If it's a complete stranger, then I don't know. They could be on drugs, or having a psychotic episode.

—What difference does it make?

—Well, I could talk them down, if I knew what was wrong with them.

—You have to *kill* them, Aster, not talk to them. You have to kill whoever is sitting across from you before they kill you. It's a very simple exercise. What would you do?

I feel like I'm missing something. I can't really do things if I don't understand them. It was like that at school. My teachers were always annoyed, just like he is now, but it wasn't my fault the questions weren't precise enough. Okay, maybe it was my fault a little, but I still want things to make sense. I don't think there's anything wrong with that.

—I don't mind training if you think it's important, but I thought you would show me how to use a *gun*. I can *shoot* someone with a gun, like *you* did. This is . . . I'm not going to get into a knife fight, sir. I'm twelve.

—As I mentioned, you do not have a knife; only your enemy does. This is the last time I ask, Aster. You need to take this seriously.

—I *am*! I am. I . . . I suppose I'd pull the knife out of my hand first. Then, if I don't faint doing that, 'cause I think I would, but let's say I don't, I'd use it to stab you. Well, I wouldn't stab *you*

you, but if it were someone else and— You know what I mean. I'm defending myself against . . . someone. Did I get it right?

Then I'd get out my ray gun—*Pew! Pew!*—or shoot lasers with my *eyes*. He'd be all: "AAAH! IIIII'M MELTIIING!" Then I'd fly away in my invisible spaceship. I can do all that, of course, because I'M AN ALIEN! I better not say that out loud; he ain't happy with me already.

—No, you did not. I would have plenty of time to stop you from grabbing the knife. Even if you did manage it, you're too small to reach across the table from where you sit.

—Tell me what I should do, then.

—You already know what to do. You just have to listen.

—I'm listening, but you just said—

—I did not say you should listen to me. I said you have to *listen*.

—Listen to whom? There's no one else here, sir. Wait, is there?

—Listen to yourself, Aster. There is a voice inside you—at least that's how *I* conceive of it—and it knows what to do. You've learned to suppress it over time because you thought it was wrong, but it *is* in you. It's like the cat.

—Londo?

—Yes. I assume he never lived in the wild. He never had to fend for himself and kill his food, but if you place a mouse in front of him, his instincts would kick in. He would know what to do even if no one in his lineage has hunted for generations. The voice is still in him, just like it is in you. All you have to do is listen to it.

—I don't know what you want me to say, sir! There's no voice. I don't know what to do. I don't know how to fight. I don't know anything.

—That's simply not true. What would you do, Aster?

—I—

—SAY IT!

—Don't get mad. I told you I don't—

—SAY IT!

—I would grab the kn— AAAAHHHHHH! WHY DID YOU DO THAT?! Take it out! TAKE IT OUT NOW!

I heard the knife dig into the wood. *Thud,* straight through my hand. Whoa. My head's spinning like I got up too fast. Cold sweat pouring out everywhere. I can't look. Crud, I don't need to 'cause I can feel my pulse against the FRIGGIN' BLADE! AAAH! I got the chills now, big-time. I can't stop shaking. I'm cold, and hot. I got a fever rushing to my brain. That's it; I'm gonna faint. I see spots. Red spots, blue spots. I see . . . I see *me.*

The knife doesn't matter. I just leave it alone. I push forward and ram the table against him. He falls backwards on his chair. Holy moly, this feels real. I lean in and flip the table sideways on his throat. His hands aren't there to stop it—he used them both to break his fall. I hear his trachea crumple. Eeew. Me and the table get back on our feet. He wiggles, gasping for air. He's dead. Now I take the knife out. . . .

Whoa.

—SAY IT, ASTER! WHAT WOULD YOU DO?

—It hurts too much! I can't talk!

—But you *do* know.

—Yes! It's not a voice. I *see* things, like a movie. NOW PLEASE TAKE THIS THING OUT OF ME!

12

Dry the Rain

We missed Christmas. Well, we didn't miss it; we just . . . I was mad. Take-that-training-of-yours-and-shove-it-where-the-sun-don't-shine mad. I didn't so much as look at him for two days, not even a little. That's hard to do in a hotel room. Somewhere in there was Christmas. I didn't mind not doing anything—he ain't exactly the eggnog-by-the-fireplace type—but it felt strange not having Pa around. I miss him. With all that's going on, I haven't thought about him as much. I think I missed missing him.

I'm still trying to make sense of what happened. I can't believe he actually stabbed me, but then, it was like . . . I was *there*, doing it. I could feel the carpet squish under my feet when I sprung up, the weight of the table. I felt my muscles tense. The weirdest part is I *knew* what to do. I knew how to kill. That's messed up, but still. I felt . . . powerful. I kind of liked it. I guess it means there's some truth to what Samael's been saying.

My hand's still a bit numb, but at least I get a break from whatever ninja boot camp he's got planned. I been reading Grandma's journals instead. Whoa. I thought *my* life was weird. Like, she was a spy! In Germany during the war. She built space rockets for Pete's sake! Grandma was *bad*. Ass. I ain't like her, that's for sure. I know how to flip a table, but she wiped out a whole squad of Nazis and didn't even blink. She was impaled! Like, I never even *heard* of anyone getting impaled before. *Bad. Ass.* She thought she was different from everyone else, but she never used the A-word in her journal. It's so much easier to swallow without the A-word. "Different" I can do. She didn't even know what she was. How does *he* know? I don't wanna talk to him, but I have a ton of questions now. Like a *ton*.

. . .

Maybe just one question. Nah, forget it. I ain't asking.

. . .

. . .

— . . . Er, sir?

—Are we on speaking terms again?

I hate letting him win like this. I'm still mad, just . . . more curious than mad, I guess.

—I don't know.

—Good. Let me know when we are.

—I—I been reading, like you asked, and . . . Well, there are these men in my grandmother's journal—she calls them the Tracker. Are they the people chasing us now?

—They are not.

—Okay. . . . Then who are they?

—They were my family. Those you just read about were my father and uncles.

— . . .

Wow. Just like that. I'm not sure there's a great way to tell someone you come from a long line of cold-blooded killers, but I might want to ease into it a little. If I got this right, though, his dad being the Tracker would make *him* the Tracker and that's, well, not good. There's even a rule for it. "Fear the Tracker.

Always run, never fight." Grandma doesn't say how the whole thing started—maybe she does; I ain't got to the end yet—but she says they been chasing us for three thousand years. She might have added a zero or two, but, that's one long-ass grudge to hold on to. Still, "fear the Tracker and run" is pretty clear. Maybe that's what I should do.

—They—my relatives, that is—and those who came before believed that your family was hiding something from them.

—Were they?

—They were at some point. Our family histories are a three-thousand-year-old game of telephone. Information gets lost along the way.

—My grandmother said they were killing us, them. You know what I mean. They weren't *asking* for anything.

—It is entirely possible that it happened as she said. It is equally possible it did not. As I said, information gets lost. The lens through which one views everything gets more and more fogged. One's motivations can become . . . distorted.

—I— Who are you talking about now? *My* family or yours?

—If I wanted to hurt you, Aster, I would have done it already.

—You stabbed me!

Asshole.

—I am sorry for that. How's your hand?

He has a point, but he's still an asshole. There's also a strong possibility that Grandma was completely out of her mind like he is. She been in the war. She could have had PTSD. Even if it's all true, she didn't have giant bad guys chasing her, or Bruce Willis. I do. That changes things a little, I think.

—It's . . . better. Still tender.

—Is there anything else you want to ask?

Come on, Aster, make up your mind. I don't know why I keep

torturing myself. What's there to decide, really? Where would I go? I don't have anyone, except for him. He's the only one who did anything to help. Like it or not, it's either do as he says or live on the streets. That ain't much of a choice when the whole world is out to get me. Besides, how bad can he be? He said the ones in the book were his uncles, and his dad. It ain't exactly fair to blame him for what they did, right? I don't think he was even born when Grandma wrote all this. If Pa'd done something bad, I wouldn't want people to judge me for it. That wouldn't be right. There's a saying even. "Sins of the father" . . . something. I suppose I don't have to decide right away. I can stay here, where there's a bed. I can read another journal. I'll have to do what Samael says eventually, but I ain't falling for that hand thing again. He only wants to teach me things. Pa always said I should try and learn something new every day.

—Yes, sir. Do we have any double A's?

—Pardon me?

—Batteries. My Game Boy died.

—I'm sure they have batteries in the hotel lobby.

—They do, but I don't have any money.

—You have money.

—I *had* forty-six bucks, but I spent it. . . . Okay, I watched a movie and I got room service when you were gone and I thought you'd get mad so I went downstairs and paid for it. Do you know how complicated it is to pay cash for a movie? Anyway, that was before you stabbed me. Now I don't care if you're mad, but I still don't have any money.

—I was not talking about loose change. You have lots of money, Aster. You only lack access to it.

—I have money? How much?

—It is difficult to say. By my calculation, your family left you around two point seven billion dollars. There might be more funds I'm not aware of.

— . . .

—Aster?

Crud. I think I peed myself a little.

13

Into the Void

Showtime.

—Excuse me, ma'am! You got a bug crawling in your hair. Farther back. A bit more. You got it. Crud, it's still there. Do you want me to do it? Bring your head down a little. Ewww. There. It's gone. Oh, it's no problem, ma'am. No problem at all. You're welcome.

One big X in blue marker, right on her chest. She didn't feel a thing. She won't find out I wrote on her until she walks by a mirror or talks to anyone. I hope Samael was watching. That was my best one yet. Kill number three! Two more and I got myself a Game Boy Color. I love learning! He said I had to work on surreptious . . . ness, sur*rep*titiousness. Sneaky stuff. I don't see how much help that'll be if I run into an eight-foot-tall killer with a gun, but my Game Boy's superold and sometimes the Start button gets stuck, so I didn't argue much.

Is it bad that I'm pretending to kill people for a Game Boy? Pa wouldn't have liked it, that's for sure. I picked a nice flower from Mrs. Bloom's yard once and I gave it to him, just to be nice. He spent an hour explaining in great detail all the care and effort it took to grow that flower, and how I'd ruined it in two seconds without even thinking about it. I felt awful, for a flower. I did kill that flower. I'm only *pretending* to kill these people now. Okay, so maybe that old lady can't afford to buy herself a new shirt. . . .

That'd be sad. I mean, writing on people's things *is* bad. I know that, but it's just a game. It wasn't even my idea.

It's kind of unfair that I have to "earn" my money to begin with since, well, it's mine, but I need an adult to get it, so . . . I even told *him.* I said it was extortion. He told me it couldn't be because *I* was the one getting money out of it. I didn't have a good answer to that, but I know he's wrong. Anyway, it ain't so bad. It sounded really dumb when he first said it, but tagging random people with a permanent marker *is* kind of fun. I think I have a knack for it. I feel like a lioness on those nature shows, sneaking up on a gazelle. The gazelle is an old lady with a walker and we're at the mall, but I like the mall. Plus there's a GameStop on the second floor.

I feel bad about that lady's shirt now. Why'd I have to think about that? I'm not gonna tell her what I did just so I can apologize. Maybe I can *buy* her a shirt. I could sneak up to her again and stuff it in her bag without her noticing. It'd be like a whole other kill, harder even. I'll ask Samael for money later. I hope I can find her again, *if* he says yes. She has a walker, so she can't be superfast. That's good.

Samael said nothing about feeling bad. He said I might . . . how did he put it? Oh yeah, "experience intrusive thoughts or violent imagery." I guess he means what happened when he stuck a knife through my hand. My heart's beating a bit faster, but that's just 'cause I'm nervous. Anyway, I ain't having permanent marker hallucinations yet. He said I need to "let my instincts guide me without surrendering to them." He talks to me like I'm Ripley about to fight the alien queen. "Fear is your friend." I'm okay with it. It's better than the "you can't do anything 'cause you're just a kid" I got from everyone else my whole life.

Maybe I *am* like Ripley a little. I read my *great*-grandmother's journal and she was a spy too! She was with the same agency

Wonder Woman works for. How cool is that? She might have killed Stalin, even. I come from a long line of spies. Well, two, at least, like Ken Griffey Senior and Ken Griffey Junior, but with spy stuff instead of baseball. And daughters. I'm Ken Griffey . . . Junior Junior. Great-Grandma said the Tracker cut her ear off, which is bad. She also said they were looking for a "sphere" that they could use to call home. Now I wonder if maybe that's why these giant killers are here, 'cause someone found the ball thingy and made a call. That would mean they really aren't from Earth, but—I don't know—all of it doesn't seem as crazy as before. I'm not sure if Samael knows about the sphere. I'll ask him, after we buy my Game Boy.

Focus on the prize, Aster. One kill at a time. Who's next? No little kids. I know it's pretend, but I don't want to pretend hurting kids. Plus it could be their favorite shirt they're wearing, like the one piece of clothing they chose for themselves, and then I'll come and ruin it and they'll have to wear ugly things all the time. Some itchy sweater with a unicorn on it. I feel bad enough as it is; I don't want to be responsible for that on top of everything. I need someone I don't like, preferably rich so they can afford more shirts.

Ohh, fancy suit guy cutting in line at the coffee shop. That's not nice. He deserves an X. Sure, you didn't know that was the line. He looks peeved. Poor him, having to wait with the little people. You're mine, now, jerk. You're *so* mine. I'm not doing the bug thing; I don't want to talk to him. I'll just run into him, pretend I wasn't looking. Faster. Faster than that. Brace for impact!

—OH MY GOD! Are you okay? I'm such a klutz sometimes.

Gotcha! Oops. My thumb got stuck in his jacket pocket. Quick! I don't think he noti—

—What the fuck? Did you just write on my fucking shirt?!

Crud! What do I do? Run, that's what!

—Sorry, sir! IT WASN'T MY IDEAAAA!

Is he chasing me? He's right behind me, ain't he? He's not. Phew! I bet he didn't want to move to the back of the line again. That wasn't fun, and I'd feel really stupid getting arrested by a mall cop. I hope Samael didn't see this. He wouldn't be too impressed. I doubt it. He couldn't have been watching me all morning, could he? I guess he could. He's leaning on the second-floor railing, looking right at me. I know; that wasn't pretty. What's he doing? Why is he making circles with his fing— NOOO! I'm not starting over! He said five kills. He didn't say *in a row*. Or did he? I should really pay more attention. . . . Crud! I was doing great!

All right. I'll do the bug thing again. That was cool.

14

You Learn

I stole a car today. Yep. I'm a car thief. I stole a car, and candy, and I played Mortal Kombat for three hours straight. I don't really *like* Mortal Kombat, but Samael bought it anyway, for the training. It doesn't count, though. I don't have to earn that one.

I get the combat part, even if it's just a video game and I'm swinging paper fans. FINISH HIM! Kitana wins! But the stealing? Desen—God, he likes words that are impossible to pronounce—de-sen-si-ti-vi-zation. It's about doing things I might wouldn't do 'cause I'm afraid or I think it's wrong. For real. I spent the day doing bad things, *because* they're bad. I started with stealing gummy bears, 'cause then I'd have gummy bears, but he didn't like that. Apparently, doing bad things ain't much of a challenge when you get something you like out of it. Like rich folks ripping off poor people because it makes them richer. That made me feel bad about the candy, so I keyed a Mercedes in the hotel lot instead. That wasn't good either. Too easy, he said. There has to be *risk*. He wanted me to *steal* it. I said no, of course. I never driven a car before. That didn't seem to impress him. There was some discussion. We settled on two games for my new Game Boy, a Sony Discman, and the new Nine Inch Nails double album.

I stared at that shiny silver car, like, forever. It's a really nice car, except for the scratch I made on the door. I think the car knew it was me. It scolded me when I got too close to it. *Pew! Pew!* I imagined it would get even angrier if I broke a window to get in. I seen people steal a car on TV. They just rip part of the dashboard off and touch two wires, but my Mercedes wasn't anything like those cars. It had, like, a billion buttons everywhere and the dashboard was supersleek. These things are really well made. I don't think you can just take pieces off like that. And there's the *pew pew*. I had to stop that first, and the blinking red light, before I could do anything. I was superscared, but I knew I had to be logical about it. Mr. Spock said: "An ancestor of mine maintained that if you eliminate the impossible, whatever remains, however improbable, must be the solution." I did that. I eliminated *all* the impossible, and what remained was . . . that this wasn't going to happen. I don't know why I wasted an hour thinking about it. I'm smart, but the only thing I know about car alarms is when Arnold lifts a car up with Danny DeVito inside it. I can't lift a car. Plus, *Twins* is probably not the most reliable source.

I found it, though, the answer to life, the universe, and everything, on a curly piece of paper sitting on the dashboard. It's not forty-two; it's nine, nine, dash, zero, one, eight, three. Bellagio Valet Parking. I went back to the entrance where the little office is, the one with all the car keys hanging on the wall. The valet was smoking a cigarette outside.

—I'm sorry, sir. Did you see a woman in a blue dress looking for someone?

—Nah. Doesn't ring a bell.

—It's my mom. . . . I kind of lost her and I can't find the car. This place is huge! I don't even know what level we're on. Do you mind if I use your phone to call her?

—Give me the number and I'll call.

That could have been the end right there. My *whole* plan

folded in an instant. But it wasn't. I'd seen that one coming. I was prepared.

—All right. It's five-five-five-oh-one-eight-three. . . . That's her office number; you want it to transfer you to her cell phone. It's easy. Just dial three—or maybe it's one first, then three—then enter the first three letters of her last name. It's Genero; there's only one, I think. *G*, *E*, *N*. Then it's—

—Why don't you go inside and call her yourself.

—Okay. Thanks!

I got the keys. I still didn't know how to drive, but I figured the hard part was behind me. I seen plenty of people who couldn't count to five and were driving cars. It ain't superhard, but there's a learning curve. I scratched the door on a big cement column backing out the car, but I'd already keyed it on that side so I didn't feel too bad. . . . I drove one floor up, very slowly, and parked the car again. Samael never said I had to bring it back. He just said I had to steal it. The door was way worse than I thought. And I dinged the other door, and the front a little. I hope whoever owns that Mercedes is a *really* bad person.

I'm not gonna lie, it was . . . exciting. I was *really* nervous, especially driving, but I was way more nervous at Sears. I think I *am* de-sen-si . . . Oh whatever. I'm getting *numb*. I never, *ever*, would have done any of that before. Pa would have grounded me for a decade if I did, but I wouldn't have thought about it even. All the kids in our neighborhood stole candy from the store. They did it all the time. Me, not once. Not even when Mr. Lee asked me to watch the register while he went to the bathroom. I had the whole *wall* of candy to myself and I never touched it.

I'm changing. I can feel it. It's not the stealing, or the permanent marker or Mortal Kombat. But Pa dying and all, the police, the FBI, the Army, and some might-be-alien bad guys chasing me, it makes everything else seem supertrivial. Grand theft auto? Who cares? I had someone's *brain* all over my face. Samael stuck a knife through my hand and we still sleep in the same hotel suite. That part is weird now that I think about it. It's like nothing really matters anymore, not like it used to. What's the song again?

> ♪♫ Nothing really matters. ♫ Nothing really matters . . . to meee! ♪

I don't know what's next. I hope it's not more stealing. That was fun, but I can't help thinking how disappointed Pa would be. I'd rather write on people some more. Pa wouldn't like that either, but it ain't *as* bad. I could paint some graffiti, like on a building or something. It's wrong enough, I think, and I like drawing, so maybe I'd be good at that. Then again, we might be done desensi . . . tizing. He might teach me self-defense, or some ninja stuff. It doesn't really matter; I'm ready for anything.

15

Down by the Water

That escalated quickly. His name is Freddie Freeman. He's a loan officer for a bank in Vegas. He likes to roller-skate, but he's not really good at it. He eats falafel for lunch every day. Same time, same place. And every night, he drives up to Lake Mead, where he abuses and tortures a little boy he keeps locked in his soundproof boat hold. Samael said he kidnapped the kid almost a year ago. Sam *found* him for me. That's what he said: "I found him for you." He been watching Freddie Freeman for days. That's why he kept going out all the time.

He gave me a whole "file" on Freddie Freeman. It's not really a *file*, just a notebook full of scribbles. What time Freddie shows up at work, where he goes, what he eats. Mostly, it's bank, falafel, bank falafel. Also, little stick figures, but I don't think they mean anything. I had one day to read the whole notebook, just one, and then burned it. One day sounded like a lot, but there's tons of notes and Samael's handwriting is really bad. Still, I got *most* of it memorized. I'm not sure I really needed to. Samael told me to come up with a plan, but he already done the stalking and the lake is the only place where he's not surrounded by a bunch of people. I said: "We should do it at the lake." That was the plan.

It's a nice lake. It's fake, though. They made it for the Hoover Dam, but you wouldn't know just by looking at it. The marina's superquaint. Money, but not, like, crazy money. It reminds me of Gulfport a bit. Pa couldn't afford a boat, but we went out a couple times with that work friend of his—what was his name? I can't remember. He had a slushy machine on the boat. I thought that was the best thing ever. I begged Pa to get one that whole summer. I shouldn't have. Pa felt bad every time he had to say no. I didn't understand money back then. I didn't get why other people had some and we never had any. I thought Pa was doing something wrong.

I'm trying to keep my mind occupied, but I keep thinking of Freddie Freeman. What's he look like? Is he big? Is he small? Friendly? Mean? I never met a monster like that. And what about the kid? I can't begin to imagine what it's like. You're alone, all the time. You can't scream or talk to anyone, except for the one person who keeps hurting you. My brain's spinning out of control and I don't have a way to stop it. Also, I can't find the boat. It's dark as a cow's guts out here. I ain't seen anyone, but I really don't want to be here long. Where's the boat? Where's the boat? There she is. The *Clever Girl.* Crud. I got the jitters now, big-time.

Samael didn't like the "we" part in "We should do it at the lake." I told him we should just call the cops, but that's not part of my training. This is. "It's just like the mall, Aster." Sure. Except it's not. I wouldn't be shaking like a leaf if it were. "You'll be doing the world a favor." Well, the world's been pretty awful to me so far. I don't think I owe it anything. I want to go back to ruining people's shirts. Stealing cars, even. I'll steal a hundred cars if I need to. "One time, then you can buy anything you want. You can have a bank card." That sounded so much better before I stepped on the boat. I don't need money. I could go back to Sears. I could! I could eat other people's scraps, sleep in the park. I don't need him. Maybe I do, a little. I don't need him *that* much.

I'm not sure why I came. I don't want to be alone, but that ain't the whole reason. I read another one of my family's journals. Her name was Annie. She was supersmart. Like she studied the sun! And at night, instead of watching TV—I'm not sure there was TV back then, but it doesn't matter—she hunted serial killers in London. It's the same with my grandmother, and her mother. Their stories were awesome. *They* were awesome. The whole time I was reading, I kept thinking: God, I wish I were like that. They were strong. They didn't need anyone. They were in control. Samael's the same. He shoots people in the *face*. Me, I feel like I'm on a dinghy in the middle of the ocean and all I can do is hold on. They're all *so* the opposite of that.

Their lives were messed up too; I know that. My grandmother didn't want to be like her mom, like all of them. She was desperate for a normal life, to be . . . more like me, I guess, but she changed her mind in the end. Good call. Being me ain't all it's cracked up to be. Even before. I loved Pa—I did—but everything else, finish school, get a job maybe you don't like, it all seemed so . . . robotic. I'm tired of feeling like this, like me. I want to be like Grandma, and Samael. That's what he wants for me. He wants me to be more like him.

"I need to know you're ready, Aster."

Am I? I don't know. I *am* on the boat and walking down the steps. There's no one here. He must be in the hold, doing what he does. It's all wood and chrome in here. You couldn't know from the outside, but he fixed up this place nice. There's a picture on the desk. Him, I suppose, and a little girl. She's a couple years younger than me. Daughter, niece, she could be anyone. She seems happy. They both do, really. I don't know why it bugs me, but it does. "He's a monster, Aster." I guess being a monster ain't a full-time job. She *likes* him. I bet a bunch of people do now that I think about it: folks at the bank, the guy serving the falafel. "How's it going today, Freddie?" "Not so bad, Bob. Not so bad." I'm okay with killing the monster. I just never thought about the rest of him.

Oh no. The door latch just moved. He's coming out. He's . . . Shorter than I thought. Something's different. The glasses maybe; he wasn't wearing them in the picture. Red flannel shirt over—is that a Bart Simpson T-shirt? It's all so . . . normal. He looks nothing like a sadistic banker. This is wrong. I can't do it. I can't, I can't.

—I think you're in the wrong boat, girl.

Crud. It's getting *real* warm in here.

16

It Girl

Father was unusually happy that night. He drove me to an apartment building not that far from our house. He did not ask my brothers to come, and for a brief moment I thought he genuinely wanted to do something with me. I suppose he did. We walked up to the third floor and he told me to open the door to apartment 306. In the middle of the living room was a man, about my father's age, gagged and tied to a chair. "It's time, Son," he said, and handed me a knife. I refused to do it. That's not true, I knew this wasn't something I was at liberty to refuse, but I stood in silence for . . . what seemed like a very long time. "Do it and you can have your goddamn puppy." I had seen this dog at the pet store—I forget what kind it was—and had begged Mother to adopt it for weeks. Still, I was younger than Aster. I froze. Father walked me to this . . . stranger, grabbed the hand I was holding the knife with, and made me cut the man's throat. We watched him bleed together. I remember wondering whether I'd really killed him. The knife was in *my* hand, but I was just a puppet. It was Father doing all the work. We never got a puppy.

I was not ready, but my father deserved some of the blame. If only he'd . . . introduced the man, given me a reason—*any* reason—why I should kill him, I might have reacted differently. My brothers and I were awed by him, but in hindsight, Father's methods were crude and inefficient. Uriel had a voracious appetite for violence, but he could barely wield a knife, even as an adult. I promised myself I would not make the same mistakes with Aster. I found a man who lives on a boat, not in some busy apartment building where anyone could walk in. I did not tie the man up or drug him. Killing a defenseless person feels . . . cheap, and cowardly, like shooting a deer that's tied to a tree. More than anything, I did not want Aster to experience the remorse I felt for murdering someone I knew nothing about. Perhaps "remorse" is the wrong word. "Disdain," maybe. I knew what Mother would think of me. I put a lot of time into making sure that didn't happen to Aster. I gave her prey a name. I made him so vile and repugnant, anyone would want him dead. I filled an entire notebook with minute details about his life to make his story feel as genuine as possible. If Aster fails on her first attempt, it will not be for lack of effort on my part. I wish my father had cared *half* as much about me.

If she can't do it, we'll try again, ideally with the same man. It seems dubious that I could find murderers and child molesters so easily. . . .

It's been ten minutes already. I told her I'd wait in the car for fif—

Here she is. What do her eyes say? . . .

. . .

. . .

—I'm proud of you, Aster.

17

Miss Misery

Crud.

—Look around, Aster. Don't be stupid. You can't run. You've got nowhere to go.

Bruce friggin' Willis is on the mall P.A. His voice is everywhere, coming through the ceiling, through the walls. Like when a kid gets lost. "Paging for Mrs. Smith; please come to the information desk." He's right about running; there must be a hundred cops in here. Uniforms. Suits. Army folks. Plus, like half the people in the mall are undercover cops it seems. That mom with the stroller is fiddling with her earpiece. The big guy by the perfume shop is talking to his newspaper. I thought they only did that in movies.

I came to buy clothes! That's it. I wasn't writing on people, or stealing things. I just needed new jeans, maybe a couple T-shirts. I was going to look at telescopes. I can pay for it now. I was looking for the right store on the big map when I saw a mall cop holding my picture not three feet away. I turned around, started walking fast towards Macy's. It's easier to lose people in a department store than in, say, the food court where you're out in the open and everyone's sitting. I had to walk *through* the food court, though. That's when I noticed there were cops and soldiers sprinkled everywhere.

It's all because of Freddie Freeman. All of it. The cops, the

Army, Bruce Willis. Even the clothes. I came to buy jeans because mine had blood on them. Everyone says blood doesn't come off, but everyone says a lot of things and you can't believe all of it. It doesn't come off. I tried hand soap, shampoo, moisturizer. And I couldn't drop bloody clothes in the hotel laundry. Hotel people know things. Maids and janitors, and garbage people, all the folks rich people don't even notice, they know *everything*. I didn't want them to know about Freddie Freeman.

I wasn't gonna hurt him. Maybe I was; I don't know. He didn't wait for me to make up my mind. He grabbed me by the arm, hard—he picked the one *without* the knife. I nicked him on the side of the neck without thinking. Not *super*deep, but deep enough. Blood started squirting on and off with every heartbeat. He was like those sprinklers on a football field. *Pfff. Pfff. Pfff. Pfff. Pfff.* Freddie, he looked at me, like: "What the hell did you do, girl?," but he didn't do anything. I froze too. The whole thing was surreal. We looked at each other while he spray-painted the boat walls. Then the spraying stopped. Well, almost. There'd be a little spurt every now and then but nothing major. I honestly thought he might be okay. He sat down—more like leaned backwards—on the bench; then . . . he died, I guess. It wasn't what I thought it'd be like. I only seen people die on TV. There's no sign or anything, no music to tell you it happened. I kept waiting for his eyes to close, but they never did. I poked him a few times to make sure, wiped the knife clean on his shirt. And I left. I was supershaky, confused. I didn't even free the kid he had tied up in the hold. Samael said he would call the police. He'll starve to death if we wait for Freddie to smell bad enough. What I done didn't sink in right away. It happened so fast. One minute Freddie was alive; then he wasn't. It really hit me this morning. Freddie didn't wake up today. He won't show up for work. He won't be happy or sad or curious or hungry. He won't say "hello!"

to the falafel guy. He'll never see that girl in the picture again. I did that. He's not a living thing anymore because of me. It won't matter what he did to that boy. They'll lock me up because of Freddie Freeman, lock me up for good.

I thought I was too young for prison, so I asked. Sam said they can try anyone as an adult in like twenty-three states. You could be ten, six years old, babies even if they did something horrible. I don't know if Nevada's in the twenty-three. Maybe it ain't. Maybe they'll take me to Walter Reed instead, disappear me like a Russian spy. I don't know which is worse. What did Samael say? "You'll spend your entire life being poked and probed like a lab rat." I can picture it. Bright lights. Glass walls. Old men in suits staring at me from all sides. Both my wrists are tied to the bed. My legs too. Guys in hazmat suits come in twice a day to draw blood. They done it long enough they stopped paying attention to me. I'm furniture now, a filing cabinet they can pluck stuff out of whenever. They start running out of veins after a while. They prick me on the ankles, between my toes. Then my blood's not enough anymore. Brain fluid. Bone marrow. I'm covered in bedsores, thin as a rake—what's the word? Emaciated. I ain't protesting anymore, but I'm too weak to eat, so they keep me sedated and feed me through a tube. Everything's a blur from then on. I'm not sure if I'm awake or dreaming, but I don't really care because both hurt the same. . . . Whoa. That's dark.

Hell no. I ain't spending my days tied to a bed, *or* in a jail cell. I'm making a run for it. Don't be stupid, he said. I ain't been doing much else lately. I'm not about to stop now. Also, they were chasing me before I nicked Freddie Freeman's neck and I done nothing wrong then, except a blood test I wasn't even awake for. I'm getting out of here. I just . . . I don't know how. Come on, Aster, think! What do I do? What do I do? Now would be a good time for those "intrusive thoughts or violent imagery," but I got nothing.

Where's Samael? Samael will know what to do. He always does. He can fix this. Pa used to fix things. A ripped backpack. When I broke the hinges of my music box. He'd get his tools and he'd fix it. He'd make things better. Samael can do that. He shoots people in the face. He can fight them. I bet he can fight a hundred of them. Maybe not, but like ten. We can make it out if we go through ten people. Where is he? He was two steps behind me not two seconds ago.

Oh good. I see him now by the elevator. I— Crud. I can't get to him. There're three cops between me and there. There's a way to get to him, I know. I just haven't thought of it yet. Sam'll know. He'll tell me what to do. There. He's saying something. I can't—I can't read his lips. Aster. He's saying my name, something my name. He's saying . . .

"Goodbye, Aster."

ENTR'ACTE

No One in Their Right Mind

The woman stumbled inside the walls of Arbailu, her face and arms seared by the desert sun. She spoke words no one had ever heard, but knowing her language would have made no difference. She had lost any grasp of who and where she was years before. She hadn't seen a living thing, spoken to anyone, for half her life and the sight of a crowd sent her into a panic. People buzzing by like insects, staring, touching. A bumped shoulder spun the world around her and she fell backwards, knocking down a merchant's stand. A piece of garment fell over her head and the woman swung at shadows, screaming, until she heard the strangest, most beautiful thing. A song. The owner of the shop she had just ravaged was gesturing soldiers away, singing a lullaby to calm her down. When she did, he gave her water and gently wiped her burnt skin with a wet piece of cloth.

The woman's demeanor, her language, her clothing, everything about her spelled "foreign," not to mention "trouble," and the authorities in Arbailu thought it wise to send her to the capital as a slave. The merchant knew she would not survive the trip to Aššur in her current state and intervened, claiming she owed him for the damage she caused. The authorities acquiesced. It was, after all, hard to imagine this woman being of use in building a temple to Ishtar, or anything else for that matter, and the merchant was willing to take the problem off their hands.

The woman had no name. She had to get one before she could enter into a contract, and the merchant offered a suggestion. The woman must have liked the sound of it, because the corners of her mouth rose ever so slightly. From then on, she would be called Nidintu, a gift.

Nidintu was a lot taller than most adults, but her mind was very much that of a child and she required constant attention, something her benefactor could not provide while tending to his shop. He enlisted a friend's help, a widow whose riches greatly surpassed his own. She tasked one of her own debt slaves to take care of Nidintu and help her function in society. Nabûa was a good man, taken in by the widow during the last famine in exchange for his servitude, but Nidintu was untrusting and an impossible student. One night, Nabûa caught Nidintu sneaking outside to stare at the stars. He sat next to her and started pointing at constellations, telling stories of the gods. That was the first time she had let him speak without running away, so he did it again the next day, and the next. He showed her the Bow of Ishtar, the Arrow. Together they connected dots in the sky to form the Bull of Heaven that Ishtar sent to fight Gilgamesh, the ear of corn of the fertility goddess Shala.

Nidintu was adjusting to her new life, but not fast enough. She had no way to repay her debt and, when her contract expired, she would become the merchant's property, something no one wanted. And so a deal was struck. Nabûa, using his master's money, purchased the debt from the merchant, and made Nidintu a free woman before marrying her. Nidintu eventually found work as the widow's accountant. She built a life for herself—numbers by day and stars by night—and found what she forgot even existed: happiness.

✲

Three Assyrian farmers stumbled upon a fragment of Sereh's ship a day outside the city, part of the nose cone filled with sensors and computer parts. This was technology the world might never see, now in the hands of common men at the dawn of the Iron Age. They would see it as magical, something from the realms of the gods. That discovery would be life changing. It could transform an entire civilization. It could, but it didn't. Finding it would change *some* lives as the metal was worth a fortune, but these people had nothing to compare it with, no *less* advanced technology that would make this appear *more* advanced. This was "fire from the heavens," very much a gift from the gods, just like every other meteorite.

The farmers had finished planting their fields and would serve as soldiers until harvest. They hoped to sell their treasure when they joined other troops in Ninua, but the metal they'd found was brittle and didn't react to heat the way good iron does. They were offered only a fraction of the price they thought it should fetch and decided to think about it over beer. The tavern keeper was an unusually short woman with an unusually large nose. When one of the soldiering farmers was caught staring for the third time, he told the woman about their shoddy meteorite to break the awkwardness. She told them of a strange man in Aššur who paid five times the usual for sky fire. The farmers were ecstatic and spent all the money they had celebrating the money they *would* have. "Remember," the barkeeper said, "they call him *Rādi. Kibsi.*"

Tereshiin had traveled half the king's lands but turned sedentary once he reached Aššur. People came and went from all corners of the empire, and he realized news traveled *to* the capital much faster than he could travel *from* it. Years of waiting had made him question that reasoning, but his patience was rewarded in spades. It began with a knock on the door. Three men in poorly fitting armor dug a bundle of wires and a piece of metal out of a bag. When Tereshiin asked where they had found their strange meteorite, the wisest of the farmers said they would tell him once they'd agreed on a price. The farmer's resolve wavered rather quickly. He left Tereshiin's shop with a fair amount of money, and a bag, heavy with the heads, hands, and feet of his associates.

Nidintu was outside tending flowers when the strange, ashen man approached her. The sounds coming out of his mouth made no sense at all. Finally, after a minute or two, he started using her language. He spoke of distant worlds and things that did not exist. There was urgency in his tone, a palpable annoyance at her lack of response. He said he'd spent *years* looking for her, became angrier when she told him he was scaring her. She asked him to leave, but he grew more insistent. Nidintu was getting louder, drawing attention from two soldiers leaning on a nearby wall. The man grabbed her arm to drag her away and Nidintu scratched him hard before screaming.

—STOP IT! NOW!

An order. The woman was a Kih. She outranked him. A lifetime of military training made Tereshiin hesitate, and the stroke that would have decapitated Nidintu stopped an ounce of conviction short of severing her spine. Nabûa rushed outside to his wife's aid and pressed as hard he could on her artery while Tereshiin weighed his rapidly narrowing options.

Kish was playing with a wooden doll when she heard noises coming from the street. The four-year-old was used to playing on her own. She was stronger than other children her age and control was a skill she was still acquiring. She had broken her best friend's nose in a bout of unbridled enthusiasm and had no second-best friend to take her place. She spent her days playing the Game of Ur against herself, or with the wooden figures Nabûa carved for her. An argument in front of her house was as much excitement as she could hope for that afternoon and she moved to a better listening post near the front door. Her heart stopped when she recognized her mother's voice and realized this was more than a shouting match over the price of bread. What came next would remain a blur in Kish's mind. Her mother lying on the ground in a red circle. Her father crying and begging the gods' mercy. A pale-skinned man staring down at her.

When Tereshiin saw the little girl, he knew exactly what he was looking at. He'd once had to execute his best friend (an admittedly low threshold to reach) because of someone like her. Several species coexisted on his home world, workers brought in to work the mines. Some species were sexually compatible; some simply could not procreate. Rare combinations, however, produced this very kind of abomination. The cells recognized the other species's genetic material as foreign. Spindle fibers formed around one parent's chromosomes just before meiosis, forcing the other parent's outside the nucleus and into the cytoplasm. The result, if it made it to term, was an exact copy of the parent with the dominant genes, what his people called a "soul stealer." Birthing one was a crime punishable by death and what remorse Tereshiin felt for striking his superior vanished into the evening air. If Sereh ever had a soul, her child was now the one carrying it. Tereshiin fought his way out of Arbailu, his sword in one hand and a screaming and kicking Kish in the other.

ACT III

18

The Facts of Life

They gave me a sedative right in front of Macy's. Two guys wearing camouflage dragged me through the mall and took me . . . somewhere in the back of a van. Then it's a bit fuzzy. . . . I remember waking up on a plane with no seats. We all sat on a long bench, like in a baseball dugout, strapped to the wall. I think I threw up, or maybe I *dreamed* I threw up, but that's a weird dream to have, so I probably threw up. Back of a van again. There was a smaller plane. That one had seats. Then I fell asleep for real.

I woke up here with a headache the size of Texas. It ain't jail, so I'm pretty sure I'm at Walter Reed. Whatever this place is, I'm in the basement. Cement floor, concrete walls, and damp like a locker room. There's a fan in the corner, but it just moves the smell around. This must have been a storage space before they turned it into the fake kid room from hell. "We'll take good care of you, Aster." I guess that's what he meant. They painted the walls pink. Light pink, like Barbie's van if you left it in the sun too long. They were in a hurry. It's the most half-assed paint job I ever seen. They dropped a shaggy white carpet right on the cement floor and put a hospital bed on top. They dressed it up so it kinda looks like a regular bed. Pink comforter, pink pillows. There's half a dozen Backstreet Boys posters on the walls. Oh no, this one's NSYNC. The curtains are a nice touch. There ain't no window, just the curtains with more pink concrete behind. I guess they didn't have time to paint the bookshelf pink. It's still hospital brown, with exactly three books in it. *Girl Talk: Welcome to Junior High!* and . . . two more *Girl Talk*. It's like the whole room came as a kit from the twelve-year-old girl store. This *has* to be the creepiest place I seen.

The door locks from the outside, of course, but it ain't being locked up that scares me; it's being locked up in a basement with no windows. That ain't for me; it's for everyone else. They want to make sure no one knows I'm here. Okay, I might have watched too many movies, but the whole thing *screams* evil government project. Bruce Willis will say I'm imagining things, but normal people don't hide children in basements if they're not doing anything wrong. I didn't get any food, so at least I know they're not fattening me up to make a dress out of me like in *Silence of the Lambs*. I suppose governments don't do that, only psychopaths. I could be wrong, though. I think they can be just as bad, except only from nine to five.

It's 9:02. If I'm right, it's only a matter of time before the colonel shows up. Coffee first, maybe, then he'll come in and tell me how completely screwed I am. I deserve it, I guess. I had some superweird dream last night. Freddie Freeman was following me around, shadowing me. Dead Freddie Freeman, of course, all chalky with a big gash on his neck. He walked like an inch behind, whispering in my ear: "You did this to me, Aster." I went everywhere with him. I was back at school with Freddie sitting next to me. I was at the mall, the ice-cream shop, always with Freddie. "You did this to me, Aster." I can hear him now, almost. I wasn't scared of him—that's the weird part—like I got used to having him around. I hope it was the sedative. I don't want to live with Freddie Freeman.

Someone's coming. Here we go. It ain't Bruce Willis, though; it's a boy. A . . . movie boy. A very hot, wavy-blond-quiff, school-captain-star-quarterback-looking boy. The kind that never, *ever* talks to the likes of me. He's a bit older than me. Fifteen, maybe. Big smile, even bigger dimples. Teeth so white you got to wear shades. I used to dream of boys like that. I dreamed I was different, different looking, different everything, the type of girl boys like that would come and talk to. An Amanda. I wanted to be an Amanda so bad. Beckett in *Can't Hardly Wait*. Jones in that old one they keep rerunning on TV.

—Hi! You're Aster, right? I'm Charlie.

—Hi?

—I got you something.

He brought cake. The quarterback brought me cake. I took it. I can't say no to cake, not when it's chocolate with chocolate frosting. Still, this is weird.

—I'm sorry. Who are you?

—Charlie! My dad works here. He said you were alone and I should come and say hi. Happy New Year, by the way!

—That's today?

I guess that explains the cake. It doesn't explain why he's the one bringing it.

—You didn't know? Yeah! It's the millennium!

—Actually, the millennium starts next year. This is just the zeroes.

—Well, happy zeroes, then. Is that a Game Boy Color? What games do you have? Whoa. Mortal Kombat. Who do you play? I like Sub-Zero.

—Kitana.

—Nice! Listen, my dad said they want you to take an MRI this morning, but I could come back later if you want.

—What's an MRI?

—It's like a big camera. It doesn't hurt; you'll see. It's just really loud.

—Are you sure?

—Positive. Hey, you know what? There's a TV and a Nintendo 64 in the break room upstairs. No one ever uses it. I can ask my dad to bring it down here. We could play games together. I know we just met, but it could be fun. What do you think?

What do I think? Do I want to play Nintendo with the quarterback? I could. I could spend my days getting poked and probed—oh, this is good cake—but I'd get to come back to my fake room every night. I could change the posters. I could play video games with boy jock here. Maybe he really likes me. Maybe he doesn't, but give it enough time . . . *I'd* like him, that's for sure. Not because of anything he'd say or do; he'd be the only person I ever talk to. Budding romance in Washington. I'd be his *secret* girlfriend 'cause no one would know I exist. He *could* have another one, a real one. I wouldn't mind much. It'd be weird at first, but it doesn't take long before anything becomes normal. "You'll feel at home with us in no time; you'll see." It's true. I could get used to this. I was getting used to being on the run and writing on people's shirts. I could be happy here even. It's not like I had much of a social life to begin with. Pa said most things are attitude. Mowing the lawn sucks because you think it does, but if you tell yourself it's a race or a game it becomes fun. I just need to tell myself, This, right here . . . This is my life.

Or . . .

—Charlie?

—Yes?

—Don't show your face here again or I'm going to hurt you.

19

The Mess We're In

—That wasn't very nice, Aster.

He's laughing. He was more serious the first time, *Fifth Element* Bruce Willis, *Armageddon* even. He's going for funny *Die Hard* now, but it ain't working. It's the uniform, I think. Or the bolt lock on the door, or the pink concrete. I'm kind of mad. I was scared before—I'm still scared—but I'm mad now.

—I'm sorry, sir, but . . .

—You can say it.

—With . . . all due respect, what ain't nice is kidnapping people at the mall. What ain't nice is keeping someone locked up in a basement and sending some *boy* to pretend he likes me. . . . *That* ain't nice. You don't lie to people like that. You just don't. Does his dad really work here? I bet he doesn't. I bet his name ain't even Charlie. . . .

—The truth, then. He's a child actor, not a really good one it seems. We thought it would be easier for you to accept your new life if information came from someone closer to your age, someone you trust. That was a mistake and I'm sorry. That said, I have no idea what his name is. It could very well be Charlie. For what it's worth, he said he thought you were "kind of cool" before you threatened him, so it wasn't *all* lies.

—Was he telling the truth about the MRI thing? He said it wouldn't hurt.

—It doesn't. It's a noninvasive procedure. Think of it as taking pictures. All you need to do is remain still.

—Like a photo booth?

—I suppose so, except horizontal, and more noisy.

—Okay. . . . I thought you were going to draw my blood. I don't like needles.

—We don't need blood for now. I wanted some of your blood because there's something very special about it—you remember what I said about your test results when we first met? Since then, however, we found a dead woman on the highway in Texas and her blood test came back the same as yours. *Identical!* Unbelievable, isn't it?

—Does that mean you don't need me anymore?

—Oh, but we do. We're going to take a look at your brain first; that's what the MRI is for. We'll take pictures and see if there is anything unique about it. We can't get them from the woman on the highway because, well, because she's dead and missing a large portion of her head. I'm sorry; that's a very morbid conversation to have on your first day. What I meant to say is there's no need to worry about the procedures, Aster. No one here is going to hurt you. What I really need *now* is for you to answer some questions. Can you do that?

—I don't know anything, sir.

—Are you certain? Because when we interviewed the people who were present on the highway, they all said that the FBI agents who were present that night had just removed a young girl, a young woman, from a car. We showed them your picture in a photo array—you know what a photo array is, I'm sure—and they all picked the same picture. Can you guess whose it was?

Crud.

—Who? Me?

—Yes, you. So you see how we might find it intriguing that two people with the same *very unique* blood anomaly—something we've never ever seen before—just *happened* to be in the same place at the same time. Did I mention that woman had two hearts? I know. That's very strange, to put it mildly.

I'm so busted. I don't know how that could be, because I ain't done anything. I was *there,* that's all. I shouldn't get in trouble just for being someplace. Also, I don't like this two-hearts thing at all. Gigantic mass murderer with a gun is one thing, but two hearts means Samael was telling the truth about that woman and if he was telling the truth about her then there's a good chance he was telling the truth about everything and if he was telling the truth about everything, then . . . Whoa. Deep breath. One thing at a time.

—I don't know what to say, sir. I don't have two hearts.

—No, Aster, you don't.

—Then you see, we're not the same at all! I told you. I don't know—

—There is also the murder case we need to discuss.

Freddie Freeman. I knew it. I watched enough cop shows to know how the rest of this conversation goes. It starts with personal questions, what food I like, what sports I'm playing. Then he asks what I was doing that night and I say the wrong thing, like, "I was at soccer practice," but I already said I don't like soccer. Next thing you know I'm wearing an orange jumpsuit, standing in front of a judge who hates me. "In the cruel and ruthless murder of one Freddie Freeman, whom everyone loved, especially that little girl in the picture, how do you plea?" Guilty, Your Honor. "You did this to me, Aster." Yes, Freddie. I know. . . . But how do *they* know? Sam called the cops, but even if they found the body, I don't think anyone saw me there that night. Maybe there were cameras. Maybe they found a hair, weird DNA floating around. It's like *Gattaca;* they know everything. All I can do now is pretend I have no idea what he's talking about, but he won't believe me. No one will.

—I'm sorry, sir. What murder?

That was *so* not convincing.

—You were there, Aster. . . . Nine FBI agents were murdered in cold blood that night. These people had families; some had children your age. Their wives, their husbands, their *children* deserve some answers, don't you think?

Phew. For a minute there I thought— Wait. Are they blaming me for this? Do they think I was in cahoots with that woman just because we both have weird blood? Like, she's eight foot tall and she has two hearts. This is bad, like *bad* bad. I ain't no lawyer, but I'm pretty sure killing nine federal agents gets you the chair, or nine billion years in jail. I can't lie about this. They know I was there. I might as well come clean. Pa always said I should just tell the truth if I got in trouble. Plus this is like the one thing I can tell the truth about.

—I don't know what to tell you. That lady came out of nowhere and she started shooting. That's all I know; I swear! I never seen her before, not ever!

—Did she say anything before she started shooting?

—No, sir. After.

—What did she say?

—I'm not sure. It sounded like . . . "*Shyeh-shyeh-shyeh.*"

—What?

—That's what she said! "*Shyeh-shyeh . . . shyeh,*" or something. I thought she was Russian.

—That doesn't sound Russian at all.

—If you say so. I don't speak Russian.

20

Daughter

I found it prudent to relocate after what happened to Aster. I thought Las Vegas was busy enough, but the authorities managed to track her within days. As for the hunters, I still have no idea how they found me, or Aster, in the first place. I can only assume there is something unique about us they can detect from a distance, a relatively short distance, I would guess, or they would have caught up to me by now. Nonetheless, I should probably not stay in one place for more than a week. Chicago seemed like a logical choice, far from my last location and large enough to hide in should my kind succeed in tracking my movements. I got a room downtown at the Palmer House, dropped my bags, and went back out to familiarize myself with the surroundings. The bellboy suggested I take a walking tour with the Architecture Foundation. I never had an interest in architecture—I never had much interest in anything now that I think about it—but I returned from the outing holding two intimidatingly large books on the subject. I was rather pleased with myself. It felt really . . . human. I sat in bed and opened one of the books. I was exactly thirty-nine words in when I reached not one, but two, conclusions. One: I have no interest in architecture whatsoever. Two: this was a blatant, not particularly subconscious attempt at ignoring the obvious.

I find myself . . . troubled—not by the constant threat of death, but from unwanted reminiscence. As much as I found her irritating, I had, it would seem, grown accustomed to Aster's presence in the short time we had been together. I daresay I developed a certain fondness for her. That realization came as both a surprise and an encumbrance. I never owned a pet—Father would never allow it—but I have heard people describe the emptiness of their home when their cat passed away and I feel an ounce of empathy I did not feel before. Perhaps it is the cat I am missing. Perhaps not. It and I were not of like mind. It escaped the moment I returned to our room after Aster was captured and I lacked the motivation to chase after it. I think it was a relief for both of us, and there are worse places to be a stray than the Bellagio.

Last night, I went for tapas at Cafe Iberico. The dining room was half-empty, but the bar at the entrance was crowded. Young girls, whose attempts at appearing twenty-one were failing miserably despite their elaborate, if painfully misguided, fashion efforts. I should have been amused, at best indifferent, but I was overcome by a bout of what I can only describe as fatherly outrage. Get back home and put something decent on. I did not speak the words, obviously, but the mere fact of thinking them was more than enough to make me feel weak and irreparably old. A night of drinking ensued. I found myself at a bar aptly called the Empty Bottle. Despite the blinding headache I experienced this morning, I took some pride in seeing no cuts or bruises on my hands. The pride would not last. I went to the store for Advil and, upon my return, found I had bought a quart of milk for Aster's cereal without realizing it. I got angry and threw the milk against the wall. I left a sizable tip on the nightstand, but it might be best to move to a new hotel before the carpet starts to smell.

It was, in hindsight, less than heroic to abandon Aster as I did. I wish I could say I thought the matter over and came to a rational decision, but I did not. *Had* I thought the matter over, I would have done the same—heroism would have helped no one in this case—but it's clear that self-preservation still ranks higher than the more noble qualities I strive to acquire. Nonetheless, I am . . . perturbed, and I fear I will remain this way for the foreseeable future. I cannot help but think that the unpleasantness I might have endured for letting her die, even the guilt of killing her myself, would have dissipated faster. I took pride in "doing the right thing" at the time, but in doing so I have only raised the bar to unattainable heights. Simply not killing her doesn't come close to "doing the right thing" anymore. As for a rescue . . .

I know who the colonel keeping Aster is. I know where he lives, where he works. It took me all of two hours to find out. Call it curiosity, something to pass the time. Knowing all of that changes nothing, of course. He has no family, no wife or children he could be bargained with. I am in no position to judge, but I found that rather sad, for him and for me. It would have been so easy. Kill the wife to show resolve, use the child as currency for Aster's release. An hour of my time and I could move on. But no. And if Aster is not returned to me, then I would have to fetch her myself, in a *military* hospital. Even if I were to lose my mind and attempt a rescue, I would not make it very far. While a violent death would certainly alleviate whatever guilt I'm experiencing, it would help Aster none. If she is to escape her captors, it would seem she will have to do it herself. That is perhaps what I find most difficult. There is nothing I can do to stop feeling this way, except to wait. It is infuriating, not to mention profoundly demeaning, to leave my mental well-being in the hands of a clueless child.

It is not impossible for her to find a way out on her own. Plenty of ordinary people have escaped from places designed to keep them in, and Aster is anything but ordinary. It is hard to imagine the little girl I met taking on the U.S. military on her own, but she is more than that. She is her mother and her mother's mother. They have outsmarted the likes of me for three thousand years. We have hunted them, killed more of them than I can count, and yet they endured. With any luck, so shall Aster. She is more resourceful than she knows, more than I know, I hope. I *am* hopeful, and angry at her for holding my thoughts hostage.

I *could,* in theory, move closer to where she's being held and monitor her situation, but I doubt it would provide the relief I'm seeking. To go from trying not to think about her to purposely thinking about her all the time seems rather counterproductive. My first instinct was right; what I need is something to keep my mind occupied. I should give Frank Lloyd Wright another try.

21

Trouble

—There is something I need to tell you, Aster. We found your mother.

Whoa. I was expecting another MRI. I don't trust MRIs. It doesn't hurt, like he said, but that thing is like a jackhammer! *TOKOTOKOTOK! BRRRRRRRRR!* It has to be doing more than taking pictures to make that much noise. The colonel looked kind of dark this morning—more *Sixth Sense*—so I thought maybe they had to draw blood. He keeps saying he doesn't need blood "for now," and I know "for now" won't last forever. I imagined a lot of things—Pa said I have a vivid imagination—but not this. "We found your mother." Well, I wasn't looking for her, so whatever. Put her back where you found her. I'd rather give blood than talk to my mother. I can do *tokotokotok* again. They can leave me in there all day if they want to. I just—

—I don't want to see her.

—What? Your mother died years ago, Aster. I assumed— You had no way of knowing; I'm . . . terribly sorry.

I guess I sort of knew. The thought *did* cross my mind when Samael said he *owed* her. Plus why else would he have her journal? That's not something you just hand out to people, like, "Hey! Here's my most intimate thoughts!" I didn't wanna know. I could have asked. I could have asked any time, but I didn't, because . . . because I needed her alive. If she's alive, then . . . then she can be mean, and selfish. She can be sad, more sad than I am. If she's dead . . . It ain't that easy to hate the dead.

—It's okay, sir. I didn't know her.

—She was a very resourceful woman. We had a hard time finding her. We knew she lived near Gulfport when you were adopted, about an hour from where you were raised, actually, but we found no trace of her anywhere in Mississippi— She didn't file taxes. She . . . didn't have a driver's license—so we expanded the search. We started looking at Jane Does. Do you—

—I know what it means.

—That's how we found her. She died only two days after Child Services picked you up. She unloaded a handgun right in the middle of Grand Central Station in New York City before she was killed. She didn't have ID, no prints on file, so they disposed of her body.

Whoa. I knew *Grandma* was badass, my great-grandma. I just— I didn't want my mother to be like them. I wanted her to be the ugly duckling, except not a swan, just ugly. I mean, why would a mother get rid of her child if there ain't nothing wrong with her? She wouldn't! If there was nothing wrong with her, then it means it was my fault; it means there's something wrong with *me*. What if— He said they found no trace of her. And they were just looking at random dead people. Maybe it ain't my mother they found.

—How do you know it was her?

—We can't be one hundred percent certain—the body was cremated—but the woman at Grand Central Station looked exactly like you. I saw the video and, believe me, the resemblance is eerie. We also found someone who matched her description escaping arrest in California some twenty-five years ago. Two women—one was about your age—broke out of a jail cell and walked right out of a police station. Again, no record, no pictures anywhere. But we showed the New York footage to some of the officers who were there and they recognized her immediately. I could be wrong, but I bet your mother worked very hard to stay out of sight, which begs the question. Why? Why would anyone go to such lengths to make sure they couldn't be found?

—I don't know, sir.

—I do. I can think of a few reasons. If there was something about her she didn't want anyone to find out, for example. If she'd committed a crime. *Or*—and that's the explanation I'm leaning towards—if someone was trying to kill her. Most people go into hiding because they're afraid.

— . . .

He knows about the Tracker. What else does he know? There's the blood thing, but does he think it's, like, this-might-cure-cancer weird, or is he all, "Your ancestors were not of this world, Aster"? Does he know Grandma was a spy? He wouldn't tell me if he did. I know how this works. It's like when I got in trouble at school and they sent me to the principal's office. He asked a bunch of questions he already knew the answers to just to see if I was lying. He's gonna ask me about the lady on the highway again, I know.

—What do you know about your father, Aster? Your biological father.

Or not. I don't know what to say to *that*. I never even thought about him. That's kind of weird, I guess, but he wasn't there. I didn't have a father before Pa.

—Nothing, sir. I never even met him.

At least, I don't think I did.

—We don't know anything about him either. We couldn't find anything. No name, no picture. We spoke to classmates of the young woman in California and they can't recall a boyfriend. There was an older boy named Brett, but he died in a car crash a month after they escaped that police station. Your mother was careful not to leave bread crumbs, but it's as if your father never existed. He's a ghost. Either he was even better at hiding than your mother was, or he wasn't there at all.

—Why are you telling me this? What does it matter who my father is?

—I told you that your blood is different from most people's. The . . . the genetic code inside your cells is very unique.

—My DNA?

—Yes. Your DNA. It uses a slightly different alphabet than everyone else. The scientists here don't know how it would interact with DNA from someone . . .

—Normal.

—Let's say "less unique." They don't know if it's compatible.

—I'm sorry, sir. You mean, like . . . sex?

—Procreation, yes. You see, if it's *not* compatible, then we can assume that both your mother and father were like you. If it is—if your mother could have had a child with anyone—then one of your parents could be "less unique." Your mother, perhaps.

He thinks my mom was the normal one? I guess he doesn't know everything. Or he's just messing with me.

—Why my mother?

—Well, as I said, we think she was hiding from someone. I believe that's why she left you behind.

—Because she was scared?

—Yes, and rightly so. I believe she left because she was afraid of whoever ended up killing her in New York.

—And you think it could be my father?!

Wow. A minute ago I didn't have a biological father; now he might have killed my mom. I guess I don't know anything either, just what Samael told me. This is so confusing. I don't know who's telling the truth. I don't trust Bruce Willis one bit, but I can't tell if he's lying or not.

—All I can say is that the only person we've met with the same genetics as yours killed several people at your father's reception and at the hospital where you were being treated, and shot *nine* federal agents in cold blood trying to get to you. It would make sense for your mother to be afraid of someone like that. Either way, I was hoping you could identify the person who killed her in New York.

Wait, what?

—You know who killed my mother?

—We have a picture of him from video surveillance. Do you mind taking a look at it?

22

Girl, You'll Be a Woman Soon

Did Samael kill her? It was one of them for sure, but they all look the same. I can't tell if it was him, his brother, his nephew, his long-lost cousin twice removed. Samael said he *owed* her. That's a weird thing to say about someone you killed. Like, "Thanks for dying! I owe you one!" Then again, Samael can get pretty weird. I'm so confused now.

My great-grandmother said they're all the same. She called them monsters, depraved animals or something. They cut my great-grandma's ear off; that's really sick. If they're all the same, then it doesn't really matter which one did it. Why would Sam save me, though? It could just be blind luck he was there. No, that doesn't make sense. Maybe there's something in it for him. They all want something from me. Bruce Willis wants my blood. The giant killer lady wants . . . *shyeh-shyeh,* whatever that is. Samael, I don't know what he wants. It could just be money, I have a crap ton of it. That's why people do bad things most of the time. Like *Heat,* and *Point Break,* and *Die Hard.* Even the third one when Hans Gruber's brother says he wants vengeance, but what he really wants is gold from the Federal Reserve. Money would make sense, except Samael didn't need me for it. He was already spending my money when we met, which isn't nice, but it also means that ain't why he helped me. It doesn't really make a difference what he wants; he hung me out to dry like everyone else when things went south.

I thought he was different. I wanted him to be different because if they're all the same, then I really have no one. Samael might be a Tracker, but he was the only person who wasn't chasing me. He's the only one who helped, and he shot that woman. He let me keep Londo even if it's pretty obvious he hates cats. Also, if they're all the same, then *we're* all the same and I'm basically my mother. I don't want to be my mother. She gave up on me just like everyone else.

So it's either my one friend killed my mom and I'm all alone or he didn't, but he bailed on me and I'm all alone. Either way, I ain't leaving this place. Not ever. No one knows I'm here. I don't think anyone would care if they did. I could disappear forever and it wouldn't make any difference. I might as well not even exist— Wait, who said that? Oh yeah, *Breakfast Club*. The point is I'm all alone. It's just m— Someone's here. I hear them fiddling with the lock.

Oh great, Bruce Willis. The guard who brought breakfast said today's Sunday. I thought there'd be no test, because of God.

—Hello, Aster.

—Hi, sir. Do you need another MRI?

—No, I . . . I had it all prepared in my head and now it seems I don't know where to start. I just came out of a meeting with the science staff and we discussed the possibility of . . .

—Of what?

— . . . This is awkward. I'm sorry I have to bring this up, Aster, but the doctors here tell me they think you're . . . able to conceive.

—I don't understand.

—They say you can get pregnant.

—I never been with anyone if that's what you're asking.

—No, I realize that. This is going to sound strange. I—*They* would like to . . . fertilize one of your eggs and let it grow for a brief period.

What's he talking about, fertilize one of my eggs? Like how?

—Sir, I don't— Are you talking about a baby? I don't want a baby.

—Of course not! This would all happen in a lab. All you—

—Tell them no. Tell them I don't want to do it.

—What I was about to say is they would grow the embryo in the lab for a brief period. There would be no inconvenience to you, except for a few minutes during the procedure. There obviously would not be a baby, as you say. The embryo would be terminated as soon as it reached—

—I said no, sir. You can draw some blood if you have to, but this is—

—I'm afraid this is not entirely up to you. There is more at stake here than you realize. A few minutes of mild discomfort . . .

They want to make more of me. I seen this before, in that bad *Alien* movie with Winona Ryder. They mixed dead Ripley's blood with the alien's and then she finds this room with all the failed experiments. There's Ripleys everywhere. Ripleys with two heads, three arms. That's it. I'm dead Ripley now. That's what Samael warned me about, not a pink room with Backstreet Boys posters. "He will dissect you when he's done." Brain fluid. Bone marrow. They keep me sedated and feed me through a tube while distorted versions of me watch me through their glass jars. . . . I'm getting dizzy now.

> . . . must bear in mind . . . some of the greatest discoveries in our history . . . small price to pay . . .

I need to get out of here. I don't know what to say, what to do, but I need to leave. NOW.

> . . . minimally intrusive . . . thousands of women every day . . .

I'll fight my way out if I have to. Samael said I knew how. He said all I had to do is listen, but I never seen anything clearly except that one time when he put a knife through my hand. Maybe if I pinch myself. Harder. HARDER.

> . . . I realize this must seem like a lot for someone your age . . .
>
> . . . you'd be helping in ways . . .

It ain't working! It doesn't matter. I'm leaving one way or another. If they shoot me, so be it. I won't care if I'm dead and they won't be able to do what they want. I just— WHY CAN'T I SEE ANYTHING! Maybe pinching ain't enough. I don't care *what* it takes; all I know is I'm leaving. My head will explode if I stay here another minute.

— . . .

—Do you understand why this is important, Aster?

Do I under—I do. He doesn't see me as human anymore. None of them do. They'll paint the walls pink and give me a speech because this is easier if I cooperate. It's convenient, but they don't care one way or another. I'm a pet. They think they can do whatever they want with me. They can't. I know what I have to do.

—I understand, sir. I understand perfectly.

—Good. I knew you would. You're a smart girl. I told them that; I did. Someone will come and get you soon.

—Before you go—

—Don't tell me. More batteries for your Game Boy.

—No, sir. I just wanted to borrow your pen for a second.

23

Spybreak![1]

Tick.

Tick.

Tick.

Tick.

Blood drips from the hole in my hand. It hits the floor like a sledgehammer and echoes off the walls. I have superhearing now. Like Spider-Man. I don't like Spider-Man. Like *Daredevil,* except I can see. I see all sorts of things. Tiny cracks in the concrete, small specks of blood whoever mopped the floor couldn't reach. Bad things happened down here, even before they found me.

I'm walking now, I think. This is weird. I'm . . . me, but I'm not. But I am? One second I'm in control; the other I'm in the passenger seat. It ain't like a movie, not exactly, more like playing Quake on the computer. I feel . . . less. There's *tons* of emotions, but they're distant, muffled. Like, I know I'm scared; I just . . . don't care much. I'm scared; I'm nervous; my hand hurts. I'm also *really* angry. Not from now—well, that too—but

1. Author's cut: If the *Lola rennt* (*Run Lola Run*) soundtrack is available for streaming in your area, replace this song in the playlist with "Running 2."

this is *old* anger. Grandma's anger or something. There's a lot of it.

—This is pointless, Aster. You can't escape. It doesn't matter what you do to me, the soldiers are coming, and they will shoot us both before they let you leave this place.

He means it. He's scared. It ain't his handgun pushing against his back. He was calm as a june bug not two seconds ago. I can hear his heartbeat now. The hair on his neck is standing up, like a mob of meerkats. He's in that moment when you're going downhill on your bike and the handlebar starts shaking. You ain't crashed yet, but you know it's coming. Skin scraping on the asphalt. Hurt so bad you try to wish it away 'cause you can't fathom getting up. He knows someone's about to die. He just ain't sure who it is.

Here they come. I see a young soldier, rifle aimed at my head. I see the shaving cut on his neck; a drop of cold sweat goes pink when it runs through it. I can *smell* him. He's scared shitless. I watch him fall to the floor when I shoot him in the knee. Wriggle like a worm, squeal like a pig. This one's no killer. Even now he's glad he didn't have to shoot. I take three steps forward and push the colonel a—

Wait. Did I shoot that soldier already, or is it all in my head?

Tak

Oh, now I shot him. I take three steps forward. Push the colonel away. I grab the soldier's rifle from the floor with my bloody hand. I'll tuck the colonel's handgun in my pants. I need one hand free for the elev—

Bright red arrow. The elevator button is lit. I must have pressed it without thinking. I know there's more than one soldier down here. I wonder where the rest of them are. I— Whoa. I'm holding the muzzle of someone's rifle. He came through the door behind me. I pull on the rifle and the soldier comes with it.

Tak

I shoot him in the foot with my other hand. He lets go of his weapon. More soldiers coming down the corridor. The colonel might be right and they'll shoot us both when it comes down to it, but they'll hesitate. I won't. I squeeze the trigger and mow through them all while they do. Fish in a barrel. They have nowhere to hide, nowhere to run but into each other. I shoot the dead again when the living hide behind them. I— Wait. That was three seconds ago. I'm in the elevator now, alone.

. . .

. . .

I hate Zamfir.

Ding. Whoa. That's some change of scenery. There's a real hospital above the secret place. One. Doctors, nurses, patients. Families. Flower delivery guy dropped his carnations when he saw the guns. Two. I only been to a hospital once before all this, but it looked just like this one. Three. The walls are hospital color. Suspended ceiling. Fluorescent lights. Everyone looks hospital tired or hospital sad. I get it—the best anyone can do in a place like this is not die. Four armed men between me and the door. Army.

Soldiers ain't made for crowded places. Folks moving in all directions. It's like a camera. Things get out of focus when someone walks right in front of it. They've got the call by now. They'll need to spot me, then wait until they get a clear shot. It's a public place, so it's not like they can just plow through the crowd. But I can. Wait! What? No! I can't—

Ding. The door opens again. People turn like before. Flower delivery guy drops his carnations again. I seen all this! Or not, maybe I'm seeing it now, only I'm not sure what now is anymo— Screams. Loud, gut-wrenching screams, the kind that makes no difference between children and adults. There's people lying everywhere, holding their wounds, holding someone else's wounds. Flower guy has a hole in his head. The floor's all blood and chrysanthemums. The walls, well, they all look like a Jackson Pollock. Did I do this?

Am I about to?

I can't . . . breathe. I'm gasping for air, staring at the gory scene in front of me. I don't know if it's guilt or panic, or . . . or someone's hands wrapped around my neck. I'm at the entrance. I don't know how long I been here, but this soldier has me by the throat. I'm staring up at him, my feet dangling six inches from the floor. There's so much hate in his eyes. He won't hate me for long. Either I'll pass out or— The colonel's handgun is in my pants. I feel the little grooves on the grip. Squeeze. Squeeze. Squeeze. I touch the floor again. The hospital doors keep moving back and forth, waiting for the dead soldier's head to move out of the way.

A car brakes hard in front. It's Samael. He's— I'm back where I was a moment ago, staring out the glass doors. There's no one, no car. Maybe it hasn't happened yet. I step outside. There. A car brakes hard in front. It's Samael.

—Get in!

—Did I do this?

—Get in the car *now*!

—Please. Did I kill them all?

The colonel comes out of the elevator. He grabs a rifle from the soldier next to him. He's going to shoot. I—I don't do nothing 'cause I been gone two seconds already. The tail end of Sam's car slams against a mailbox as we turn the corner. I hear gunshots behind us, but none of them hit. I— Whoa. I'm back in front of the hospital.

—Get in the car now!

What do I say again? Oh yes, I know.

—Please. Did I kill them all?

24

Porcelain

—I'm sorry, Aster. I didn't mean to wake you.

—It's okay. I wasn't sleeping.

I'm afraid to close my eyes. All I see is dead people on the hospital floor, flower guy with a hole in his head. The eerie part is none of them feel real, not like Freddie Freeman does. Freddie shows up in my dreams. I can touch him. I feel the fat under his skin when I press my finger on it. I see the sweat on his upper lip. He leaves footmarks on the carpet and I watch them disappear when he's gone. He's real. Sometimes I can hear him when I'm awake. The bodies in the hospital all feel like mannequins. Plastic. It's like I'm looking at them on TV. I was there, but I wasn't.

—You should really get some rest.

—I can't. You never answered my question.

—What question?

—Did I kill all these people?

I don't know why I'm asking. I watched myself do it, sort of. It was my hands on the gun, my finger on the trigger. I don't want it to be true, but that doesn't change anything. There's no big mystery here. It was me. I did it.

—You did well, Aster.

I did what? That scared me just then. Deep chills. He *means* it. He thinks that was the right thing to do. Respect your elders, don't get in a car with strangers, shoot a whole bunch of people at the hospital. Now I know Grandma's journal ain't just a story. Sure, maybe he ain't like his dad and brothers, but he's definitely the Tracker. I don't know why I'm surprised. I seen these folks on TV, they buy a lion as a pet and then they act surprised when they get mauled 'cause the lion was all cuddly the day before. You can't take the lion out of a lion. I knew that. Maybe it's not him I'm scared of. Maybe I got the chills because I agree with him. He said it, but I thought it first. I did good.

—I don't even know how I did it. There were, like, a dozen soldiers there, with guns and all. I cut through them, like . . .

—You were trapped, caged like an animal. You did what you had to do to get out.

What I had to do. That's true, I guess. That's what I had to do to get out. I just don't know if I *had* to get out. If someone is going to kill you and you kill them, it's called self-defense. It's . . . justifiable. But what if they're not going to kill you? What if they just lock you in a pink room and make you do things you don't want to do? Is it still okay? And what if it's not just that person you have to kill but a whole bunch of people who never did anything to you? It wasn't self-defense lying on the hospital floor. It wasn't . . . Okay. I could have stayed. I'd still be alive. *They*'d still be alive if I done what they asked. I might could have, if they'd stuck to needles and brain scans, but put a *baby* inside me? Why'd he have to say that? I don't know if it's worth killing all those people over, but I don't feel as bad as maybe I should. That's what I feel the most bad about, not feeling bad enough. Also—

—The thing is, I didn't do nothing. Not really. I just watched! Well, no. I was there, but . . . It's really hard to explain!

—You did what any of us would have done.

Any of *us*. He means I did what *he* would have done. Like what he did on the highway. *BAM!* In the face. He thinks we're the same. My grandmother would disagree, but after what I just did, it's hard to argue with him. Don't mess with the Kibsu. It sounded really cool when it was Grandma killing Nazis. Now that it's me shooting florists, I ain't so sure anymore.

—We're . . . *bad*, aren't we, sir?

—I find it best not to think of it in absolute categories.

—Are the police going to think of it in absolute categories?

— . . . For what it's worth, Aster, I am sorry this happened to you.

I'm in so much trouble. There's like a billion witnesses. Whoever ain't dead saw me do it. I bet it's on camera. Regular cameras, even! Not the top-secret basement ones no one's supposed to know about.

—I'm screwed, aren't I? There's no going back now.

—It was never an option, but what exactly were you hoping to go back to?

—I don't know. Something other than jail? I thought they might put me back in that basement if they caught me, but now . . . I'll be on the six o'clock news, the front page of every newspaper, every— Wait. We just watched the news. It wasn't on TV just then. How come they ain't talking about it? You'd think—

—I suspect they prefer to control the narrative. They already have every level of law enforcement looking for you. There is no need to complicate things by letting everyone else know who you are.

—So . . . what do we do now?

—That is a good question. I have to assume they have me on camera, so neither of us will be safe in public anymore. It shames me to say I have also lost track of the hunters.

—What does that mean?

—It means we have to run.

—From . . . everyone? We could stop them, sir. The hunters, giant people, I mean. There's only three of them.

—There'll be more. Hundreds. Thousands. Millions. There's no stopping them. The best we can do now is hide and enjoy what little time we have. Treat every day as if it were your last, Aster, because it may very well be.

I don't want it to be my last. That's like the one thing I know for sure. I don't know why, my life sucks and people want to kill me, but I really, *really* want to live now. I never given it much thought before, no more than anyone else, I guess. There's this thing inside me. It's awoken and it's telling me to live. Survive at all costs, like Grandma said.

—Sir?

—What?

—I want to read my mother's journal.

25

Godless

I thought I wasn't good enough. More trouble than I was worth. Like an old, ugly cat that throws up everywhere until one day you've had enough and drop it off at the SPCA. You know they'll probably put it down, but you tell yourself they won't. They'll find a home for it, someone who'll love the ugly cat more than you did. It's for the best, really. Or maybe you just leave the door open and let it fend for itself at the Bellagio. "It will be happier there than on the road with us, Aster." Poor Londo. I thought moms were supposed to love their children. And if you love your child and still get rid of it, there must be something terribly wrong with her. That's what I liked most about Pa. He picked the ugly cat at the SPCA. He *chose* me. It didn't matter where I lived or how much money we had. I felt wanted with him and that's the only thing that mattered.

I thought it was my fault. I thought . . . I thought if I'd been someone else, someone better, she'd have kept me. I thought if I'd been like Nicole . . . That's why I pushed her, I think. Plenty of kids messed with me before she did, but she rubbed me the wrong way more than anyone. Little Goody Two-Shoes. Everyone liked her. I mean *everyone*. Jocks, nerds, teachers. Nicole was the ultimate Amanda. I was watching her smile her way through life and I thought my mom would have liked her more than me. I just—I couldn't. I felt bad when she broke her wrist—I did, a little—but I kinda hoped that one small thing would make her whole life take a turn for the worse. Like in *Run Lola Run* when Lola trips over the guy with the dog and then she finds out her father's not her father and Manni gets hit by an ambulance. I didn't wish anyone dead, nothing that bad, but maybe she couldn't be a world-famous ballet star or something.

I thought I was broken. It never occurred to me, not one bit, that my mother felt the same way. She thought *she* wasn't good enough, that she didn't measure up. She did, though, measure up. She *wasn't* broken. She couldn't see it sometimes, but she was just like *her* mom. Lola was badass too. Like the other Lola, but this time she leaps over the guy with the dog and she saves Manni. She was superbrave. Then she lost *her* mom and she was . . . lost, like I was. Having to save the world *and* being a mom while bad guys are chasing after you, that's a lot to handle. I only have the bad guys to deal with and I'm tired all the time.

She wrote a ton of things about me. Apparently, I didn't talk, like at all. She said I didn't trust her. For real, she thought it was her fault. I was a *baby*, Mom? Maybe I was, you know, *shy*, or busy thinking of ways to reach the top of the kitchen table. Babies are weird, though. I can relate. One time I went to work with Pa 'cause I was suspended at school and this lady I never met asked me to watch her little girl for a bit. Longest five minutes of my life. I don't like babies. They make you feel dumb, even if *they're* the ones who can't do anything. Like, you can tell they ain't happy about something, but they won't tell you what. You keep scratching your head, but they're *babies*! They don't know what's what, so maybe they want to fly, or they're peeved 'cause you ain't turning into a dog like they want you to.

It's kind of funny. I thought I was a bad child and Mom thought she failed at being a mom. That part's mostly sad, but maybe we really *are* the same person. And maybe I was a bad child and she wasn't the bestest mom, but now I know she cared. She wanted to protect me, from . . . from the pressure, from the Tracker, from going through what she gone through. She wanted to give me something. A gift from her to me. She wanted me to have a regular life. She thought that was bigger than anything—me getting that life—bigger than being together, bigger than *her* life. That's why she gave me up. She had one shot at the Tracker and she took it, for me. It didn't turn out good, but she tried. She thought it was worth it. That *I* was worth it.

My mom fought a *wolf*. Like, a real wolf, with her bare hands. Waaaargh! Take that, you . . . furry beast! I read about people who got *mauled* by a wolf, people killed by a wolf, lots of people running from wolves, but I never seen anyone who won. I bet they talk about it all the time in wolf town, that time Barnaby got its ass whooped by a wild human. That was my mom, y'all! Oh, and she found the sphere! The gizmo the Tracker's been after for like a million years. She used it to lure him in and . . . I guess this whole mess we're in is sort of her fault. *Our* fault, maybe, since she did all that because of me. I should probably be mad at her still. She tried her best, but pretty much everything she did turned out bad, like she might have triggered the end of the world. That's not nothing. Whatever, I don't care. Right now there's only one thing that matters.

I ain't broken and my mother didn't hate me.

Oh, and my real name's Catherine. It ain't a bad name. There's Katharine Hepburn, though it's spelled different. Catherine the Great. I mean, it says "great" right in her name. I can sort of see myself as a Catherine. Yeaaaah. . . . Thanks, but no thanks. I been an Aster longer. That's the name Pa gave me and I ain't taking that from him. I am Aster, daughter of Lola, and I ain't broken.

ENTR'ACTE

Like Father, like Daughter

The child had done nothing wrong, Tereshiin thought. She was a mistake, but she was someone else's mistake and it seemed cruel to make her pay for things she did not do. She was also the closest thing to an ally Tereshiin could hope for, and he chose to raise Kish as his own. He taught her about *their* ways, *their* planet. He spoke of cities so tall they reached above the clouds, flying chariots and ships that sailed between the stars. Tereshiin's words were like magic spells, each reshaping Kish's world in complicated ways. The sun was now a star, the Earth a giant ball zipping through endless space. The universe Tereshiin offered her was so much greater than the one she knew. Even her place in it was better. She wore a necklace that could save the world, *a* world among many. She could turn this boring planet into the magical realm in Tereshiin's stories. All she had to do was train and do as he asked. Though she was never presented with a choice, she was eager to help, intoxicated with purpose and the promise of adventure.

It is incredibly easy to turn a child into a killer. They look to adults to help refine the broad strokes their emotions are painting. Take away their toy and their first instinct is violence, until someone teaches them to dial down their response. All one has to do is not teach them and harness their most primal instincts instead. Before she turned nine, Kish had fought two men at once and prevailed. Tereshiin had offered her a long sword to give her more reach, but the child always preferred short blades. Swords were like stilts for the arms, she said, useful at long range but all the clumsier in close quarters. There was something more intimate, more real, about a knife wound. People kept fighting after losing a limb—the will to live is strong—but one well-placed stab under the arm brought resignation to the bravest of men.

For six years, they traveled together, to every town, every outpost within reach of where part of her mother's ship was found. They combed the desert for almost a full year, cursing the wind for erasing a day's work in minutes. The citadel of Arbailu kept coming in sight, a periodical reminder of the short life Kish left behind. But time, like the wind, erases everything, and the vivid memories that woke a child up at night were now blurry sketches in the young woman's mind. Her mother's face was the only image that remained clear. Calm water, a polished blade, all the things that reflect light conspired to make sure she could never forget.

The past did not matter, not hers anyway. Tereshiin said it a thousand times. He was her father now. Her mother was a lunatic at best, a traitor at worst. She'd abandoned her mission, traded the fate of an entire world for a life as dull as it was meaningless. Kish was hovering between anger and shame on the road to Arrapha when their horses reared, startled by four men blocking the path ahead.

Tereshiin was first on the ground. He didn't wait for the thieves to make demands and decapitated the first man within reach without warning.

Kish got off the chariot and took her knives out of their sheaths behind her back. She let the fever take control as she'd always done and ran to the closest enemy, a brutish-looking man wearing cheap leather armor. Kish never stopped running. She slid between the man's legs and jammed her blade inside his pelvis. When the man fell to his knees, she kicked him forward to retrieve her weapon and saw a shadow merging into hers from behind. She swung her other blade without looking. She knew she hit a neck just from the feel and turned to face the man she'd just killed. Only the man wasn't a man, not yet. He was tall for his age but still very much a boy. He was perhaps a year older than Kish, two at most. Both of them seemed to recognize each other's youth at once. The boy looked at her with a mix of sadness, puzzlement, but also something tender. Kish felt it too, though she could not have put it in words. Some form of kinship, compassion for another child growing up in a violent world.

Tereshiin wiped his sword on a dead man's tunic and told Kish it was time to leave. "In a minute," she said. She and the boy stared at each other, time slowing down with the boy's breathing until it stood completely still. Kish felt a sudden rage against the man she'd killed first, thinking he was the boy's father.

She kneeled on the man's chest and stabbed at his eyes. She removed his nose, plowed through what skin was left on his face until Tereshiin grabbed her from behind and stood her up. Kish turned to look at him, her face covered in blood.

—He was just a boy, Father! He didn't have to die like this!

—It doesn't matter, Kish. Now come before someone sees us.

Kish climbed on the chariot and didn't speak for the rest of the day. She kept thinking about what Tereshiin said, unsure of what he meant by "it." What didn't matter? That he was a boy? That his father brought him? That he died? That *she* was the one who killed him? Every one of these things mattered to her. She wanted to know which ones shouldn't. She wondered what was wrong with her for not knowing when it all seemed so clear to her father. Kish was angry at herself, but that anger soon turned towards the dead boy. She hated him for upsetting her like this, for making her feel weak.

She would never tell her father, but she thought about that boy almost every day. Every time they entered a new town, saw new people on the road, she hoped someone would speak of a missing boy and his father. She wanted, needed, to know his name. She needed to know why he did not matter.

ACT IV

26

Flower

2001

Gotcha.

I'm getting better. I didn't think I'd ever catch one when I started. The little buggers are *fast*! You have to aim where the fish will be, not where it's at. I get it now. That took long enough—we been here almost a year—but I finally got the gist of it. You have to think like a fish. Visualize, *be* the fish. I'd make a pretty good fish, I think, except I can't swim. I can . . . *not drown*, that's about it. I'm more like a cat than a fish now that I think about it. I wish we had a cat. The closest thing we have are geckos and I hate them. They're cute and all, but they poop on the walls and they wake me up at night. How can something so small make that much noise? It's like a pterodactyl lives in our house. I miss Londo. He didn't scream at 3:00 A.M. and he pooped in a box.

I miss people too sometimes, not anyone in particular, people in general. There ain't many here. This is where Filipinos go when they want to get away from everything. They're right. Everything ain't here. It's just a few nice folks and a whole lot of pretty. It's great, but I wish there were a mall. Just a tiny one, with good jeans and a game store. Running water would be good too. There is, but like half the time, and pretty much never when I want a shower. I think it knows. Ooooh, Aster's coming! Turn it off! Turn it off!

We ain't spending a dime, which is funny because I have all

this money. Samael says it draws attention and we don't want that. Sure. There ain't a lot we could spend it on, anyway. I been wearing the same five T-shirts for a year. They're super worn-out, but I look kinda tough, so it's cool. I think I look like Sarah Connor with sunglasses on. Samael says I don't but he's wrong. Maybe he's thinking of the first movie. All in all, we have a pretty good life. Just about everything we need is right here. We're like Tom Hanks in *Castaway*, but with a nice little house—on stilts! Our house has legs—that's cool—and a big TV. And chicken. I ain't seen the movie yet, but I'm pretty sure Tom Hanks doesn't have chicken.

I pick up urchins at low tide in the morning. Sam eats them. I can't do urchins for breakfast, but I like looking for them. That's usually when Andre shows up. He's like a hundred years old, but he takes his boat here every morning looking for *wakwak*. We have a lot of *wakwak*. They're gross, long worms that gobble sand in one end, take out the nutrients, and expel the "clean" sand out the other. The butt end is always on top, so we can see little mounds of sand poo growing everywhere. Andre digs the worms out and cooks them. Our whole beach is sand poo, so he visits a lot. We usually help him dig—he's *really* like a hundred years old—and he gives us rice, or *wakwak*, *after* he's prepared it. It ain't bad when Andre makes it. I think he marinates them first? Whatever he does, we tried cooking it ourselves once and . . . Ew gawd, I can't even.

Anyway. We're safe. Safe as can be, I guess. Sam thinks the giant people need to be close by to find us and Bruce Willis will look everywhere else before he gets to this place. Even if they caught up to us, it's 360 degrees of escape route. We have a boat and we can sort of defend ourselves. We don't have an underground weapons cache with rocket launchers like Sarah Connor, but we have a shotgun, and I can throw things now.

Axe, knife. I can hit a target at forty feet with that fishing spear. I ain't eight foot tall, but I'm a little buff. I wouldn't mess with me if I were . . . not me.

Sam's a lot better at training me. Or maybe I'm better at being trained. Anyway, we're pretty efficient. We get bored in the afternoon, so we're both pretty eager to train every day. We throw things. We push things . . . hit things. I *really* like throwing stuff. I never would have guessed. My mother said she liked playing darts, so maybe I get it from her. I think I like the sounds more than anything. There's something supersatisfying about a knife blade splitting a coconut, oh, and that deep *thunk* the axe makes when it bites into a tree. I love that. Sure, *wakwak* and exploding coconuts ain't exactly how I saw my life at thirteen, but hey. Lemons, lemonade.

I'm not sure how much Sam likes it here. I never hear him complain or anything, except for the heat. He can't stand the sun, but he seems fine with our routine. He does his thing; I do mine. We train for an hour or two, talk for a few minutes at dinner, and that's it. He goes into his room and I don't see him till morning. He sure likes his alone time. I don't even know what he does in there. The TV's out here and I ain't seen him with a book, like, ever. Yoga, maybe. Yeah, I think not. . . . He says he doesn't want to bother me 'cause I sleep on the couch, but he goes to bed at like *eight*. He ain't the social type. He might have been, before—I don't know—but not now. The man has *issues*.

I think he feels responsible. He sort of is, but it's not *all* his fault. Fifty percent, maybe? Okay, 60, but he didn't send the colonel after me and he didn't kill all those soldiers at the hospital. He— It doesn't matter whose fault it is, even. It is what it is. I just wish we were doing something about it. "Enjoy what little time we have." That's hard to do when the whole world's against us and there might be a bazillion giant people on their way. Also,

I don't want a little time. I want *a lot* of time without Bruce Willis and the FBI and eight-foot-tall aliens. I want my life back. I don't want to just sit here and watch the world burn, but Samael won't lift a finger to stop it.

Well, I will. I have a plan.

27

Hard to Explain

Ewww. My hands are all—bweaaaah. My armpits are at it too. It ain't that hot today; I guess I'm more nervous than I thought. I got this plan, and it's a good plan, but I need Samael's help and I ain't superconfident he'll go along with it. The problem is he really has to because I can't do this on my own and there's really no use in having a plan if you can't do the things in it. I thought I maybe could, for like a minute, but then the minute was over and I'm still thirteen and I can't even buy a plane ticket to get out of here. I have to beg Samael to buy beer, so it's pretty clear I ain't saving the world by myself. Being a teenager really sucks sometimes.

I just have to convince him, except that's not really my thing, convincing people. Even Pa said I'd never have a career in sales, and he was always superencouraging. Like "you can do anything you set your mind to, Aster, except sales." He was right. I think something's either a good idea or it's a bad idea. How you present it shouldn't make a difference if it's a good idea. Right? Right. It's like cake. Many things are like cake but this in particular. No one would buy bad cake because the box is pretty. You only care about the cake. Unless maybe it's a gift, but, really, who gives cake as a gift? Crud. I *am* nervous. Oh good, Samael's coming. Might as well get this over with.

—Hi.

—Hi? When did we start saluting each other?

—I . . .

—Never mind. Is something the matter, Aster?

—No, sir. Well, yes.

—Can you please stop calling me sir? We have lived together for over a year.

—Yes, s—I mean, Samael. I— You know how, like, the world might end and everyone is out to get us?

—I am aware of our situation, yes.

—I been thinking about it and how we could maybe make things better and now I have a plan.

—You have a plan to stop the end of the world.

Is he making fun of me?

—I . . . Yes.

—Is that all?

—Well, no, there's more. Not a lot more, but I'd like to not be a fugitive for the rest of my life, and— Do you mind if I just read it? I wrote it down. I think better when I write things down.

— . . .

Right. I'm not sure he wants to hear it, but no one ever says: "Yes, I mind," when someone says: "Do you mind?" Focus, Aster. Focus.

—Okay. . . . It's not a hundred percent finished but—

—Please, read.

—Right. Here we go. Number one: get rid of the bad guys.

—To which bad guys are you referring?

—The supertall alien ones.

—I told you several times, Aster. More will be coming. Hundreds, thousands, millions perhaps. You and I cannot "get rid" of them all. No one can.

—I know. That's number two: make it so more *ain't* coming.

— . . .

—You ain't gonna say anything?

—I thought I would let you finish.

—Oh. . . . Thank you! Number three: stop the colonel from chasing us.

— . . .

—Sir . . .

—Yes.

—Say something!

—I was waiting for you to describe how you plan to accomplish all this.

—Oh. Yeah. Well, number one is easy. I mean it's not *easy*, but it's not complicated. We do—you know—like you did last time. *Bam!* In the face!

—I . . . Please continue. I am rather curious about what comes next.

I think that was sarcasm.

—Okay, number two is a little bit more complicated.

—I would imagine.

That was *definitely* sarcasm.

—These folks that are coming, like you said, they're coming because of the signal that sphere sends. The one my mom found.

—Sent, past tense. It is no longer transmitting. And I can only assume that is the reason for their presence.

—But it could transmit again, right? You can turn it back on.

—Yes.

— . . . How? Is it a button?

—Does your plan require a button?

—No. I was just curious. Anyway. I was watching *The Hunt for Red October* again—we really need new DVDs—and at one point the Russian submarine fires a torpedo at the *Red October* and it's going to hit, but then the *Dallas*—that's the American submarine—moves in and the torpedo follows it and then the guy says: "RELEASE COUNTERMEASURES! EMERGENCY BLOW!" and they release these flares and the submarine shoots *out of the water* and the torpedo gets confused and goes chasing after something else. And I thought: we could do that! RELEASE COUNTERMEASURES! We take the sphere, turn it on again, and send it away.

—Away from where?

—Here! The planet. We could send it into space, with a rocket.

—I admire your enthusiasm, Aster, but as far as I know, rockets only fly a few hundred miles. I fail to see how sending the sphere from Earth to . . . almost Earth would be helpful. Besides, they already know where the signal came from.

—Not just a rocket. We could put it on a *probe*. My grandmother figured out when the planets were all lined up and then they sent the Voyager probes in the seventies. They went pretty far, and that was twenty-five years ago. I'm sure they got something much better by now. And I know there ain't no guarantee, but there's a chance they'll go chasing after it, even if it's just for a while. It's worth a shot, ain't it?

—I—

—Come on! Do you have a better idea?

—I do not, but that doesn't mean— What about number three? How do you plan on getting the authorities off our back?

—I'm still working on that one.

—Of course.

—I said it wasn't a hundred percent! And two out of three ain't bad. I'll think of something while we take care of one and two; I promise.

He thinks this is stupid. It *is* stupid. No, it's not. It ain't perfect, but it's a plan. It needs some fleshing out, sure. Most plans do, don't they? I ain't seen lots of plans before, but they can't all be superdetailed right from the start.

—I appreciate the time and effort you spent on this, Aster, but—

—No but! Please, Sss-Samael? I gotta do *something*. We been here a whole year, like you said. I can't spend the rest of my life waiting for the world to end, or for the Army to show up on our beach like it's D-Day. That's not a life. And I could be wrong, sir, but I don't think you want to stay here either. You can't stand the heat and I *know* you don't like *wakwak* that much. So please. *Please*, say yes.

—. . .

28

Come on Let's Go

I was looking forward to our time here. I thought nature and a simple lifestyle would help relieve some of my stress and anxiety. I even started meditation, with some success. I have, thus far, been able to control my violent instincts and I have hurt no one in over a year. No blackouts, not a single drunken brawl. I take some of the credit, but in all fairness this island makes it relatively easy. There is no one *to* kill or fight with. Except for Aster. Aster is always there.

I do, from time to time, see my hands wrapped around her little neck and ask myself whether it is real or my imagination running wild. I am ashamed, *profoundly* ashamed, by the thought, but part of me would enjoy watching the life drain out of her. Perhaps fortunately, she is small and somewhat innocent. The emotional payout for strangling her would obviously pale in comparison to the guilt, but that does not make her any less annoying.

Our home is smaller than the hotel room we lived in. It's . . . quaint. Aster loves that the house is on stilts. I do not share her fascination with it, though it does keep wildlife from entering uninvited. The view is nothing short of spectacular and we are on the beach the moment we step off the porch—*gallery*, as Aster calls it. Our home would make the envy of most vacationers. I suppose it does, for the handful who venture in our cove. But we are not vacationing. We live here, the two of us, in this small, claustrophobic cubbyhole. And Aster . . . Aster is in the living room, and in the kitchen because it's the same room. She is there when I wake up, when I eat, when I go to sleep. She chews loudly, walks loudly. And she talks, incessantly. She asks questions about her mother. She asks if I was involved in her death, whether I saw it happen. I have tried my best to stick to the truth—it is much easier to remember than fabrication, but I cannot be honest about everything. The lies accumulate, everywhere. They take up space in a house already too small and make Aster's presence more irritating than I thought possible. She . . . *forces* me to lie, to be a lesser man. I want to take that shame and shove it down her bony little throat until— There it is again.

It is, I tell myself, not *entirely* her fault. I am in dire need of a hobby. There is nothing to do here. There is no challenge, no thrill. There is no compelling reason for me to get up in the morning, to breathe in, and out, and in, and out again. I *have* suppressed my violent urges. I have done so well, in fact, I seem to have suppressed the rest of me. Self-care was first to go. I do not care to bathe, or brush my teeth. Each feels like a project, something to be pondered and prepared. I do it only to maintain a semblance of normalcy, and to delay the losses that are bound to follow. Self-respect, self-esteem, self . . . everything.

And so while I believe Aster's "plan" is absurd, bound to fail, and utterly useless, it is with a deep enthusiasm and a renewed sense of purpose that I have agreed to join her. I doubt she can find a way to send the sphere to outer space. I doubt it would change anything. Frankly, I could not care less. I know nothing can be done about the trove of people chasing her, but we *can* kill the hunters who landed. I can.

I realize the endeavor presents a certain ethical conundrum. On the one hand, these people are my kind. Aside from Aster, they are in fact the *only ones* of my kind. On the other, I do want to kill them. I *really* want to kill them. I can do it guilt-free—they *are* a danger to everyone—but there is a refreshing simplicity to my kind's violent nature, a clarity of thought I am only beginning to notice. Humans kill. They exploit, treat each other like cattle. They are capable of destruction on such scale I sometimes find it difficult to believe our people could do worse. Yet they do all that while claiming the moral high ground. They cling to the idea that it was their smarts and ingenuity that made them the dominant species, as if killing was not the mother of human invention. I have no doubt *Homo sapiens* would have bludgeoned every rival with rocks had it not been able to create better things to kill with. I am astonished by the mental gymnastics these people will perform to reconcile their actions with their idea of good. For all their faults, my kind kills more honestly. That is precisely why I have to stop them, but it is also the reason I am eager to do so. This changes nothing, of course—I will kill them all—but I find it philosophically interesting.

I can hardly contain myself. I do not wish the end of humankind and there is objectively some form of altruism in what I am about to do. That said, I also long for the danger, the exhilaration, the unbridled fury. I feel more alive now than I have in years. I have prey.

I am, to a manageable extent, morally disoriented by the situation. That is only normal. What brought me here in the first place is the desire to stop killing, to better myself based on my understanding of good and evil. I realize now that the act of killing itself was never the problem; it was the *guilt* I experienced for killing selfishly. It did not help that I murdered my own family, but that is beside the point here. I felt guilt for wanting to kill then and feel none for wanting the same now. One could thus reasonably conclude that what I do does not matter at all. I know that killing my brothers was wrong, but *at the time* I truly felt saving my mother was worth it. It would be foolish of me to dismiss the possibility that I am wrong again, but the odds of being right seem greater when trying to save an entire world.

Either way, I truly hope I get to use a knife, to plunge it in their throat and turn until their head dangles. I wish to hear their spine separate, to feel the blade hurry when there is no bone left to resist. I want to shove my arm inside their chest and rip out their organs one by one. I—

Breathe. . . .

Unfortunately, my prey will have to wait. Our first order of business is to go to China. Aster wants to solicit the help of a longtime friend of her family. I agreed to accompany her. I have no desire to visit China, but one should never look *too* eager when it comes to murder. It is not entirely clear to me if it is Aster or myself I am trying to convince.

29

Make It Happen

It wasn't supposed to be like this. I played it in my head a hundred times and— He was supposed to say yes! "Yes, Aster. It will be my pleasure," with a Chinese accent. Then I smile and I'm superproud because Qian Xuesen likes my plan and he's ridiculously smart and he knows this stuff better than anyone. We drink tea and it's the best tea ever even if I don't like tea and he starts talking about specific impulse and things I don't understand. *That's* how it was supposed to go. "Yes, Aster. It will be my pleasure." Not . . . this.

—Mr. Qian, I—

—Please, let me finish. There is something . . . very unique about you and your family, Aster, and, somehow, the deep connection I felt with your . . . great-grandmother—have I been alive this long?—survived the passage of time, as if my friend's essence was passed on, intact, from one generation to the next. I feel the same bond, the same . . . fellowship, now, with you, as I did so long ago. That is what I feel. What I *know* is there is a child I've never met before sitting in front of me making irrational demands.

—It's not irrational, sir! I just . . . I can't tell you why, only that it's important.

—Why can't you tell me?

—I just . . .

I don't know what I was thinking. Yes, I do. I was thinking this would work because it had to. I was absolutely convinced it would work because if I had doubt— If I had doubt then I'd start thinking about it and I'd realize this idea of mine made no sense at all. I mean, I knew it didn't make a lot of sense, but neither does eight-foot-tall people with two hearts, or my family being "not of this world," or Pa dying, or my cat living at the Bellagio. So *yeah*, I thought I'd meet Qian Xuesen at a teahouse, ask for a rocket *and* a space probe, and the former head of the Chinese space program would say: "Sure. What color do you want it?"

I got off the plane with my pretend father and it felt like I'd won already. I could see it. I only seen Beijing, but China doesn't look like China, at all. There's all kinds of modern buildings, big roads, like *big* big. Neon signs and pink Ferraris. I seen two already! Oh, and there's malls, lots of malls. It's *so* not the China I imagined. What Beijing *does* look like is a place where you can get a rocket and a probe. For real. I could smell success, and roasted pork, and sweet . . . something, hoisin sauce, and sesame oil. Samael and I ate twice already. I ate a ton because every corner of this city smells like food and maybe I was celebrating getting my own spaceship a little. HOW? How did I convince myself this could *possibly* end well? Also, why didn't Samael stop me? I'll turn fourteen next week, so I'm not a child anymore, but this is, like, a lot. He's old and he's kind of responsible for me. He's supposed to know these things. "I'm sorry to tell you, Aster, but asking for rockets from complete strangers is not acceptable behavior." How hard would that have been?

Xuesen doesn't even know me! He met my mom for like five minutes and that was twenty years ago. Now here I am asking for favors. It ain't like I'm asking to borrow his car either. I *did* say I could pay for the rocket, but that made me sound even crazier. I don't even know if he'd have done it for my great-grandma, the one he actually knew. *They* were close. They wrote to each other for decades and I could tell how much he mattered to her when she talked about him. I get a sense *she* thought he would have helped. I'm not sure how, but I get these . . . supervague thoughts that ain't really mine, or at least they don't feel like they're mine. I'm probably wrong about that too, or I'm not, but *she* was wrong about him.

It doesn't matter anyway. My great-grandma ain't the one asking him. I am. Why would he help me? Why would he risk everything, maybe his life, to help a kid—technically, a teenager, but still—he never met. Even if he *did* want to help, which he doesn't, he's *super*retired. He'd have to ask people to do things. *Other* people who never even heard of my great-grandma. Maybe they owe him a favor, but I don't think you can owe anyone a rocket. He might have to involve the whole Chinese space program, and the government, and . . . I suppose what I'm asking is a little bit like treason, if you're a glass-half-empty kind of person. They may have pink Ferraris, but I bet just talking about this could land him in jail for what's left of his life. They could be listening in right now, with spy satellites or bugged teacups. Half the people here could be party members keeping tabs on him. I don't know what a party member is supposed to look like, but that guy over there keeps staring at me. Crud, they all are.

I'm scared all of a sudden. Like, *super*scared. I was sure he'd say yes, and I can't really handle him saying no, but now I realize it doesn't have to stop at no. I'm a fugitive blabbering nonsense to one of the most important people in China. He can have me arrested. Like, in a minute that whole room could be filled with soldiers and then I'll be tortured in a basement somewhere because they'll think I'm a spy. My *whole family* were spies! And if I don't die in a Chinese jail cell, they'll hand me to Bruce Willis when I have no fingers left so I can rot in some *other* basement. The worst part is I can't explain anything, to anyone, ever.

Crud. I'm in *wayyyyy* over my head. I bit more than I can chew and now it's all going to get real and I can't do anything and I think I'm having a panic attack.

—Aster, are you okay?

—I . . . can't . . . br—

It's like someone's tightening a vice grip around my neck. What did I do last time? I did the flower thing, but I can't breathe at all, plus I passed out anyway. I think—I think I'm gonna pass out.

30

La Valse D'amélie

Music. Happy, romantic music, like in those movies where the man walks through a crowd and asks the woman to dance. Like *Dirty Dancing* at the end, except superold when people dressed like vampires all the time. Or maybe the ballroom scene in *Beauty and the Beast.* Yes, that's it. I'll dream about that. The room looks endless. Shining gold everywhere. The music is playing. I'm all alone, until I ain't and Belle takes my hand. We're dancing. Let's start from the beginning again. I . . . can't. I think the music's real. I was dreaming, but now, not so much. I was . . . Crud. I was having a panic attack, in China.

Soft light. It's nighttime, I think. Late evening, maybe. I'm on a couch. Parallel little green lines six inches from my nose. I like corduroy. It looks like a bamboo forest. Where am I? I'm not sure I want to know. This blanket is supersoft. I think I'll just stay here and wait for the world to end.

—Oh, you're awake. Are you feeling better, Aster? You gave us quite a scare.

That's Qian Xuesen. I guess I need to turn around now. Yep. Qian Xuesen, in a big old fancy chair. There's a gigantic bookshelf behind him that makes him even more intimidating. He's like a million years old and wise and all. That was intimidating enough. I don't know what I'm supposed to say now. Hi? No, that's weird.

—The music. It was beautiful. Was that you playing?

—I do sit at the piano every day and pretend I know how to play, but if what you heard can be described as beautiful, it must have been my wife, Ms. Jiang. This is Ast— Where is she? She'll be back.

—Yes, sir. I— Where am I?

Please let it not be his home.

—This is my home. I thought you would rather wake up here than in a hospital answering questions from the authorities. I hope I did not presume wrong.

Oh crud. I sputter nonsense at him, then start hyperventilating, making a scene in a public place, and he has to drag me to his house and watch me drool on his couch for God knows how long. I am just . . . mortified. I don't really care about saving the world, now. I just want him to stop staring at me. I want to go home, wherever that is.

—No, sir. Very, very not wrong. I—I better leave now. I'm sorry for everything, sir. I'm terribly sorry. Thank you for everything.

—Please! Sit. You need to rest.

—I'm okay. I really need to find my friend, the man I was with.

—He's in the kitchen, enjoying my wife's soup. I can bring you a bowl if you want, but first I would like you to answer one question.

— . . .

—Earlier, you asked for my help in finding a rocket and a deep space probe. Those are—even *you* will recognize—rather unusual demands from a teenager, or anyone for that matter. You must have known I would ask questions, but you never told me why you require those things, only that it was important. I will ask you again, Aster. Why are you so interested in sending out a probe?

—I can't tell you, sir. I'm sorry.

—And why is that?

—'Cause it ain't something you tell people. You'll think I lost my mind.

—Please. I promise I will not judge you.

Fine. It's not like I have any pride left to wound. He probably thinks I'm nuts already.

—Okay. . . . Here we go. The U.S. Army is chasing me because they think I'm an alien—or *half* alien; they're not sure. My ancestors—Mom, Grandma, my great-grandma; you met her—they didn't know what they were either, but it don't matter because right now there might be some really bad aliens on their way here and I'm doing my best to lure them away, but for that I need to send something as far from Earth as possible and I don't know how and that's why I'm here. . . . I forgot to breathe. I know this sounds completely crazy and you never seen me before in your life, but my family trusted you more than anyone and I had nowhere else to go. So . . . I came to you.

— . . .

—And now I'll leave! Like I said, sir. I'm terribly sorry.

—Did you know that in two years my country will launch its first manned space flight? We will not be first in space, obviously. I doubt many will talk about it outside China, and yet we have spent years preparing for this, spared no expense. Do you know why we do it, Aster? Do you know why people build rockets? Part of it is simply the challenge. We strive to go to space for the same reason people climb Everest. Because it is there. Part of it is curiosity, scientific or otherwise. There is so much out there we do not know, so much more than this world, hidden behind a black curtain. The unknown is tantalizing, like a locked room no one is allowed to enter. But I believe there is another reason, one we never talk about. Humans, every single one of us, are profoundly lonely. We fill that void as best we can, with relationships, with art, with God, but it is never truly filled. When we look up to the night sky, when we stare at the stars, each of us, deep down, wishes we were not alone in this vast and cold universe.

— . . . Okay.

—I am simply wondering, now, if my connection with your great-grandmother was not, subconsciously perhaps, an attempt at filling this existential hole. . . . But back to the matter at hand. Even if I wanted to help, I am no more in a position to do so than I was earlier today. I sincerely doubt any one individual is. That said, you suggested sending something into outer space. Is it very large?

—No, sir. It's a ball, about yay big.

—Am I, then, correct in saying that you do not *really* need a deep space probe, merely that this object be attached to one?

—Euh, yes, sir. It doesn't have to be *my* rocket either.

—In that case, I would suggest you take a look at NASA's New Frontiers Program competition. Two of the projects considered are missions to Pluto if I'm not mistaken. Either would be suitable for your purpose, I believe, as both missions are set to continue beyond our solar system. Both projects are also reasonably advanced. If one were to be selected, it could foreseeably launch within the next . . . four to six years.

—THAT LONG? Sir?

—These things take time, Aster, and the planets need to be in certain positions. To start a new project now would take decades. . . . All of this, of course, is academic if the project is not selected in the end. If I were in your position, I would approach one of the teams—my choice would be the one at the Applied Physics Laboratory—and offer them whatever assistance they need.

—Okay. I can do that. . . . Where is that, sir? The Applied Physics . . . thing?

—At Johns Hopkins University, in Baltimore.

—Baltimore?

—Correct. May I suggest, given your age, that your . . . *companion* be the one to approach them? I fear that most people, unfortunately, would be reluctant to listen to a young person such as yourself. I would also refrain from telling them what you just told me.

—Of course! Thank you! Thank you so much for believing me!

—I never said I believed you. It will take some time for me to digest what you said and I may never know whether I believe you or not. With that in mind, there seems to be little risk in helping you succeed, and a potentially high reward if what you mentioned is true. If you wanted to bring something *to* Earth, I would object on the grounds that it could be dangerous. I do not see the danger in removing something *from* it.

—That makes sense. Now I know what I have to do! This can work, right? I'm so excited. Thank you! Thank you! Thank you! I'd hug you if I could. Can I? Hug you?

—Yes, you can.

31

Blue Monday

I stepped on the remnants of a club sandwich this morning. I didn't notice the half-eaten fry stuck between my toes and left a trail of ketchup all over the tan carpet. Aster said it looks like the scene of a very small crime. There are some advantages to the nomadic life our predicament imposes, but living out of hotels is evidently not conducive to a healthy lifestyle. Our room looks like it belongs to an unruly rock star. Aster leaves her dirty clothes everywhere—on the couch, on the television stand—and the floor is a minefield of unfinished plates we've learned to navigate. I've hung the "do not disturb" sign on the door. I am ashamed to let even the cleaning staff see what we've become. Mother taught me to pick up after myself and I have, to this day, taken pride in keeping a tidy home. She would be unimpressed. Regardless, it took all the willpower I had to remove the fry from between my toes, so we'll probably just move.

I am . . . under the weather. I've had the same headache—perhaps it's a migraine; I do not know the difference—for more than a week. I don't have the energy for anything, even the most mundane tasks. If I didn't know better, I'd say I was coming down with something. None of us has ever fallen ill before, so I assume—"hope" is a better word—that this will pass quickly. Perhaps it has to do with this charade I have been putting on. I am pretending to be the son of a recluse plutocrat fulfilling his father's dying wish by sending his ashes to outer space. To that ridiculous end, I am sponsoring a mission to Pluto and beyond to the tune of $5 million. I thought writing a check would be sufficient—moving Aster's money around is hard enough as it is; fake signatures for fictitious people running pretend foundations—but to impersonate someone with this preposterous backstory . . . The chitchat, the handshakes. We were never comfortable with social niceties. They insisted we meet, then talk, and talk, and meet. "Yes, Mr. Anderson. Thank you so much, Mr. Anderson." I do not know why Aster insisted I call myself Thomas Anderson, only that I had to. My brothers and I were named after angels; an apostle's name seemed appropriate, but I cannot quite picture myself as a Thomas. John, perhaps. Matthew. Yes, Matthew.

The scientists were all very courteous and professional, charming as far as scientists can be. I thought about killing them the entire time, but I can hardly blame them for it. I blame my current indisposition. And Aster.

I feel . . . misled. I agreed to Aster's plan because the only part of it that seemed remotely feasible was the one where I get to hunt again. I assumed, wrongly, that the hunt would come first. "Step one. Get rid of the bad people." That *is* what she said. There were other steps, I realize, but it is clear to me that the numbering implied priority. One should come before two. Anything else is illogical. Thus far, I have traveled around the world and shook hands with half the world's scientific community. I barely had time to *look* for my prey and even that is a tedious, vapid process. I am no closer to a kill than I was on our island, but this is not our island. This is Baltimore. This is Beijing. This is . . . too many people.

I am seldom left alone. There are people everywhere, crowding every street, elbowing each other at bars and cafés. There is always someone within arm's reach and I so desperately want my arm to reach. And grab at their throat. And stab at their neck. I take no pride in it, but I can deny my genetics for only so long. Those who came before me, all of them, got to enjoy the hunt until they died or retired. I strive to better myself, and indeed I have, but the wheels are already in motion. I *will* hunt. To wait for it only to indulge a child's astronomical pipe dream is cruel and unusual, not to mention profoundly demeaning.

I have, of course, said nothing. It would mean admitting to Aster that I only agreed to help her with her space project because I thought it would never happen. I was certain our trip to China would nip this in the proverbial bud and that we could move on to better things upon our return. That meeting was, alas, not the reality check I hoped it would be. I continue to believe that no sane person would think this was even remotely possible. Whether I'm right or wrong is somewhat irrelevant. I only want to hunt.

I clearly underestimated Aster's motivation and her ability to rally others to her cause. I don't know why. She has, to some extent, rallied me to it. It pains me to admit it, but I have come to seek her approval. It's not so much that I like her—she can be incredibly annoying—but to see myself in a positive light through someone else's eyes is highly validating, and something I haven't experienced since childhood. Though it is at times immensely frustrating, I am increasingly aware that the role of father figure I've come to play in Aster's life brings me pride and satisfaction I could hardly find elsewhere.

And in her defense, Aster is not stopping me from hunting; she's the one who suggested it. She is . . . excited about this silly space endeavor, but she too wants to fight. Her training, though incomplete, has awoken a part of her she did not know existed and now the beast wants to be fed. I will not let her kill my prey, of course. They are mine, and she still lacks the necessary control to rein in those newly found instincts. She would slaughter everyone in sight if let loose during her fevers.

I made a promise and I intend to keep it. I only hope I get to hunt soon. Whatever attachment I have for the girl will soon be dwarfed by my violent appetites. I am reasonably confident I can stop myself from hurting her, but if this drags on, I will undoubtedly feel compelled to leave her behind. I pray it doesn't come to that, for she would not survive very long if left to her own devices.

32

Bang

Whoa. Too much math. I thought rocket science was cool—it sort of is—but it's all equations and now my brain's turned to mush.

—Samael? Can we go to the movies tonight? . . . I know you don't like to, but I want to see *Donnie Darko* or *Mulholland Drive* and both are rated R, so . . . I mean, they'll probably just let me in, but if they don't I'll have taken the bus all the way there—

—Quiet, Aster. I've found one.

—One what?

—Prey.

33

High and Dry

Samael found one of the giant bad people. Well, he found a newspaper article on AltaVista. A very tall man completely destroyed a police car after beating down the two policemen who tried to arrest him. No pictures, but how many gigantic people with superhuman strength can there be? It seemed like a good bet anyway, so we hopped on a plane and boom! Berlin. I can't believe we're here already. Beijing took forever—I couldn't feel my butt for a week—but Europe is superclose as far as continents go. I watched *one* movie after we ate. Just one! They had *Amélie*. Whoa, that was good, and subtitles are great on a plane because you can't hear a thing with the cheap headphones they give you. There wasn't enough time for another—they stop the movie like a hundred times when you get close to landing—so I read maybe a hundred pages of *Life of Pi*. I bought it at the airport because I liked the tiger on the cover. I thought it'd be like *Free Willy* but with a tiger. Nope.

Europe is nice, though. It's different, but not. Every house looks like Dracula could live there, but everything works more or less the same way as home. I don't feel incompetent like I did in China. I could be European! *Guten Tag! Oui! Oui!* I thought there'd be snow, though. No snow. It's just cold. I wish I knew where Grandma grew up. I could visit if I knew, after we've done what we came to do. I'm sure it's changed a lot since then, but it'd be nice to see some of the things she saw. I feel like I know her some already, but this would feel more real.

Also, it would give me something to think about, 'cause I'm a bit nervous right now. . . . Okay, I'm shitting bricks. I ain't over what happened at the hospital and these giant people scare the hell out of me. This is my plan, though, so . . .

—Samael?—See, I didn't say "sir" this time.

—Consider me impressed.

—So, I was thinking and . . . How do we do this? Do we just walk around the city and wait for him to come to us? You said they could detect us somehow.

—No, we do not. I know precisely where to find him.

—You do? Where is he?

—I don't know what he does during the day, but he sleeps at a homeless shelter in the basement of a church in Friedrichshain.

—That's . . . very precise. How do you know all that?

—I have been browsing through German chat rooms on Yahoo looking for anything unusual. I found one dedicated to foreign languages. Most people were simply looking for someone to correspond with in another tongue, but there was someone who identified himself as a priest asking if anyone recognized the language of an "abnormally large man" who barely communicates. He was, I assume, looking for an interpreter. He sounded a few words as examples of the man's speech, which no one recognized.

—Does he say, "*Shyeh-shyeh-shyeh*"?

—Not that I remember.

—Okay, then. When do we leave? I'll be honest, I'm scared a little right now, so maybe I should eat something before we go. I think better on a full stomach, but I also get sleepy sometimes, so—

—There is no need for you to be scared. I will go alone.

—What? You don't want me to come with?

—I do not.

—But sir, Samael, you said—

—What did I say?

— . . . Okay, so you didn't say anything, but you watched me pack and, like, we were on the plane together? I mean, that's why we came here, to fight this guy, right?

—*I* came to kill him. You came because I did not feel comfortable leaving you alone.

—But now you do.

—For an hour or two. You are the last of your kind, Aster. The very last one. I will not risk your life unless it is necessary.

—Why? I mean, you're the last one too!

—I am stronger and better prepared. And I am not. I have a cousin, or at least I think I still do. My father's brother had a child he kept hidden from my family. He would be about my age.

—You never met him?

—No. He does not know what he is. From what little I've learned, he's lived a fairly normal life. I did not wish to take that from him.

—I understand. But I don't have a normal life. I have a super messed-up life, same as you. Besides, what have I been training for this whole time? You spent a whole year teaching me stuff.

—And if one of these hunters ever finds you, you will have a fighting chance. But you are sitting this one out.

—I—

—It is not up for debate.

Sitting it out . . . I didn't do all that so I can sit things out and let him do all the work. That's not why I threw things every day until my arms went numb. I didn't do wax-on-wax-off with him for nothing. I didn't steal cars and . . . I didn't kill Freddie

Freeman so I could—"You killed me for nothing, Aster." Shut up, Freddie!—so I could sit in a hotel while he risks his life. Two against one is better. It's not superfair, but neither is fighting someone half your size. He's gonna get himself killed, I know it. He's gonna die, and then I'll be . . .

—What if something happens to you? What am I supposed to do then?

—Survive, Aster. You're supposed to survive. I will see you when I return.

—You're leaving now?! Wait! Sam—

. . .

It's the second time he leaves me. Mom left me once and she died. If he doesn't come back, I—

How long he been gone? Eight seconds? Hell no, I ain't staying here. He doesn't want me to fight, fine. I ain't sitting on a bed doing nothing while he gets his head ripped off. I . . . I'm going to see Berlin. Berlin's cool. It's *old*. Like, the restaurants here are older than the United States. When they signed the Declaration of Independence, the place across the street was having a two-for-one on sausages. Plus, I seen tons of people my age—well, close to my age. That's it. I'm going out. I'm going to get drunk. I never been drunk, not real drunk. Sam won't let me have more than two beers, but he'll probably be dead in a couple of hours, dismembered or something. I'll be alone. Then I'll probably die. Getting drunk seems like the proper thing to do. I just need to find a bar that'll let me in. How hard could that be? It's Tuesday. I have a big pile of D-marks. That money won't exist a few months from now. I might as well bribe someone with it.

Berlin, here I come.

34

Dead Leaves and the Dirty Ground

[Good morning. I have General Groves on the line for Colonel Veilleux.]

—This is Colonel Veilleux.

[Thank you. I'll put you through.]

— . . .

—Hello?

—Ben? You there?

—Yes, ma'am. How can I—

—It's this damn phone; I never— Hello? Can you hear me?

—I hear you fine, General. What can I do for you?

—I just got a request for reserve troops out of Devens. It's got your name on it.

—Yes, ma'am.

—That's it? "Yes, ma'am"?

—I . . .

—What the fuck do you need fifty HUMINT officers for, Ben?

—We're close, General. Real close, but I need more men. There's too much ground to cover, too many leads. Interrogations alone—

—Stop right there. Don't tell me you're still running around chasing that girl. It's been over a year, Ben. You need to let it go.

—I can't.

—Yes you can. Let the FBI handle it. I have a meeting with the secretary of defense on Monday. I'm sure he'll want to discuss your case. Last thing I need is you running AWOL.

—I thought I'd been cleared.

—Cleared? You pinned all this on a dead guy, which is . . . probably the best you could do, but that just means they won't court-martial. They can still fire your ass. You owe me a report, by the way.

—You've seen my report. You've had it for months.

—Oh, that thing. I threw it out.

—What? But—

—Come on, Ben! You and I go way back, but you've got to give me something more than a blood anomaly if you want my help keeping your command. Unless that kid can fly and shoot lasers out of her eyes, it doesn't explain how she broke out of a secure facility under your watch.

—She killed my men.

—Yes, she did. That's the problem, in case you can't see it. A twelve-year-old girl killed a dozen highly trained soldiers. IN YOUR HOUSE! This is a shit show, Ben, and it's not going away because you said Private Whatever-the-fuck-his-name-was broke security protocols. You need to cut that Samuel Gerard bullshit, get your ass back home, and right that ship of yours before you sink with it.

—Did you show them what I gave you?

—Show who?

—I don't know, SecDef, POTUS.

—NO!

—Why not?

—'Cause if I had, you'd be chock-full of Thorazine by now,

drooling over a straitjacket. "Nonhuman attributes." Did you read it out loud, Ben? It sounded a whole lot like you were talking about little green men.

—What would you call it? I have an eight-foot-tall woman inside a freezer with two hearts and some really messed-up DNA.

—I'm sure lots of people have two hearts.

—No they don't.

—Ben, I'm telling you, as a friend. You don't want to go there. Not with the shit you're in. Besides, you're not even looking for giant people with two hearts. Find me one of them, preferably alive this time; then maybe we can talk. Right now you're chasing your tail trying to catch a fucking teenager.

—She's not—

—She was in middle school, Ben, right before you kidnapped her! A regular kid. Sleepovers and whatnot.

—You saw the footage.

—I did, but since the interesting part's from a lab Congress doesn't know exists, it's not going to help you much, now will it?

—Still, I—

—Hey! I'm talking to you. I've given you a *lot* of leeway and I rarely ask questions because . . . because I don't want to know, but I'm telling you now, Ben. Leave the girl alone.

—No.

—What'd you just say? It's that damn phone again. Sounded like you were refusing a direct order, and I know you wouldn't do that.

—SHE KILLED MY MEN!

—Watch your tone, Colonel.

—You weren't there! She killed them all. She shot them like it was nothing, like . . . like she was popping balloons at the fair.

— . . .

—I'm sorry, ma'am, I—

—Two.

—What?

—I'll give you two intel guys. Off the books. Say they're doing patient surveys or something.

—Two isn't—

—The words you're looking for right now are "thank you" and "General."

—Thank you.

—And you get your butt back to Walter Reed. You got to at least make it *look* like you're doing your job.

—I will.

—Today.

— . . . Yes, ma'am. Right away.

35

Dissolved Girl

I think I'm drunk a little. I had three beers. I never had three beers and they're BIG, supertall beers. They're like a flower vase. Maybe they *are* vases. "Boss, we're out of glasses!" "Just throw the lilies in the garbage and give her the vase. She's American; she won't know the difference." I had no trouble getting in. I didn't even need to bribe the guy with a giant Mohawk. Maybe I look older. No, I don't. I think they were happy to have a third customer.

"You did this to me, Aster. You killed me for nothing."

He won't stop talking. The worst part is I grown used to Freddie Freeman. He ain't much of a conversationalist—conversationist? He says the same thing over and over again—but he keeps me company. The barman here doesn't speak English. This is all wrong, I know. A year ago, I was scared of everything. Now I'm talking to a dead man and I'm angry 'cause Samael won't let me fight giant aliens. What is *wrong* with me? I— My head is spinning a little. I *like* this . . . I think. That's crazy, ain't it? I don't *like* being chased by Bruce Willis, and people trying to kill me. I don't like that. That's . . . bad. But I gotten used to the—what's the word? Bigness. Ha-ha! I am tipsy. Intensity? It's like I'm in a movie. A year ago, I was just a kid with no friends getting suspended from school. Now I have a family of maybe-alien spies, and I'm a fugitive and I have tons of money and I can steal cars and throw things and it's hard to go back to normal after all that. Part of me wants to. *All* of me feels superbad about it. Pa gave up a lot to give me that life I don't really want anymore. My mother *died* so I can have that life. Ingrate! Yeah. *That's* how I feel. Pa got me a bicycle for my birthday one year. Mine was too small and beat up from throwing it down everywhere as if Pa could just buy a new one whenever he wanted to. It was a *nice* bike. Pa had the shop build it for me. Used, but with good parts. *Way better* than a cheap new bike he could have gotten at Walmart, but I didn't like the color. All I saw was the burnt orange and the tiny scratches, and then Pa's face when he realized he gone through all that trouble and I didn't like it. All he wanted was to make me happy and I wasn't happy. Like that. That's how I feel, only a thousand times worse.

But I'm in Berlin. It's okay to enjoy that, right? Pa'd be thrilled if he knew. Not about the beer, but he never been outside the country either. I wish I'd known I had all this money. We could have gone places together. I could have bought him a house, like Ritchie Valens with his mom. We could have gone to the Rib Room in Norleans. I ain't even sure he ever ate there, but that was his definition of fancy, the thing you compare every other thing to. Things we couldn't afford were "like a night at the Rib Room"; the best meals were "as good as the Rib Room."

It's almost ten. I bet Samael's at the church now, waiting for giant bad guy to show up. Maybe he has already. Maybe Samael doesn't have a head anymore. Nooo! Don't think like that. He'll be fine. Where will they fight, though? You can't fight in a church; that's just wrong. Sean Connery said so: "You are safe only on Holy Ground. None of us will violate that rule. It's tradition." They can't fight on Main Street either—Main Straße or whatever it's called. They'd need a dark alley where no one's watching. There could be one right there, I guess. Otherwise they'll have to walk around together looking for a spot. That's awkward. I don't even understand why Samael wants to fight. He could just . . . *BAM!* In the face. He could use one of those sniper rifles and shoot him all the way from the *other Straße*.

I should have gone with him. I could help; I could be bait even. I'm still mad he left me beh—

Oh, the door's opening. A *fourth* customer. HOLY MOLY! It's one of them! It's . . . Cold sweat pouring from everywhere. I feel the blood rushing to my head. *Hot* sweat pouring from everywhere. I'm heating up like a donut in a microwave. Big, giant lady standing in the doorway. I can't quite see her face, this place is emo dark, but she's a lot younger, this one. Leather jacket. Leather pants. Kind of like Arnold in *Terminator* 2 after he takes the clothes of a big guy at a biker bar. How'd she find me? Who cares? I gotta run. I wanted to fight them, but that was before. Now I'm too drunk to fight, and sober enough to know it was a dumb idea to begin with. Run, Aster, run. My mom didn't and she got herself killed. There's nowhere to run *to*, though. There's no door, except for the one I came in, and it's right behind her. Fire code, anyo— Whoa. I'm dizzy.

I smash two beer flower vases against the bar, grab one in each hand. My heartbeat shoots through the roof while I run at her with everything I got. I cross the small dance floor, jump on the pool table, and leap at her, arms first. I smash my hands against her temples. The glasses explode like fireworks, but a chunk of them digs into her br— Wait. Did that happen yet or is it about to? It hasn't. I haven't moved an inch. It's . . . not happening at all.

Come on, brain. Think of something else. I run at her and . . . and I got nothing. Why? It worked at the hospital. It worked when I got my hand stabbed. It worked not five seconds ago! Except it didn't happen for real, but it was working in my head. Why'd my instincts shut down all of a sudden? I even stopped sweating.

I'm in danger! I'm supposed to sweat when I'm in danger, and fight and . . .

Maybe I can talk my way out of this. "Hi! Me, an alien? Oh, you have me confused with someone else." Okay, that's stupid, but it's not like she has my picture in her pocket. Then again, she hasn't stopped staring since she walked in.

I think . . .

I'm pretty sure I'm about to die.

36

Big Time Sensuality

I'm sitting ducks. I have *no* brain. I can't move my arms, or my legs. It's like my whole body's been dipped in concrete. I don't want to die. I *really* don't want to die like this. I feel like a piñata waiting to get smashed. Crud, she's coming. Veeery slooowly. There's a strobe light on the dance floor. She inches forward with each flash, like a stick person in a flip-book. Here she is. I can touch her. Well, I could if I could move my arms. She raises hers, puts one hand on the back of my neck. I pee. She—WHOAAAAA! She kissed me! Half cheek, half lips, like she ain't sure about it. It's oddly gentle, careful, like when you ask for a taste of someone else's ice cream and you don't want to leave spit all over it. Our lips get stuck together. They stretch a little when she moves away. Pop. It's my fault; my mouth's superdry right now. This is so weird.

Wait, she's back at the door. I guess none of it was real. Except her, she's definitely real. Oh. And the pee part. What do I do? I can't just shove a broken glass into her brain *now*. I mean, what if she saw it too? There's no reason she would, but the whole thing felt so . . . She's coming, again. Slow, just like before. The strobe turns on. Flip-book. It's all the same! No, something's different, but I can't put my fing— Oh, I know. I can move. I'm moving. I'm walking towards her. We're both on the dance floor now. Or we're not and she'll reappear by the door in a minute. How do I know what's real?

She takes her jacket off. She— Whitesnake, really? Three-quarter sleeves. She's really into that eighties thing, or she robbed the first store she came across after she landed. It kind of suits her, though. Her hair's lighter than I thought, kind of like mine, but she's got really short bangs. She reminds me of someone. I know; she looks like Laura in *High Fidelity*. Just . . . huge.

We're . . . circling each other. I think that's what we're doing. I'm near the door now. I could make a run for it, but I ain't turning my back to her. Also, I don't *want* to run. I don't know. I could be hallucinating, but I think her shoulders are moving. Yeah, she's dancing, sorta. Our circle is getting smaller. *Holy moly,* she's tall! I can see her face more clearly now. She's *super*young. Older than me, but not *much*. Sixteen, maybe. If they age like us, that is. If they don't . . . well, if they don't, she could be six hundred years old. Honey, I blew up Yoda, but prettier. Are those freckles? Yep. Freckles. Alien freckles. I'm . . . hypnotized a little. She's got gigantic eyes and semi–Brooke Shields eyebrows to match. I guess her eyes are normal size for her head, but from down here they look humongous.

We're superclose now. I can't really see her face anymore, except for her nose holes. I guess she's looking at the top of my head. I don't know what I look like from above. Why do I even care what I look like? I ain't— Well, I *am*, *kinda*, but I'm not flirting with giant alien girl who may or may not be trying to kill me. I mean, I never even been with a regular person. Pa always asked if I had a boyfriend, any chance he got. I think he was waiting to have *the talk*. I told him I wasn't into boys yet. That was sort of true. He wouldn't have understood. Pa loved me, but this would have been a tad harder to swallow than the Sears catalog being canceled and he never got over *that.* Oh God, she's moving her hips now.

And I thought *I* was in good shape. There's half an inch of her showing below her shirt and whooo! She is *ripped.* Xena can go get dressed. It's a good thing we ain't fighting; she could fold me into a paper plane. At least I don't *think* we're fighting. I'm pretty sure. You don't dance with someone and then rip their head off, do you? Samael said they're vicious hunters, but this one doesn't seem so bad. Unless it's a trick. They semiflirt with people and make them self-conscious; then they eat them or something, like Natasha what's-her-name in *Species.* I let it happen 'cause this feels oddly intimate, and unsettling . . . and then there's tentacles coming out of her. Bwaaaargh!

Or not. Call me crazy, but I think she's just as nervous as I am. Even with the music, I could swear I can hear her heart beat, one of them. *Papoom. Papoom.* Maybe it's mine I'm hearing; it's racing like a pig at a sausage factory. AAAH! She raised her arms in the air. She's just dancing, but for a second I thought— Crud! I peed again! I can't do this, whatever this is. I don't really want it to *end,* but . . . I feel like I'm playing with a wild tiger . . . while juggling knives, on a tightrope . . . above an alligator pit. It's a bit much. . . .

The song's over. She's grinning at me. Cute alien girl is grinning at me. And off she goes. Really? Just like that? Now I'm standing in the middle of the room like an idiot and my pants are all wet. I changed my mind. I liked it better before when we were dancing. Oh, she's at the bar. I think she's getting us beer.

37

Eighties Fan

Crud, she's in my bed. OOOOH CRUD. Headache. *Big* headache. And she's in my bed. I thought I might have hallucinated the whole thing. Nope. She's real. Twice my size real, and sort of spooning me. She has to, I guess, 'cause she doesn't fit in beds. But I can see my *pants*. They're on the back of the chair! I'm having a panic attack. I don't remember what happened. Think, Aster, think. I tried to talk to her, but she just kept smiling, and drinking. She dragged me back on the dance floor, and then more beer. We took a cab. Yes, I remember the driver making fun of us. We made it to the hotel. She made a weird gargling sound when we walked in—I don't know why I remember that, but it really made an impression. Then what? I took a shower! Yes, 'cause I was full of pee and that's why my pants are there and when I came out she was sound asleep. Oh. My. God. Nothing happened.

Except for the kissing thing. It was in my head, sure, but maybe it was in *her* head, and if it was in both our heads then it *kind* of happened. And the dancing. It was . . . playful. Like, she was holding back and I was scared shitless. And now her arm's wrapped around me and it's *really* heavy. And she has weird skin. Not that I went out of my way to touch it, but she's holding me like a teddy bear, so. It's soft, just . . . not the regular kind of soft? I don't know what's weird about it. It's thicker maybe? Whatever.

I don't want to think about it anymore. I ain't done anything, but it feels like I done something. I peed in my pants and flirted with an alien. My life's completely messed up. . . . What am I supposed to do now? I don't think I can handle cute alien girl awkwardness, but I can't just leave; this is my room. Plus she's superwarm and it's freezing outside the covers. I'll just stay here all day, I guess, and do nothing.

. . .

I need water, and aspirin, lots of aspirin. That's what I get for trying to keep up with her, I guess. She drinks like a fish and she's twice my size; that means I drank like two fishes.

. . .

My head's itchy. So is my leg; it's getting numb . . . and I think I need to pee. Hell no. I can hold it in. I ain't waking her up. I don't think I can do small talk right now. I don't even think she speaks English.

On the upside, I guess it's safe to say she's not trying to kill me. I imagined them all walking around with a shotgun, tearing through cops like the Terminator. She's pretty well adjusted, if you don't count the Whitesnake shirt. If Sam's right about when they landed, she been here for three years. She must speak *some* German if she bought beer. She had money to *pay* for the beer, so maybe she works someplace. Sure, she could have robbed someone right after she tore him in half, but I think she's employable. I'd hire her. Oh no! She's moving! Noooo! Noooo! Nooo!

—*Het braghah shaht.*

That's . . . not German.

—Hi! . . . I don't think I told you my name last night. I'm Aster.

—*Saa shiinseh shreh.*

—Is that your name? Saa . . . something? You're nodding. Saa what? Just Saa?

—*Hagh shahghasht huh.*

—Huh. I'm sorry, I don't understand.

—*Shahghasht.*

This is gonna be hard. What's she doing? She's . . . squirming. Contorting? Dancing! She's horizontal-dancing!

—Dancing! Yes, we danced.

Big smile. Oh crud, I snorted. She's funny.

—*Shyesecht het?*

Shyeh-shyeh-shyeh I know this one! That's what the giant lady said on the highway. I think. I'm pretty sure.

—I don't know what that means, ma'am.

Did I just call her ma'am? I did. I called her ma'am. Gawd, I'm nervous.

—*Kannst du mir helfen?*

Now *that's* German. I can do German. *Noch ein Bier bitte* . . . Okay, that's all I know.

—Wait for me *one* second. One?

— . . .

One finger. Why would she think that means one second? I need the German book. Where's the book? Where's the book? WHERE IS IT? There! What'd she say again? *Kant. K. K.* Where is *kant*?

—There's no *kant*! No. *Kant.*

—*Kannst. Kannsssssst.*

Oh, with an *s*. Also not there. I could swear I seen that word, though. "Useful Phrases," maybe. Come on! Come on! HA! *Kannst du mir bitte das Salz reichen*? Can you please pass the salt? Informal. Sure. We did spend the night together. What did she say? *Kannst du*, can you . . . something, *helfen. H. Hamburger! Hedgefonds. Helfen!* Yes! It's a word. It means . . . "help." "Can you help me?" She's asking for my help. Cute alien with bangs is asking for my help! Oh my god. That means the giant lady on the highway was asking for my help. Then she lost her face. What do they want help with?

—You want *me* to help you? Help you with what?

— . . .

She's just smiling. That's adorable, but not helpful.

—*Helfen!* Help. *Me, helfen you,* with what?

How do I gesture "what"? Raise my shoulders, hold my hands up, palms out. Pouting lips. Wow. I never noticed how weird a shrug is before just now.

— . . . *Jagd.*

She's tapping her chest. *Yagd.* What's that? Yak. Yankee. No, *yagd.* Oh I know! They write it with a *J. Jagd.* . . . Got it. It means . . . "hunt."

—You're hunting?

—*Nein! Jagen* mich!

—Someone is hunting you! Chasing you. The other giant person is hunting you? You have no idea what I'm saying, do you? The other one. Big, tall, like you. Here, in Berlin. Tall. Supertall. No, not you. The *other* one. What's other? . . . *Andere! Andere* supertall!

—*Mein Bruder.*

—*Bru—* Brother? The other one's your brother?

She wouldn't run from her own brother. I guess they're both running from someone else. Maybe they're fugitives like— Wait. Her brother. Oh crud. It's her brother! NO! NO! NO! NO! NO! This is not good! I need to find Samael.

38

Du Hast[2]

Here he is, standing tall. I can tell he was ready for a chase. He's fidgeting, like a sprinter waiting for the pistol to go off. Do not worry, my friend; I will not run. I think he knows. He's smiling now, and so am I. I've waited patiently for this moment and I intend to savor it. I take out my knives. The sound of the blades brushing against their sheath sends shivers through my spine. I do not know which god to ask, but I am asking, begging. Please, let him not carry a gun. I want this to last. Yessss. A blade. His is long and curved. This is perfect. We are gladiators, staring at our breath and the inevitability of death. Darkness is our arena, silence our acclamation. Only the moon came to watch. She throws glitter at us, snowflakes bright as silver prickling at our skin. There is no confidence, no bravado. We may triumph or perish, but it matters not, for here is but one certainty. We were made for this.

Breathe. I cannot wait any longer. I run at my prey. He has more reach than I do, so I must keep him close. Breathe. I can feel the fever rising. Breathe. Here it comes. I let the urge take over. I feel the burn rushing through my veins. The weight on

2. Author's cut: If the *Lola rennt* (*Run Lola Run*) soundtrack is available for streaming in your area, replace this song in the playlist with "Wish (Komm zu mir)."

my shoulders is gone. I am relieved, light as a feather. I soar at him. I am raptor. He is prey.

The eagle spreads its wings, wide as the sky. The wind swirls. The raptor whirls. His blade comes down hard, but the eagle is gone. He swings at shadows, panting, while death flies circles around him. The eagle's legs stiffen. It strikes, claws out, unannounced. The wound is shallow, the surprise much deeper. The prey pauses, dazed. It gazes at the graze.

Straight stance, arms lowered. My prey wishes to fight no more.

—COME ON! FIGHT ME!

Pride echoes from the eagle's bill. It lets its might be known. The prey's blade rises, its owner resigned. The eagle dives, talons forward, enlivened by the smell of death. This is the moment I hav—

My arm. He's faster than I thought. It's a deep cut, but I can still move it. Parry. Parry. Step back. Now breathe. . . . Breathe. My arm hurts like hell. It *burns*, like it's on fire. *Yes, fire.*

The phoenix rises from the bird's ashes. Flames dancing, twisting. It cannot be touched. It screams, loud and angry, setting the world ablaze. The firebird unleashes its wrath, spits fire at its foe. The prey steps back, its confidence seared. The phoenix spins faster, faster still, a burning tornado too bright to look at. Oh no. Chest pains. I haven't felt like myself for weeks, but now is really not the time for—

AAAARGHH. His blade dove straight into my side. I didn't see it coming. I didn't feel it cut through skin, or flesh, or fat. I only felt my rib being cut in half. That, I felt a lot. The earth is trembling. It's my legs slowly crumbling under me. I can't control it any more than I can stop what's coming. I'm on my knees, watching the life drain fast out of me. I'm leaking like a sieve. I see the blood pooling under me. I feel its soothing warmth spreading across my shirt.

This is how it ends. Finish it now, my friend. . . . He's not. He's enjoying the moment, but he'll come for the kill soon enough.

The smell of metal tickles my nostrils. Pungent. It's *my* smell, my blood. I am iron. I am . . . machine. Yes. A steampunk warhorse from a forgotten time. He's coming. Breathe! Steam builds up. Pressure rises. Heat rushes through my broken carcass. More pressure. More heat. The thick black oil softens. Rusted gears break their ancient bond and turn. Slow, still slow, but the engine burns hot. The horse comes to life. Forward. My iron hooves stomp the ground. Steady, deliberate. Pistons marching to the drums of war. CHARGE! The horse rears up on its hind legs. Cannons blazing. Sharp hooves slashing at whatever dares near.

I hit his neck. Not hard, not deep, but enough.

He raises his hand to cover the wound.

Full stop.

We both know. It was just a reflex, trying to stop the bleed. I would have done the same. I would have left myself open. I would have lost.

I dig both blades into his gut.

He nods.

I pull up as hard as I can.

Our eyes meet. I once took pleasure in this, watching the life leave someone's body. Not this time. I hold his gaze out of respect, so he does not die alone. He was a good prey.

. . .

My knees bend as I let his body fall. I fear this may have been a draw.

ENTR'ACTE

A Horse of a Different Color

Rumors of the supernatural sent Tereshiin and Kish north into Nairi. It was nightfall when they reached a small settlement on the shores of the upper sea where they hoped to spend the night. They had traveled for two days straight and Kish was looking forward to a good night's sleep and respite from the constant pounding of the road. An old man greeted them just outside the village and offered his blessings. Kish saw nothing suspect about the man, who fit her definition of the generic villager to a T. She did notice her father's facial expression when the stranger stepped closer to their chariot. Tereshiin affected a smile, and thrust his sword into the man's heart before he could say anything.

Kish was shocked, and angry. Her prospects of finding sleep in that village had just fallen to the ground and she voiced her discontent rather vehemently. Tereshiin slapped her. He went on about an ancient war on their world, the deaths of billions at the hands of a merciless enemy. Kish asked what this had to do with an old man in Nairi, but Tereshiin ignored her. Kish didn't understand. The man lying in the dirt was frail and small. He looked nothing like the ruthless warriors Tereshiin had described. Perhaps the man was only half-human, like her. She analyzed the man's features but found nothing conspicuous. His skin was of familiar color; his eyes were very much eyelike. He had very thin eyebrows, but that hardly seemed alien enough to merit suspicion, let alone death.

Kish pleaded for an explanation, but Tereshiin didn't care. He took a wide stance in the middle of the road and held his sword forward. His eyes were wide but unfocused, as if his mind had abandoned a sinking ship.

Silhouettes in the distance grew larger and larger. Most of the villagers were unarmed, but they died just the same. Tereshiin slaughtered men and women alike. He hacked at people who were already dead. None could ever die enough to satisfy his rage.

Kish noticed a young boy, four or five, running to his dead mother.

—Father, there's a child coming!

Tereshiin was still fighting grown-ups but had no intention of stopping there. He would kill every living thing in that village. He would kill their dogs, burn their houses to the ground.

—He does not matter. None of them do.

This time she understood what her father meant. The words resonated in Kish's head, amplified by each stroke of Tereshiin's blade until they were too loud to bear. The boy did not matter because he was different. His family did not matter because *they* were different. Who else was different? Was Kish? There was but one logical conclusion, one that burst into Kish's mind like a star going nova. *No one* mattered, not a single soul, including her.

They had killed before only to save themselves. She'd killed because she had to. That wasn't true, she realized, horrified. She'd killed people who were running away. She'd killed people who begged for their lives. She'd killed people who didn't matter to save others who did, like her father told her to. One by one, the ghosts that woke her up at night showed her the future she'd sought. She saw corpses, as many as the stars, rising from the ground to form the great cities Tereshiin spoke of. She saw herself standing on the shores of the Idiqlat, stepping on skulls to reach the scarlet waters.

She saw herself playing with a wooden doll.

She hears noises coming from the street and moves closer to the door. A scream. She knows that voice; she's heard it her whole life. She pulls the door open and steps out. Her mother is lying on her back, arms wide. There's shade on both sides of her head, one darker than the other. Her father kneels and places his hands on her mother's neck. Another shadow stretches in front of her. A man, looking down, his sword still dripping with her mother's blood.

She remembered not just that day, but all of it. Memories rising from the desert sand like a scorpion unearthing itself. Every taste, every smell, running her fingers through another man's beard. She remembered the lullaby her mother sang to her at night. "Someone sang it for me once," her mother had said. "I was scared, and I heard a melody. I was thirsty and hurt. A stranger gave me water, and gently cleaned my wounds. *That* is why I'm here now, with you. Every bit of joy we have, we owe to a stranger and a song." Her mother had been born elsewhere, but it was the people here who saved her. Kish was alive because of people who did not matter. She was one of them.

Tereshiin ran out of adults to slay. He walked up to the boy and held his sword high. It came down with strength and fury, but it never touched the boy. Sparks lit up the night as two blades collided, one held by a man who had raised a killer, one by the woman who called him Father.

ACT V

39

Evil Angel

—We have to kill her, Aster.

—No!

—Yes. We have to kill her and we have to do it now, while we can. She's a killer, Aster, built for one purpose only. She's a danger to you, to me, to everyone who crosses her path.

—She's not! I slept w— Next to her, Samael. If she wanted to hurt me, she—I was sleeping! As in unconscious, not moving, probably snoring— Oh crud, I was snoring. My point is she could have killed me a hundred times, but she *didn't*.

—And she might not hurt you tonight, or tomorrow, but one day she will and every minute we let her live takes us closer to that moment.

—She's all alone, Samael—you saw to *that*—and she's scared. She's scared of everyone, except us. Well, me, at least.

—She has no reason to be scared of us.

—You just said you want to kill her.

—I meant that you are half her size and I can barely walk. She may be young, but neither of us would last a minute against her.

—You fought her brother.

—And I barely survived. Were it not for a serendipitously located drugstore, I would have bled out and we would not be talking today. It will take a while for my bone to mend, but my skin should be healing by now. It isn't. I am in no condition to fight her. The simplest course of action is to kill her while she sleeps. I give you my word it will be painless.

—She won't hurt us! That's not why she's here. She's a fugitive, and she's asking for our help. You don't kill people who ask for help, that's just wrong, and you definitely don't kill people in their sleep! Seriously, who *does* that? She *needs* us, Samael.

—She told you that?

—Yes! Well, not exactly. She said, "Will you help me?"; then we talked some more and she said a lot more things, but I didn't get all of it. I think she's a deserter, something like that. The three of them were. You know what that means, right?

—Nothing. It means nothing because you have no idea what she said or whether you can trust her. However, if she said what you think she said and was being truthful, it would mean her people now have even more reason to come here.

—That's . . . not what I was going to say.

—I figured as much.

— . . . I was going to say it means we have more time to send the sphere away. I mean, before we thought they were here already and now they're not, so maybe they don't know where the signal came from. Maybe they never even heard it. Either way, it means my plan has a better chance, doesn't it?

—What's her name?

—What?

—This entire reasoning of yours is based on the assumption that we can trust her, so I'm asking you to consider how well you know her. Do you even know her name?

—Saa.

—Just Saa.

—Yeah. I think. What? Her English ain't that good. She speaks alien and German, and both are sort of the same to me right now.

—Fine. Let us assume for one moment that she's telling the truth. What do you suggest we do with her?

—What do you mean?

—I mean the U.S. Government found the body of her . . . associate on the highway. Let me rephrase that. They found the body of a woman of unusual height and size, whose anatomy suggests she isn't human. There have been incidents involving people of unusual height and size all over the map. They will put two and two together if they haven't already. You believe she was a fugitive on her world. I can tell you with absolute certainty that she is one on this world.

—So are we!

—Indeed! You saw what the authorities had in store for you. What do you think they will do to her when they catch her? And believe me, they will. I changed my appearance as best I could. You cut your hair. With all the resources at our disposal, we barely manage to stay under the radar. What can *she* do? Where can she hide? There is no future for her. None. Not here, not anywhere. I know you like her, Aster, but she is a liability to everyone who comes near her and every second she spends in this room puts us both at unnecessary risk. We have to k—

—Stop saying that!

—Me? You said so yourself, Aster. That *was* your plan, was it not? Step one. Get rid of the giant bad people. Well, there she is. She's the last one.

—SO AM I! So are you. I know, you have a cousin, but that's close enough. We're Alabama red-bellied turtles, all of us.

—I beg your pardon?

—Turtles. They're like yay big. I read about them in the paper. They only live down south, and with global warming and the sea rising, the marshes they live in are disappearing. I collected money at school for them, gave up my whole allowance for two weeks. There's only a thousand turtles left. Maybe it's ten thousand; I forgot.

—Your point being?

—I ain't killing the last one!

—We're talking about the alien woman now, not the turtles, correct?

—Yes. We're keeping her.

—She's not a pet, Aster. She's the apex predator in a world more dangerous than you and I can imagine. She doesn't belong here.

—We're keeping her. For now, at least.

—I strongly—

—It's Christmas! We can talk about this after the holidays, but we're not murdering anyone on Christmas Day. That's like superwrong.

— . . . I used to love Christmas. It was perhaps the only time our family felt . . . normal.

—Does that mean—?

—We should relocate. Somewhere remote where we won't draw attention.

—The three of us?

—Yes, the three of us.

—Thank you! Merry Christmas, by the way.

—Merry Christmas to you too, Aster. . . . I didn't buy—

—It's okay. I didn't either.

40

The Shining

2002

Oooh, Caaanada! Terre de nos. I forgot. French is hard. We couldn't stay in Germany, so we been hiding in a tiny tiny Quebec town near the U.S. border. It's called Frelighsburg. I'm pretty sure that's a German name. Is that ironic? I don't think I know what "ironic" means anymore. Everything here is tiny. There's tiny old buildings, tiny streets, tiny mountains all around. And it's all white. I wanted snow, well, I got snow. It goes above my head in places. This has to be the prettiest place on Earth—okay, maybe top ten, *if* you stay inside. Outside, it's cooooold. *Evil* cold. You go outside and the air rushes into your nose and stabs you with minuscule shards of ice. I didn't know you could freeze from the *inside* of your face. I don't understand how people survive here. Maybe they don't. Maybe half of them die of scurvy every year. We went out twice. The hotel owner, Jean-Pierre, loaned us all snowshoes so we could walk in the woods. I never even heard of snowshoes before. They're cool, but they're definitely not shoes. We walked for like two hours. I hurt everywhere when we got back. My hands, my feet, my nose, my ears. Oh God, my ears! And then, OH MY GAWD. It turns out freezing your toes hurts like hell, but it's nothing compared to *un*freezing your toes. We stay inside now, except to get food, and beer. They make their own. It's *way* better than German beer.

Samael's gone for a few days. I been watching TV—they have

HBO—and fighting with Saa. You have to say it like you're trying to gargle. *Saaaargh.* She still speaks her own language, sometimes. I'm not sure why. She knows I don't understand any of it. She's supersmart. It's only been two weeks, but her English is getting way better. She knew like two words when we got here. "Food." She used that one a lot, though it sounds more like "foot" when she says it. She eats *all the time*. And "fight." Well, she said "fart," but she said it right before we tussled, so I figured she meant "fight." She still does it. She just . . . she pushes me for no reason, then I say: "Hey!" and I push her back, and then she says: "Fart"; then we tussle. I know she goes easy on me, but it still hurts. We had a pillow fight once. She liked that. I sprained a finger, but it was fun. She wrecked that pillow, though. There were feathers everywhere. Samael was mad. He made us pick them up one by one. Saa didn't like that. These two really don't like each other. Samael thinks she's evil and she— Well, Samael came up with a far-fetched story about the police shooting her brother, but I don't think she bought it. . . . There's *tons* of feathers in a pillow. I was surprised. You'd need like a dozen ducks just to make one. Maybe they're geese, whatever. I feel bad for ducks now. We have eight pillows in our room and there are a lot of rooms. There's more hotels, and houses. *Everyone* has pillows.

Saa never talked about that night in Berlin. Either she wants to forget it or she ain't got the vocabulary. Me, I ain't got the vocabulary. She likes me; that much I know. Maybe the tussling is good enough. We tussle a lot. I . . . I feel awful. Samael was half-right. I didn't think of her as a pet, but I didn't think of her as, well, like me. She is, though. She's just like me, except she's huge and says weird things, but I see it in her face. She's sad sometimes, even when she smiles. She gets lonely when I'm not around. She gets lonely when I'm around. I really wish she were happy. I wish I could help with that, but Sam's right; she can't go anywhere. I guess she's *a bit* like a pet. She's stuck in a cage, which sucks, and she'll die if she ever gets out. I think she knows; that's the worst part.

My whole plan is on pause now. Most of it, anyway. I still don't know how to get Bruce Willis off my back. There's Saa to deal with now, and then there's George W. Bush. I didn't plan for him. Our Pluto mission won the New Frontiers competition. That wasn't much of a surprise because the two finalists were missions to Pluto and we gave money to both. There was one in Colorado that was backed by JPL, and the folks in Maryland Qian Xuesen said we should talk to. That's the one that won. Anyway, that was last November. Now the *new* administrator at NASA, the one George W. Bush put in, decided not to include it in next year's budget, which pretty much nipped the whole thing in the bud.

It's not over, just . . . harder, but then again, everything is, so . . . I threw money at it. That's my new thing, apparently. We gave *thirty million bucks* to the project to keep them afloat while we lobby every expert in the field to tell NASA they should really send the probe up. Samael is down in Maryland to sign some papers. I bet he hates me right now.

I told him we should get them to change the name while we're at it. I mean, we're paying. He looked at me funny. I think that meant no. Still, they called it *New Horizons*. It's not the worst name in the world, but it's kind of—I don't know—obvious. It's like calling it *Superfar* or *Never Been There*. I'd have called it Venetia, for Venetia Phair. She'd have loved that.

In 1930—her name was Burney back then—Venetia's grandfather read about how they discovered a ninth planet in the solar system. He told her, and she said they should name the planet

Pluto, after the Roman god who could make himself invisible, 'cause, you know, the planet was hard to find. Her grandpa liked that and he wrote to the astronomers who'd found the planet. They liked it too, enough to use the name. It's supercool. She was eleven and she got to name a planet. I wish I could do that.

41

We're Going to Be Friends

Saa hasn't said a word all morning. She keeps staring out the window, like she's waiting for something, someone.

—Everything okay, Saa?

—*Mein Bruder. Er fehlt mir.*

—I don't know what that means.

—I miss him.

—Were you two close?

—*Ja.* Always together. He . . . protect me.

—He was older than you?

—*Zwei Zyklen.* He was . . . seventeen.

—Seven—Wait, what? You're fifteen years old?

—Fifteen my years. Different, maybe.

Whoa. She's a year older than me. Well, one more rotation around *a* star. That could mean anything, I suppose. Mercury goes around the sun in eighty-eight days; Neptune takes 165 years. She could be older than the pyramids, or the biggest toddler ever. Nah. I say we're the same age, almost. It sure felt that way back when . . . There was this . . . carefulness in her kiss. Not like I'll-be-gentle-'cause-I'm-twice-your-size carefulness—although there's probably some of that too—but it felt like "I have no idea what I'm doing, so I'll go slow." Of course, the kiss was all in my head, so maybe she's fifty-five and divorced three times. It felt real; that's all I know.

—Saa, when we met at the bar—

—Dancing!

—Yes, we danced. But before that, I—

She's grinning. She knows what I'm talking about. Gawd, I'm self-conscious again.

—*Yesherat schiire.*

—That ain't German, right?

—*Nein.* Drinking from the same cup. Sometimes your . . . *Denken* is my *Denken*. My head, your head, same thing. *Es ist normal.*

—You mean our people are telepaths?

—I don't know . . . telepath.

—We can communicate with our mind?

—No. We cannot control. More like . . . gas.

—Gas? I don't— Oh, you mean like a fart?

—Yes. It just happens.

—Ha! Well, you kissed me in your fart.

—Maybe it was your fart.

My fart! Hell no. It was totally her. Fine, I can't stop looking at her, but I peed my pants when I first saw her. I don't think you can pee your pants and kiss people in your head at the same time. Still, we're telepaths. . . . Oh my god, giant lady on the highway. She gave me her hand. She wanted me to go with her. I thought I was losing it. I guess what I saw was real. *Yesherat schiire.* Brain fart. Giant lady wanted my help and she got shot in the face. Now I feel bad for getting her killed. Then again, she gave Pa a heart attack, so maybe she deserved it. How'd she know where to find me, though? I was hitchhiking in the middle of nowhere. I don't know how Saa found me in Berlin either.

—How did you know I was at the bar? You never said.

—*Detektor!*

—For real? What does it detect? People like us?

—*Ja.*

—Can I see?

—*Detektor.*

Cool. Alien iPhone. It's just a blank screen with two red dots in the middle. I guess that's us. I wish I knew what it's searching for. DNA, maybe. Saa and I don't exactly look alike, but that machine thinks we're the same. This is so weird. Whatever they did to us to shrink us down to size, I'd be as tall as she is if I been born . . . one of them.

—What's it like, on your world?

— . . .

Was that a shrug? I think that was a shrug.

—You don't know?

—*Nein.*

—You never seen it?

—*Ich war ein Baby.*

—I don't understand. I thought you said you were a soldier.

—I am born soldier. Long mission. Long trip. They send children. *Unser Kommandant*, she take care of us, not want us to die.

—That's why she took you here?

—*Ja.* Hiding. *Kommandant* be back soon. Looking for you!

Oh crud. She doesn't know. Sam said there were three of them. Saa, her brother, and that Gigantor woman dropping FBI agents in the rain. I don't know what to tell her. I could tell her the cops shot her, or the Army. They would have; they just never got the chance. This is so messed up. Samael killed her brother, her commander. Might as well have been her mom the way she tells it. I don't want to lie to her, but I can't exactly tell her the truth either.

—Saa, there's something I need to tell you.

— . . .

She knows whatever comes next ain't good news.

—Your commander. I think she found me.

— . . .

Oh God. Her shoulders dropped. She's tearing up like a four-year-old who got lost at the fair.

—I'm so sorry, Saa. She found me but the Army was there, the ones who locked me up in a basement. They found me at the same time. She tried to help, but . . . There were just too many of them. There's nothing she could have done.

—*Sie ist tot?*

—Mm-hmm.

Totally *tot*. Everyone she knows is *tot*. She said she was a baby when she left; that means she ain't never met anyone else her own kind. I'm the closest thing she has to her race, to family. I'm the only red dot besides her, and Sam if he were here, but he wants to kill her, so . . . I'm the only good red dot. Whoa. I'm having a hard time breathing right now. I'm not ready for this. I'm not ready for any of the things that are happening to me, but I can't be responsible for another person, a gigantic, impossible-to-hide, fifteen-year-old person who eats like a college football team at an all-you-can-eat buffet.

—Aster?

—What?

—*Ich werde okay sein?*

— . . . Of course you're gonna be okay. We'll take care of you; I swear.

—*Vielen Dank.*

—You're welcome, Saa.

Poor thing. She's in big trouble if I'm all she's got. I can't even take care of myself. I'd be long dead if it weren't for Sam. Maybe he'll warm up to her. I hope he does, or she has no chance in hell.

42

A Perfect Day Elise

—Please, have a seat, Mr. Anderson. I trust you're having a pleasant day.

—As always. I very much enjoyed the tour. Your facilities are quite impressive.

I imagined all of it burning with everyone inside, especially my guide, who spent every excruciating moment filling my brain with technical minutiae. Part of it is my fault. I woke up with another migraine and a stomachache—but the guide truly deserves some torment for putting me through this. Ironically, she kept talking about tolerance. Only two microns, she said. I dared not ask what a micron of tolerance is, but I know I do not have that much left in me.

—It was the least we could do, Mr. Anderson. It's not every day a private citizen sponsors a research program to the tune of thirty million dollars. Speaking of, I do have some questions regarding the object you wish us to take on our journey to Pluto. You said it was a spherical container.

—It is indeed.

Please do not make me talk about it. I beg of you.

—And it is made entirely of titanium.

—If that's what it says in the proposal—

—It is. It's just unusual for something to be one hundred

percent titanium. There could be hinges, closures made of another mater—

—My father was an unusual man.

—Yes. Speaking of, you said his ashes will be inside the container.

—In a small plastic bag, yes.

It sounded absurd coming out of Aster's mouth but not nearly as much as it does when I hear myself say it.

—Is it sealed?

—The metal container or the bag?

—Both.

Dear Lord . . .

— . . . Yes?

—I'm afraid this might be a problem. You see, if any air remains inside the—

—Oh! You meant hermetically sealed? Then the answer is no. Nothing is sealed.

—Great. I'm terribly sorry. Even with private donations such as yours, we'll still have to meet NASA's requirements if we want our probe to sit on their rocket.

—I completely understand. Will that be all?

—I only have a few more questions. How much does the container weigh?

—I thought I included that information in my proposal.

—You did. You said the container weighed nearly four kilos, but there was no mention of the ashes. Now, forgive me—I have limited knowledge on the matter—but I assume the weight of one person's ashes is not negligible.

—How much?

—I'm sorry?

—How much can the entire thing weigh? You said four kilos before. Can we agree on four kilos?

—That would only leave room for a few ounces for your father's ashes.

—It's fine. He wished for his ashes to be sent into space. He never specified how much of them.

—Are you certain? It seems a little—

—We weren't that close. Now, if we are in agreement, I can have the funds transferred over to you today. Would that be acceptable?

Thirty million dollars is a small price to pay to put an end to this charade. I admire Aster's enthusiasm, but it's not as if this has even the slightest chance of working. I only agreed to help out of guilt, and a misplaced sense of responsibility.

—Yes, sir! Very much so. Let me . . . just get the paperw— Oh my. This isn't something you see every day.

—I'm sorry, what is?

—In the parking lot. There must be five hundred troops. The police are there too. Have a look.

As Aster would say: crud.

—I will take your word for it.

—I hope it's some kind of military exercise, but you never know these days. Perhaps you should wait before leaving. I will get us some coffee.

—That's very kind of you, but I have had too much already. Do you mind if I use the bathroom?

Breathe. Where is the staircase? Breathe. I can almost feel it.

43

Let Forever Be

They don't serve poutine for breakfast. I don't see why not. It's got potatoes and cheese. They can just throw an egg on top and call it breakfast. Saa likes burgers. "HAM-booh-gah," she says, always smiling. When they ask what she wants in it, she just smiles more, like they gave her a compliment. "Give me everything!" she says. Me, I'm all about poutine. They have different fries up here. Their fries are really thick, and brown, and soft. They speak French, so they must know. I'm not addicted at all. I can stop eating poutine anytime I want. I'll probably have to when Samael comes back.

Saa ain't here either. She's probably at the bar if it's open. She's not allowed to go out on her own, but I let her go to the bar. It ain't right keeping her in like that. I just hope I didn't lose her. I suppose I could check on her, but I like this quiet. There's French *Working Girl* on TV. I seen it often enough I don't need the words, and French Sigourney Weaver is funny. They're in the elevator now. It's coming. Say it! Get *le* bony ass out of *le* sight! Yay! Go, Tess! I used to watch this with Pa. He really liked that movie. He liked pretty much anything with Joan Cusack. I think she reminded him of his wife. I seen pictures from way back when they got married and she kind of looked like Joan Cusack. Plus he'd get teary-eyed every time she had a line and *Working Girl* ain't exactly a Greek tragedy. I get emotional when she gets her own office, though. Oh, there it is. "I expect you to call me Tess. I don't expect you to fetch me coffee unless you're getting some for yourself . . . and the rest we'll just make up as we go along, okay?" *Oui! Oui!*

I feel superselfish sometimes. I *am* selfish. I just don't know if it's normal. I made this plan to maybe save the Earth. That's what I said, but, really, that's not why I did it. Saving the planet, I mean, that's just *too* big. That's . . . way bigger than me, and I know there's a part of me that thinks I can't do it. But I'm still doing it, because what that part of me really wants is to lie down and watch TV. This, right now. That's what I really want. Watching an old movie without being afraid someone will kick the door in and lock me in a pink basement. I'm exhausted. I need quiet, and old movies. And poutine. I mean, I have more money than I can count. I'm like Batman or something. I should be able to eat fries smothered in gravy and watch *Working Girl* whenever I want.

Seriously, I'm fourteen years old. I shouldn't have to worry about Bruce Willis, and the Army, and what happened to Samael, 'cause he really should be back by now. And where's Saa? She been gone for the whole movie. I shouldn't have to worry about Saa. . . .

Okay, fine, I'll go look for her.

44

2 Rights Make 1 Wrong

I found Saa. She nearly froze to death, hiding underneath the gallery. She was crying, rocking herself back and forth like those polar bears at the zoo. I asked what was wrong, but she pushed me away. Then I asked louder and she pushed harder. I hit my head pretty hard on concrete. It wasn't her fault; I just wasn't ready for it. It hurt pretty bad, though. I felt the back of my head. She calmed down for a minute when she saw the blood on my fingers, long enough for me to take her inside.

I put her under a hot shower, clothes on and all. She wouldn't let go of me—I still have the marks on my arm. I sat on the floor next to her and let her squeeze me. She's twice my size, but for those twenty minutes she was smaller than me, a scared little kid trying to hide from the world in a neck too small. I told her what she wanted to hear. It's going to be okay. I told her over and over. It could have been true. It didn't matter; I knew she needed to hear it.

We ran out of hot water pretty quick. I helped her take her wet clothes off and wrapped her in thick hotel towels like a fluffy mummy. I picked her favorite clothes from the drawer. She has like four shirts, but she goes for AC/DC every time if it's clean. The kitchen was open, so I got ham-booh-gahs from room service. That helped. Food always helps, but I think us sharing it was a big part of it. The two of us eating the same thing without talking. I even ate faster than usual so we'd finish at the same time. We wiped the ketchup off our hands, like a ritual. Then—I don't know—it was like someone flipped a switch inside her head. One second she was a sobbing mess; the next she was sitting straight with the usual half a grin on her face.

I asked: "*Was ist passiert?*" "I'm sorry," she said. She took my hand and walked me to the owner's office downstairs. She told me she got into an argument with Jean-Pierre; I forget what about. Whatever it was, she wrung his neck like a washcloth. He was lying facedown—well, faceup, really—but his chest was against the floor. I never seen anything like it. I never seen anyone with their head backwards, obviously, but he looked . . . terrified, like he been given a glimpse of hell. Whatever Saa turned into, I know it wasn't human.

I was scared of her right then, real scared. I stood on my toes, fists clenched, ready to pounce if she came after me. No Kibsu Spider-Sense, more like I'm stuck in a cage with a tiger. It didn't last. She looked at me all puppy-eyed, like she'd knocked over a vase. That gets me every time. Plus she was standing like ten feet away, and when there's nothing near her for size comparison she really looks like a little girl. "*Shyesecht het?*" she said. Will you help me? She said it softly, half whisper, half sigh. I did. I helped her. I didn't have much of a choice—it was either that or run away before Samael comes back, but I wanted to help. Maybe that's not the right word. She didn't want help. She wanted me to *erase* this, to have a . . . mulligan—is that what it's called?—a do-over. She wanted to pretend it never happened. I wanted it even more than she did.

I closed the door. We wrapped Jean-Pierre in the bloodstained carpet and Saa carried him upstairs to our room. I told her to stay there. Stay. Stayyy. . . . She put him in the tub, closed the door, and turned on the TV. *JAG* was on. Whatever, she seemed fine with it, so I left.

There are many steps to pretending a murder never happened. I figured I'd start with the ones I knew how to do. There's a closet full of supplies across from the office. I keep getting toilet paper from there. I grabbed every cleaning product I could fit in my arms and went back in. I scrubbed everything. I scrubbed the floor, the walls, under the desk. Pencils, magazines, things I found in the trash. You'd never tell someone had their neck twisted backwards in there. There ain't a print left either, ours or anyone else's. You could have open-heart surgery in that office.

I'm going back to our room now. I wish I didn't have to. I really wish Samael were here. There are many steps to pretending a murder never happened and I really dread the next one. I seen people get rid of bodies in movies, but they're usually professional, with all sorts of body-ridding equipment. We don't have flesh-eating chemicals in our room. We have tiny shampoo bottles, and some hand lotion that smells bad. The hotel has electrical heating, that means no furnace, and it's minus infinity outside, so I don't think digging's an option. There's always *Fargo*. . . . I doubt they have a wood chipper waiting in the yard, but I can probably rent one, spray Jean-Pierre all over the snowshoe trail . . .

Even if I manage to grind him into pulp, someone'll look for Jean-Pierre at some point. I'm not sure he's married, but I bet he has friends, an overprotective sister who keeps checking on him. Today's Thursday; the staff'll probably want to get paid. Like, I really need Samael to come back soon so we can leave. He's gonna be mad, though. There'll be all kinds of "I told you sos."

I'll tell him it's my fault, what happened. It is. I shouldn't have let her go alone. When kids drown in a pool, you don't blame the kids; you blame the parents who left them unsupervised. That's me. I left Saa unsupervised.

"You did this, Aster."

I know, Freddie. I know.

45

There Goes the Fear

—You can forget about sending the sphere on that probe, Aster.

Samael's back with more good news. I'm going to ask, because that's what people do, they ask, but there's really no point. Everything I need to know was in that sentence already. I can forget about sending the sphere on that probe. It's short. To the point. What comes after "Why?" could be the most interesting story ever, or it might be something boring like: "They canceled the project." It could be a million different things, but none of them will change the meaning of that first sentence. I ain't sending the sphere on that probe. Asking why is just morbid curiosity at this point. Still . . .

—Why? What happened?

—I had a rather unfortunate encounter with a military acquaintance of yours.

—The colonel? For real? How'd he find you?

Samael came for me at the hospital and now he's paying for it. They know his face. Now they know more . . . they know he's interested in that probe.

—I don't know how he found me, but he brought a small army with him this time. I was fortunate enough to evade capture, less fortunate in that I cannot show my face in public again.

—I'm sorry you had to run. Did you have to kill anyone?

—I did indeed. It appears my physical woes are worsening. I was in the stairwell, about three floors ahead of the soldiers chasing me, when my left leg suddenly stopped moving.

—For real?

—It went lifeless in an instant, as if someone cut the wire connecting it to the rest of me. Two men caught up to me after I fell. Their death was . . . unavoidable.

—You didn't tell me you were sick.

—I have had frequent migraines for months now, some chest pains, but nothing like this until now.

—What do you think it is?

—I don't know. I've never been ill. No one in my family ever has, as far as I know.

—Maybe you should see a doctor.

He can't, I know, but it seemed like the right thing to say.

—We do not see doctors, Aster. You of all people should know that. Enough about me. I trust you and Saa managed to stay out of trouble.

I don't want to say it. He'll be mad, sure, but also if I say it I'll remember and I don't want to remember. Not finding him like that, not . . . ewwww. I'll just put my head down and point to the bathroom.

—Over there.

—What's over there?

—Just . . .

— . . . Aster, why is there a dead man in our bathtub?

—Saa got into an argument with Jean-Pierre.

— . . . I see. Why is he cut in half?

—Please don't be mad! We . . .

—Yes?

—We tried to cut him into smaller pieces, you know, to take

him out without looking like we're taking him out, but I couldn't find tools. I checked everywhere! There's a shed even, but there's nothing in it. The only thing we had was the steak knife that came with room service. It doesn't cut very well, but Saa felt bad about what she did, so she tried anyway and . . . that's what we ended up with. And he's not really *in half.* If you pull on the legs, the rest of him kind of follows. . . . Anyway, I told her to stop before she made even more of a mess.

—What about the crime scene?

—His office. But that one's okay. I cleaned it all up. There's no blood, no prints, no nothing. We just . . .

—I will take care of it.

—You're not mad?

—I'm not mad at you. You did reasonably well under the circumstances. I realize I should have taught you how to dispose of a human body before. I will teach you now.

—Oh, it's fine; I—

—That was not a suggestion. I am not doing this alone.

— . . .

—Please stop crying. . . . For what it's worth, I *am* sorry, Aster.

—Why? It ain't your fault Saa killed Jean-Pierre. You weren't even here.

—I'm not sorry because Saa killed a man. Well, I am sorry she *did,* but I know how much it all meant to you: the probe, sending the sphere into space, stopping the colonel. You had a plan and now it's gone. I'm sorry that you—that *we* failed. I truly am.

—Thank you, Samael.

Who said anything about failing? That ain't why I'm crying. Mom wrote how it broke her heart when she left me to go fight the Tracker. Hardest thing she'd ever had to do—that's what she said—but she did it anyway because she had to. She knew what she had to do to get what she wanted and she didn't hesitate. I wish I were like her. I wish I were brave like she was, 'cause I know what I have to do—I know all of it now—but I ain't like Mom. I hesitate.

46

Lose Yourself

You had a plan and it's gone. *Pfft.* I didn't count on the colonel catching up to Sam, but it's not like we were ever going to put the sphere on that probe anyway. There'll be a million people inspecting every millimeter of it a thousand times over before it launches. It'd take them about a minute to figure out the sphere is, well, anything but whatever we said it was. I suppose I could have told Samael, but I'm not sure he'd have done his part if he knew. He hates acting.

I have a plan. Sarah, my great-grandma, she *always* had a plan. I'm trying to be more like her, except younger and not a spy. Like those chess masters who can see ten moves ahead, but they can't really see ten moves ahead 'cause that's quadrillions of possible moves, but they see the most probable ones. I don't really like chess. I want to be like the guy in that heist movie, with the painting, in the museum. Crud, I forget his name. The . . . bowler hat and the green apple. James Bond's in it, and Rene Russo. I like Rene Russo. Anyway, he's really good at making plans. I don't think I'm *that* good, but I can read. I crammed through everything there is to know about that mission. I feel sort of bad for not sharing everything, but I get only one shot at this and there are too many moving parts already.

The New Horizons people didn't get my money, though. That's not good. I still need the project to get funding. I don't like it, but I'll have to trust the scientists at the NRC. They're preparing the—whatsamacallit—Planetary Science Decadal Survey right now; it's like a ten-year grocery list for space stuff. It comes out this summer, so we'll know soon enough. They'll want to go; they have to. Pluto's the only planet we've never seen. If we don't go, it's like watching *A New Hope* and *Empire Strikes Back* but not *Return of the Jedi*; skipping dessert in a five-course meal; turning football off at the two-minute warning. That's enough, Aster. It'll work.

It better work, because that's the only plan I have. I think I'm doing all right, though. I ain't never done a plan like this. Even if I had, things don't always work out the way you want. Take weddings. People want theirs to go well, so they plan every little detail like a year in advance. They even hire a *wedding planner.* Like, that's all they do, these people; they plan things. Even then, even with someone who makes plans for a *living,* all it takes is some rain, or some uncle getting drunk and falling on the cake, or the groom getting E. coli, and the whole thing goes to hell.

I don't like weddings.

They tweaked the mission specs based on the sphere being attached to the probe like I wanted. That's good, but I don't want them to change it back now that they know it won't be there. I need to fatten that probe a bit; two or three kilograms will do. We can't go anywhere near these people anymore, but I think I know how to do it. I'll write a big check to the University of Colorado. They want to build this . . . Ha! I have no idea what it does. Something about space dust? Whatever it is, it will go on the probe if they manage to build it and I bet it'll weigh a couple kilos. It's supercool. As a bonus, I get to make some students happy. Students will design it; they'll write papers about it. If it launches, they'll have students monitor it for *years,* analyze the data on . . . the thing that it does? It's so awesome, I'm kind of jealous. I wish I could go back to school and go straight to college, in Colorado. . . .

I'm excited. I worked superhard on this and now I can see the finish line. I did the paper part of the plan: writing things, reading things. I did more math for this one plan than in my entire life before that.

Now comes the tricky part, the one where things go boom and my life's in danger. More in danger, I mean, 'cause my life's pretty much always in danger nowadays. I'm scared a little. I think that's normal. If the probe thing doesn't work out, then there's just no probe and I have to come up with something else. If *this* part of the plan doesn't work, then I get a bullet in the head, or I explode! I could do both. I could get a bullet in the head, then explode. Whatever. My point is the stakes are way higher.

It's like when Neo faces the three agents at the end of *The Matrix*. I forgot he gets shot first. That's bad. I don't want to do that. Maybe when Arnold fights the liquid metal guy and saves Sarah Connor and her son. Except he gets melted afterwards, so not that one either. *Léon: The Professional*. He fights like a million cops and— Crud, he dies too. *He* explodes! Why is there no movie that ends well? Oh, I know! *La Femme Nikita*, that's the one! It's perfect now that I think about it. Her life was a big mess like me and she had to train and then kill some people. Samael can be the guy in a suit. Plus she gets her life back at the end. *And* she doesn't explode, or get melted. Yeah, I want to be like *her*. She's superbadass and she speaks French. *Oui! Oui!*

47

Time for Heroes

Saa rolls down her window. The crisp of winter rushes inside the van and she watches her breath plume into the cold air. She grips the wheel tight, tighter. Her right foot pushes down. The engine roars louder and angrier until she lets go of the brake. The tires spin for a second before she's pushed back against her seat. A soldier's head turns when the van jumps over the curb. He calls for help on the radio, but it's too late. *Bang! Bang!* He fires twice as the vehicle speeds past him. Saa watches the building get larger and larger, until the whole world is nothing but red bricks. She lets go of the wheel and screams her last breath: "HAM-BOOOOO-GAAAAHHH!"

—Aster?

— . . .

Maybe not like that. I don't want anything bad to happen to her. Maybe she can climb in through a window like a cat burglar. A big window? Okay, so it'll be hard for her to just sneak in, and she stands out like a sore thumb, but she's smart; she'll figure it out. Yeah! She's *super*smart. She can do this without getting herself killed.

—Aster, will you please answer when I'm talking to you?

—What? What?

—Have you seen Saa? I've checked her room, the hotel lobby. I cannot find her anywhere.

—It's okay, Samael.

—It is most certainly not okay. We can hardly afford another one of her homicidal tantrums. I know you care for her, Aster, but if I find anyone in less than perfect health lying in the bathtub, you will be disposing of two bodies instead of one. I want that to be very clear.

—No, I meant I know where she is. She went to Washington.

—She— Why?

—I asked her if she'd go and—

—You *asked* her to go to Washington.

—Yeah. . . . You know how I got out of Walter Reed hospital? Of course you know, you were there, but anyway, they still have all my blood samples and brain scans and all that stuff. They have that dead alien from the highway. My grandmother, my great-grandmother, well, all of them, they said not to leave a trace and I thought—

—You wanted to get rid of the evidence. I understand that part. What I do not understand is how you could possibly think *Saa* was the right person for the job. She can barely order food. How will she even get to Washington? More to the point, what do you expect her to do when—*if* she makes it?

—I got her a van. I rented it.

—I seriously doubt she knows how to drive.

—*She does!* She's pretty good, actually. And I got her forty canisters of acetylene. And—

—ASTER! This will never work.

—Yes it will! . . . It *could*!

—Even if it did, blowing up a government building is . . . It's a mistake. Saa will get herself killed, which, in and of itself, isn't such a bad thing, but it will only make your situation worse. The Army will think you're working together. You will add domestic terrorism to your already enticing résumé. The colonel will be all the more determined to find you and this time, mark my words, he won't send you cake and ask for a brain scan. They will shoot you on sight, Aster, and that's not the worst part.

—It's not?

—No it isn't. The worst part is they will shoot *me* on sight because they already think *we* are working together.

—We *are* working together. . . .

—All the same, I would rather not add bullet holes to the ever-growing list of my physical woes. It is one thing to risk your own life, but you put all of ours on the line as well.

Samael is right. I *think* Samael is right. No, he is. Bruce Willis'll want to kill me more than he'll want to study me. He wants to kill me and Saa more than anything, I bet. He won't stop thinking about it. When the new Red Hot Chili Peppers came out, I wanted *that* more than anything. I asked Pa if I could do some extra chores. I stared and willed the grass to grow faster so I could mow the lawn again. I stuck my finger in every pay-phone slot hoping for loose change. I checked under the cushions at the coffee shop and ran out before they asked if I wanted anything. There wasn't a minute in the day I didn't spend thinking of ways to get what I wanted. That was just a record. I put a gun to the colonel's head, killed a bunch of his people, and now I'm going to burn down everything he has. Well, not me, but still. He'll be obsessed. He'll see me everywhere, even in his dreams. He's going to lose his mind. Good.

—I'm sorry, Samael. I guess I didn't think it through. We'll be fine, though, won't we? They won't find us if we're careful. Saa might not do it. Like you said, she can't do much on her own. Maybe she'll get hungry and rob a White Castle instead. She might just go around the block and come right back. Don't be mad at her if she does. That was all my idea. Just tell her I made a mistake.

—You can tell her yourself. I think it is best if she and I keep our interactions to a minimum. I also have to leave for a few days.

—Me too! Where are *you* going?

—I have a personal matter to attend to. My flight leaves this evening.

—Mine's in two hours! I really have to go. If Saa comes back before you leave, just . . . promise me you won't get into a fight with her.

—I will do my best. Where are you flying to?

—Back to China. Wait, what if Saa comes back and we're *both* gone? She might just leave!

—I wish we were so lucky. I only hope she returns before doing anything that cannot be undone. Sending her to Walter Reed was irresponsible, reckless.

—I know. I'm sorry.

—I expect more from you, Aster.

—I'm *very* sorry. I gotta go now. Bye!

. . .

Come on, Saa. Burn it all down.

48

Quelqu'un M'a Dit

Liebe Aster,

I wanted to say a few things in case I don't come back from Washington.

Samael told me your father died because of my commander, that it was because of her that you are being hunted. I know why you kept this from me and I appreciate that you tried to spare me some guilt. I am truly sorry. I know it does nothing to bring your father back, but I am, even if I will never really know what you lost. When my brother first told me what a parent was, I didn't understand. I belonged to the state like all the children I knew, but I was a month old when they dropped me at the academy and I have no recollection of my parents. My brother did his best to share with me the blurry images in his head. I never knew whether those memories were good or bad, only that I envied him for having them. I can never give back what my commander took from you, but if I can help you reclaim even a fraction of it, I am obligated to try. I am bound to you in more ways than one.

I come from a warring race. That's what my commander told me. That's why we came here, so we could live. I was so excited to see this peaceful world, I never gave any thought to the violence I was bringing to it. I also never imagined that it would not want me. The people here are small and frail, but they dish out a different kind of violence, more subtle, more heimtückisch. *They fear and hate anything different, and I can never not be different. I see myself through other people's eyes and I don't like what I see. I feel ugly, undesirable, except when I'm with you. I like the way you look at me.*

I'm not sure there's room for me here, or anywhere for that matter. I'm also a terrible specimen of my own race. We are bred to be fearless, and I'm not. I'm terrified. I'm afraid of what I can do. I'm afraid of dying, today. I'm afraid of so many things, but the one that scares me most is that you'll get hurt because of me. That's why I'm going to Washington. I'll never have a normal life here, but you can. If I can help make that happen, even a little bit, it's well worth taking a bullet or two. Besides, these Arschlöcher *killed my commander. I have to make them pay.*

I will see you soon, I hope. If not, just know I'm glad I found you.

Saa

49

Heartbeats

I had not been to Prague in twelve years, not since I saw my own hands wrapped around my mother's throat. I dared not show my face again, but I thought I would . . . observe from time to time, watch her from a distance to remind myself of our time together. I almost did, once, but the memory of our last encounter was too fresh and I turned the car around on my way to the airport. I told myself I would try again, later.

Later never happened and now it is too late. I swore I would never go near my mother again, but here I am, holding her tight for fear of dropping her. I do not know what to say, if I should say anything at all. It matters little, of course. She is but a pile of dust in a cardboard box. Nonetheless . . .

—I am sorry, Mother.

. . .

No. Nothing. . . . I thought saying the words out loud might make me feel better, but I only felt silly for talking to a box. I never understood what people meant when they said they were looking for "closure." I believe it might be what I am looking for now. The funeral was a letdown, to say the least. Her friends—her new friends—were there. They'd put up pictures of her throughout her life. None included me or my brothers, not a single one. It wasn't exactly a surprise, but it did not make me feel all that welcome. I introduced myself as her longtime accountant. When everyone left, I collected her remains. I thought I might feel "closure" then, but all I can think about now is that my mother is in a cardboard box. The weightless bag of ashes inside is all she ever was. Her smiles, her hugs, her sorrow, her pain, it's all in there, in a lunch bag. Perhaps she was a bit more than this, I'm sure whoever collects the ashes never really gets it all. This is *almost* my mother . . . maybe a dash of someone else. It's almost any of us, even the likes of me. When the time comes, I too will fit in a lunch bag. It all seems so . . . pointless. It also makes me glad I never had children. They might bring about some joy, a sense of accomplishment, but they too are temporary. In the end, it's just more lunch bags. More boxes. Ugh. I find the universe increasingly . . . disappointing.

Except for Aster. She is the one thing in my life that never disappoints. She left for China without so much as an explanation, but even halfway across the globe, Aster is never really gone. Case in point, I was watching the news on the plane and half of it was Aster's doing. A fire broke out in the basement of Walter Reed Army Medical Center and consumed the entire west wing of the main building before it was contained by firefighters. Oddly, it is not the crime itself that filled most of the conversation, but the terrible living conditions patients had to endure in many of the hospital's buildings. Not only did Aster succeed in erasing her presence there; it now appears some greater good may come about as a result of her foolishness.

Saa, against all reasonable odds, performed her duty well. I would not have trusted that woman to boil water. Aster trusted her with erasing all traces of her, perhaps with her life, and that trust was somehow rewarded. There is nothing about our tall alien friend that should inspire trust. She's a killer, a predator completely unfit for, well, this entire planet. She is deceitful, dangerous, *and* incompetent. Objectively, this was a terrible idea. And yet Aster saw something in Saa, something I evidently missed. Perhaps most importantly, Saa literally risked her life for someone she barely knows. From her perspective, it was an even worse idea, but she chose to do it. I cannot tell if I am more impressed with Aster's intuition or her ability to inspire others. I did not teach her either of these things, so they must have been in her already.

I look at her and I see so much of myself, not the person—we are different beasts, she and I—but my influence. She is what I made her to be, what I wish my father made of me. I sometimes forget she's also her mother, all of her ancestors. They are the canvas I painted on, the stone I carefully chiseled. The *David* is, after all, still a piece of marble. One *could* say Aster was always there and all I did was chip away the excess material. . . . Perhaps the metaphor is not entirely adequate. What I did is objectively more akin to training a dog, but that image is not quite as satisfying.

Whoever deserves credit for Aster being Aster, I cannot help thinking Mother would have liked her. It's an easy thought to have coming out of my mother's funeral, and an easy thing to say since everyone seems to like Aster, but they share—shared—the same . . . quiet strength. That is perhaps the only quiet thing about Aster—she never shuts up—but I believe she and my mother would have enjoyed each other's presence very much. I know Mother wished for a daughter when she was pregnant with me. I can hardly blame her after what my brothers had put her through. I would have enjoyed having a sister, someone who didn't look exactly like me. I wonder now what our lives could have been like had we not been . . . what we are.

This is ridiculous. Our lives would not be our lives if we were someone else. I am evidently more shaken by Mother's death than I care to admit. I suppose carrying her ashes everywhere is not helping, but it would have been bad form to drop her remains in the trash at the funeral home.

. . .

I will do it at the airport.

50

The Scientist

This is so weird. I only been to China once. Like, I know absolutely nothing about the place, but it feels superfamiliar for some reason. Well, I know the reason. It's 'cause I been to the exact same places. I landed at the same airport. I took the same route on the same kind of cab. I'm about to meet the same person in the same teahouse. I'm sitting at the same table even. The whole country's an airport, a cab, and a restaurant. It ain't that hard to get comfortable with. Also, I keep moving all the time, so my definition of what feels like home is a little skewed. Here he comes, through the same door. . . .

—My dear Aster, I did not think I would see you again so soon. When you last came to China, I—

—I'm sorry, sir. I'm terribly sorry to bother you like this, but I need your help again.

—Do not be sorry. You are always welcome. To be perfectly honest, it feels as though you never left. Our last conversation has occupied my mind incessantly until now. It would seem the only thing stronger than the existential questions you raised in my mind is the profound joy you and your family have always brought me. I presume you were unable to convince the New Horizons team to attach your device to their probe.

—Yes. Well, no. It won't be on the probe, sir. All I wanted was for them to include the weight in their calculations.

—I'm afraid I do not understand.

—Well, I never cared that much about the probe. It's the rocket they'll send it on that interests me.

—An Atlas V if I'm not mistaken.

—Yes, but with a third stage added. The rest of the rocket won't go anywhere, but the third stage will also be on an escape trajectory out of the solar system. I might have gotten the math wrong, but I think it might even get to Jupiter before the probe does.

—That is brilliant. So you want to hide your device inside the third-stage rocket.

—Oh no. Well, that's what I wanted at first, but then I read about it some more and it's *really* tiny. There's not enough room.

—I see. Then I'm afraid I don't have a solution for you. . . . Unless . . . Perhaps you could use the adap—

—The adaptor ring that attaches the rocket to the probe. Yes, sir, that's what I thought, but it won't fit either. The ring is a *tiny tiny* bit too small. Seriously, like this much. That's why I wanted the probe to be heavier. If I got them to add a few kilos to the payload, they would use the Star 48*B* as the third stage for the rocket instead of the "regular" Star 48. That one carries an extra eleven kilograms of propellant and it's a tad larger. Not much, but just enough to fit what I want to send out inside the ring.

—This is . . . impressive. If I may ask, how do you know all this?

—I bought the company that makes it. Oh, you mean how do I know about the third stage and all that? I read all the technical details and the service manuals. They'll give them to you if you just ask. But I didn't know there were that many companies. I thought, like, NASA made the rockets, but no! They buy them from someone, and the third stage is made by someone else and they subcontract parts of it to a billion other companies. I bought the one that makes the adaptor ring. Just that. Well, they make other things but not for the rocket. . . .

—You bought it.

—Yes, sir. It wasn't that much. It's a small company.

— . . .

—Sir, please say something.

—I do not know what to say. You appear to have thought of everything. I am, therefore, confused as to why you require my help.

—Well, the thing is, I can read the manuals and the budget requests and all that, but I don't know how to make things for real. I don't know how to machine aluminum and I can't ask thirty employees to make a second part with a secret compartment inside it. All I *really* wanted when I bought the company was the key to the warehouse so I can switch the crates before they deliver it to NASA.

—And you believe I can help because . . .

—Because you're really smart and you know how rockets work and you must know people who can make things like that and not tell anyone. I'll pay for it, of course. I have money. Also, you're an adult. It's a lot easier to get things done when you're an adult.

—Perhaps your friend, the one who accompanied you, could—

—He can't. He knows nothing about this kind of stuff, plus he has some health problems at the moment. I have another friend, but she has her own issues. I need *you*. Will you help me?

—Aster, I—

—Please?

—Before you interrupted me, I was going to say . . . yes. I will gladly help you. I can inquire with certain Russian entrepreneurs who will make just about anything for a price.

—Will they ask questions?

—Not if you do not want them to, but I suspect that will also have a price.

—YES! Thank you so much! Can I hug you again?

—Not so tight; I— Thank you. May I ask a favor of you in return?

—Yes, sir. Anything you want.

—This device of yours, it comes from another world.

—I think so, yes.

—Would it be possible for me to see it, perhaps to touch it?

—That's easy. I brought it with me. And the plans for the ring, and my necklace has to be in there. That's also from—like you said—another world. Here, you can hold it. Well, you can do more than that. You'll have to take it home to send to those Russians. Just . . . don't touch the sphere with the necklace. That's like the one thing you can't do.

— . . .

—Why are you crying, sir?

—Oh, Aster. Since the dawn of time, humanity wondered if there were others, whether gods or aliens lived high in the sky. Here, in my hand, lies the proof we have been looking for all along. These two objects are irrefutable evidence that we are not alone. Each could be the most significant discovery in our species's short history, and here I am about to help you get rid of them for eternity. . . . I will ask you this, Aster. I will ask you once and never mention it again. Are you absolutely certain this is what must be done?

— . . . Yes, sir, I am.

—How can you be so certain?

—I feel it in my gut?

—That is . . . good enough for me. Now, shall we order some tea?

ENTR'ACTE

The Path

Their fight in Nairi left Kish without a right hand. The sword she'd picked off a dead man broke on Tereshiin's first blow. The second blow went straight through her wrist. The third never came. Tereshiin had forgotten how much Kish loathed swords. He remembered, eventually, when his gut spilled out. He ran when the villagers came for him, holding his intestines with both hands. It was the last time Kish would see Tereshiin. She hoped her feelings would one day sort themselves, but the thought of him would always conjure a mess of emotions.

The mother of the little boy Kish had saved took care of her arm and dressed it. She did it with a smile, as if pitting dates for the night's meal. This wasn't the first time violence had entered her home and it wouldn't be the last. Kish was offered to stay but politely declined. There was somewhere else she needed to be.

It had been fourteen years since she'd seen inside its walls, but Arbailu was just as she left it. The hum of the crowd at the market, the smell of roasted lamb and fresh kidbei. Even the old fruit lady, whom four-year-old Kish believed was born this old, was still scolding children for running through her stand.

Kish's excitement morphed into uneasiness as she approached the house she grew up in. She didn't recognize the gray-haired man sweeping the pavement, but his smile and tears left little room for speculation. Both were still speechless when Nidintu ran outside and hugged her younger self. Her embrace lasted for an eternity, not nearly enough time for Kish's heartbeat to slow down.

There was too much to say, too much to ask. Kish had no idea where to begin, but her mother knew.

—Come inside and eat some dates. Nabûa, will you run to the market and see if they still have milk?

Milk and dates was exactly what Kish needed and the words started pouring out of her. She told her mother about where she'd been, what she saw. Nidintu ran her finger up and down the scar on her neck while Kish spoke of the man who upended their lives.

—He said we're not from this world, Mother. He also said we were . . . exactly the same, like two clay copies from the same stone.

—You *are* exactly like me! Your father almost had a heart attack when he saw you. I remember the day you were born like it was yesterday. I knew there was something special about you. But you are very much of Earth, my love. Even your name should tell you that.

—Kish?

—Kish is what *I* call you. You are *Kishar*, granddaughter of Tiamat, and goddess of the Earth.

They talked until sunset, and Nidintu prepared her daughter a bed. Kish was moved by the simplicity of her mother's life, but she fell asleep knowing that quietness fit her no more than the clothes she wore when she last saw this house. She woke early the next day with the same bittersweet certainty. Her mother was sitting by her side.

—I was watching you sleep. Come. There's something I need to show you.

—Now?

The women walked to the neighbor's house to borrow a horse and chariot, then rode north to the Zabu ēlū, about four leagues from the city walls. They found a secluded spot on the river shore, with a giant oak tree casting shade on a lone patch of grass. Kish joined her mother to help when she started digging at the base of the tree. Every muscle in Kish's body tensed when her fingers brushed against the smooth, round shape.

—Is this what you and that man were looking for?

—Yes, Mother. But I thought—

—No, my love. I don't remember anything. Your father and I traveled through here once and I recognized that tree from a dream. I thought—it was more a feeling than a thought—I once hid something here.

—Did you know what it was?

—Not really. Just . . . something that needed hiding.

—What will you do with it?

—Me? That is for you to decide.

. . .

—I can't stay with you, Mother. Not after we found this.

—You never could. You and I both know it. The Rādi kibsi was looking for paths in the sky. He will look for you, now. You *are* the path.

—I can't do this alone, Mother.

—Alone? You will never be alone, my love. If everything you told me is true, then you are me, and I am you. I can never *not* be with you.

—I don't want to leave you.

—Good! We have to return this horse! And your father is cooking lamb for us tonight. You can leave tomorrow, or the next day or the one after.

—And do what? I don't know what I'm supposed to do.

—You are the path, Kish. His, but also yours, and mine, and

everyone else's if you're up for it. You can help shape this world. Make it whatever you want it to be.

Kish spent nearly four months with her mother and father. Then one day, not unlike all the others, she felt ready. She never said goodbye. She just smiled and her mother knew.

—Tell Father I love him.

—He knows, but I'll tell him anyway.

—Thank you.

—Where should I look when I think of my daughter?

—East, Mother. You should look east.

—To the sunrise. I like that.

ACT VI

51

Mr. Brightside

2004

I thought I could find solace in the grass fields of Scotland. I suppose I did. Aster was done with her space endeavor. All we had to do, she said, was wait. We did. We waited for nearly two years in Scotland. I'm not entirely sure how we settled on a destination. I think Saa had something to do with it. To be honest, I was glad to help Aster while I could, but also relieved this plan of hers was coming to an end. I looked forward to settling into a quiet life away from everything. Scotland certainly fit the bill. It was . . . peaceful. We stayed in a small house looking down a cliff, surrounded by an endless sea of green. There wasn't anything for Saa to hurt, except for us and a handful of sheep. I must admit, I grew fonder of our tall friend over the past few months. I wouldn't go so far as to say I enjoyed her presence, but I got . . . used to it, the way people get used to cold weather, or the sound of trains rolling past on a nearby track. Perhaps coming to terms with my own mortality has helped me mellow out. Perhaps it was nature that did it. I *had* hoped nature would fix more than my temper. It has not. I pee blood now, every day, six times a day. I know little of medicine, especially when it comes to my kind, but I know this can't be good.

I doubt Salt Lake City will be more salutary. I had never been, nor had I considered going, to Utah before now, but this is where the rocket is made, so here we are, awaiting a piece of technology

Aster had manufactured in China. Or is it Russia? I forgot. She has a tendency to explain things in one breathless, long-winded sentence, and I sometimes stop listening midway through.

Where the thing was made is not particularly relevant. What matters is that Aster has found a way to send the sphere away from this world, one that she never shared completely until we were all herding sheep in the middle of nowhere. I wish she had been more forthcoming, but the sting of deceit pales in comparison to the sense of pride I felt at her accomplishments. This was *my* doing as much as it was Aster's. I . . . *made* her. Before me, she was ordinary, just one more face in the crowd. She was one of them. Look at her now. She forged a plan and marched forward, never looking back. She hid things from me not out of malice but because she thought the truth might hinder her plan. I understand all too well. This was a cold, calculated move, one she would have been incapable of making before I met her. I have seen my creation spread its wings and take flight. Aster may not be my daughter, but she is my legacy.

I can only imagine what she will accomplish in her lifetime. I wish she did not have to spend it running from the authorities. She could change the world if given the chance. She could *rule* it if she wanted to. She will not want to, but I have no doubt she will thrive in her time. She has the will and the resources, and I have given her the skills she'll need.

I do not have much time left, but I have done what I set out to do. I saved Aster. Sending the sphere away may prove futile if our kind is already under way, but if they are not, every mile traveled by that rocket will make Earth that much safer. It is not a perfect ending, but it is as much redemption as anyone could reasonably hope for, and likely more than I deserve. I find it difficult to quantify redemption. I can count the number of people I killed with my fingers . . . and some toes. Numerically speaking, saving a greater number of people should make up for it. Saving the world, if that's what we're doing, would certainly eclipse whatever errors in judgment I made in the past. On the other hand, the guilt I feel for killing my brothers is greater than their number would suggest. Perhaps the price to pay for that is also greater. Similarly, I take more pride in keeping Aster alive than I do in potentially saving the world. The fact that I was the one to endanger it might have something to do with the discrepancy, but I am struck by the utter lack of objectivity involved in determining one's worthiness. I suppose it is not for me to decide whether I've paid my debt or not, but I feel more at peace now than I have since tending our garden as a child.

A garden. Perhaps Aster would find it as soothing as I did. Now that I think about it, I am surprised I never brought it up before. I am no longer able to fight, or run, or do any of the things that were part of our routine in the Philippines, but this we could do. We could spend time together in the yard every day—we'll require a yard. I think Aster would enjoy caring for other living things. She might even learn to stop talking all the time.

Speak of the devil. She and Saa are waving at me. I believe it is time to go. I may be debilitated, but Aster doesn't know how to drive and I refuse to sit in a car with Saa behind the wheel. . . .

52

Neighborhood #1 (Tunnels)

Eighteen months I been waiting for this. Wait, no, *twenty* months! In Scotland! Not the have-a-pint-in-Glasgow, *Here's tae ye!* kind of Scotland, no. We lived in nothing-but-sheep-and-grass Scotland where Saa couldn't kill anyone. It was nice for about a week; then I started *wishing* for an alien invasion. Gawd, it was boring. We never saw anyone, ever, except for the old man who delivered our food each week. I talked his ear off every time. He had a hearing problem, I think. We had a wooden TV from the dark ages. No reception, of course. There *was* a DVD player, just no DVDs, except for *Tony Little's Gazelle* and we didn't even have the Gazelle. I never—not in a million years!—thought we'd be there that long, but customer service ain't exactly five-star in the world of Russian counterfeit rocket parts. Live and learn, I guess.

But here it is, in a crumbling warehouse filled with gas canisters. My little spaceship. Well, spaceship adaptor ring. To be honest, it's not the most awe-inspiring thing I seen. . . . It looks like one of those exercise saucers for babies, but without the seat or the fun things attached to it. It's shiny, so there's that. The Russians did a good job. You can't tell the sphere is encased inside the frame. My necklace is in there too, about half an inch from the sphere. Xuesen even fixed my design. There's no mechanism now, just enough give in the structure for the necklace to touch the sphere when the rocket's last stage separates. It feels superweird to get rid of it. My family managed to hold on to that piece of jewelry for three thousand years and I'm just going to shoot it into space. "See ya!" That necklace is the only thing I got from my mom. I still have her journal, but she didn't *give* it to me. Samael did, right after he stole it. That necklace was Mom's most precious thing in the whole world, and it was *her* mom's most precious thing, and her mom's mom's. My whole family would be so mad. Whatever, they're not here. I'm the one dealing with this mess and, well, you gotta do what you gotta do.

This feels supersolemn. The three of us are staring at this metal thing, like we're waiting for it to speak. I know why it matters to *me*. I put a lot of effort into this. This is how I save the world, maybe. This is how I have a tiny little chance at maybe saving the world, for a while. It doesn't sound that great when you put it this way. Still. This is my plan. I'm kind of proud. I'm allowed, ain't I? Mostly, I'm surprised I made it this far.

I understand why Saa ain't talking. This is a big deal for her too. If this doesn't work and her people come, *our* people—it's so weird to think we're the same species—they'll kill her if they come. They might kill everyone else as well, but they'll kill her first. They'll make her suffer. My plan, for what it's worth, is her only shot and she knows it. Samael, well, he's polite enough not to ruin the moment. I suppose that's something.

This is the last we'll see of it. We're shipping it today, in a big wooden crate. It'll stay in storage somewhere until they assemble the third stage. The van seemed superbig a minute ago, but it's going to be tight. I got to take these bags out first. All right, time to close that crate. I never used a nail gun before. How does it—AAHHH!

—I'm fine! I'm fine. Just, scared a little . . . That ought to do it. Saa, you want to give me a hand to lift it? On three. One. Two. Threeeee.

Crud, it's heavy. I'd have asked Samael to help, but he can barely walk. It's in. I just hope I'm strong enough to p— Oh, right, *Saa's* strong enough to push it. Close the doors and . . . *voilà*. I'll tap twice on the van to let Sam know it's loaded. I always wanted to do that.

—Is anything the matter, Aster?

—No, why?

—Why did you hit the van?

—Oh. It's . . . Never mind. You have the address, right?

—Yes, Aster. I do. I will see you at the hotel when I get back.

—Drive safe!

There. It's done. I already switched the crate numbers in the computer. When they assemble the rocket, this is the one they'll get. I done it! I'm crying a little. Well, almost crying, like when you're on the cusp and it just hurts your throat real bad. I wish I— WHAT THE HELL?

—Saa! What'd you do that for?

She threw a basketball at my head! I don't know where she found it.

—Wasn't me!

Oh, sure, it wasn't you. It's just the two of us in here now. I'm sure she thought I'd catch it, but still, *ouch!* Oh, she's laughing at me now. Fine, I'll play with you. It's hard to stay mad at Saa. I tried a bunch of times. It's that big grin of hers; it gets you every time. It doesn't work on Samael, but I don't think he's as hell-bent on killing her anymore. Maybe he knows he can't fight her in the shape he's in. She'd kick his ass with one arm tied behind her b—

What's happening? She heard something. Yes, I hear it too. Car after car pulling up around the building. I think the cops are here. No sirens, but we can see the red lights flashing through the little windows in the garage door. The Army can't be too far behind.

Whoa. Head rush. I'm sweating like a sinner in church. Kibsu instincts kicking in. Saa too. She's pacing like a caged animal. She just grabbed a crowbar from the floor.

—Saa! What are you doing?

— . . .

—Saa!

—I'm going to kill them all.

53

Butterflies and Hurricanes

Aster is dead.

I crossed paths with a dozen police cars less than a mile from the warehouse. I nearly turned around, but there was little I could do to help Saa and Aster in my current state. I . . . convinced myself they had already left and kept on driving. Then everything disappeared. . . . I felt the ground shake. The flash in the rearview mirror blinded me instantly. I hit the brakes as hard as I could to stop from crashing into whatever was in front. It took a moment for my eyes to adjust. When I looked back, the column of black smoke was towering over the entire cityscape. That building was filled to the brim with explosive materials. *No one* could have survived this. Not the police. Not Saa. Not . . .

Aster had her whole life ahead of her. There is so much she could have done with it. What a waste. It wasn't supposed to end this way. Aster . . . Aster wasn't my daughter, but I felt I was leaving something behind because of her. I killed my father, my brothers. I ended my bloodline after three thousand years, but I did not fear death because a part of me would live on, through *her.* Now I will die alone. I will cease to exist and no one will remember or care that I ever did. The loss isn't all mine. Every one of Aster's ancestors gave their life to ensure the next generation survived. They all died for nothing. They lived for nothing. When my heart stops, an entire species will have disappeared from this world, and no one will know. I do have a cousin, so maybe there is hope.

I should have died in that warehouse. Five more minutes and I would have. Five minutes and I would be lying dead next to Aster. I would have welcomed that fate given the chance. I get to live a little longer, but it hardly seems like a prize. Perhaps it was my destiny to bring Aster's plan to conclusion. Had I died, that plan would have gone up in flames like the building we were in. The Army would have the sphere. All the work Aster put in would have been lost, her training and efforts a complete waste of time. It wasn't. I delivered the crate as planned.

She did not die in vain. I should find comfort in that.

Sometimes I feel the universe is toying with me, as though we're all puppets in some sick show. Aster could have died yesterday, or last year. She could have been caught. I could have crashed into a wall when the building exploded. She did not, and neither did I. A million different things conspired together to make sure Aster's plan worked. It was, as they say, "meant to be." The universe would not let Aster live, but it wanted her plan to succeed. I wonder if anything we do matters at all. If things are . . . *destined* to happen, then free will is an illusion. Time is an unstoppable wind and we're nothing but pinwheels pretending we all want to spin. Was killing my brothers a mistake or was it also "meant to be"? Did I have a choice? Would the pain I carry around be any less real if the answer were no?

I don't know which is worse: a universe with intent and cruelty, or one of complete and utter randomness. I can bow to the former, pray for what might pass as mercy. In that universe, my fate is punishment, justice handed to me by a wicked existence who revels in humbling everyone to the point of humiliation. I can *hate* that universe with unbridled passion because there is something to hate. One cannot hate a random universe with the same fury. It robs you of that precious right. It hurts you just the same but eludes blame for its fickleness because it never once cared about you.

Aster is dead. Was it by design? Or did a cosmic roll of a quadrillion dice lead to the most improbable outcome? Neither seems particularly satisfactory. I never had faith in a high being. I never believed in luck either, but the odds of my being alive when everyone else died were . . .

What *were* the odds? What were the chances I would escape just in the nick of time? Come to think of it, I did not *escape.* I left the warehouse because Aster asked me to. I left a warehouse full of explosive materials moments before it blew up because she told me to leave. I went where she told me, *when* she told me.

. . .

We all did. Aster picked that warehouse. She chose the location, the time. I left at her request and delivered the crate on schedule to an address of her choosing. . . .

. . .

Everything was *precisely* as Aster wanted it to be. . . .

54

This Fire

All this waiting is driving me mad. So is Saa running in circles, swinging her crowbar at people who ain't there. The police have been here for an hour, but no one's talking. They just want to make sure we don't go anywhere. Someone else is coming and I have a pretty good idea who it is. He'd have told them to stay put. He'd have insisted. "Don't move a *finger* until I get there!" This is personal to him, like Samael said. I ran away twice and put a gun to his head. Saa, well, Saa blew up his life's work. I wish I could have seen that.

GAWD, I'm nervous! What was that movie Pa really liked? Al Pacino robbing a bank. Anyway, he didn't look that nervous and he spent way longer than that inside that bank. I wonder if they'll just bust through the door and storm in. There's no hostages, nothing to negotiate. Still, I bet he'll ask nicely at first. With this many cops, there are bound to be news crews around by now. No one wants to look like a raging maniac on TV. I wouldn't. Oh. I think we're about to find out. There's more people coming. Big trucks from the sound of them.

—Aster, it's Colonel Veilleux. I know you remember me.

—YES, SIR! I DO!

—Good. As you can see, we have the building surrounded, so I'm going to keep this simple. I want you and your friend to come out the front door with your hands above your head. Will you do that for me, Aster?

"As you can *see*"? I can't see *anything*! The little windows are too high; I can't— WHOA! Saa lifted me like a sack of spuds and sat me on her shoulders. Crud, he wasn't kidding about us being surrounded. Every cop in town must be here. There's a SWAT team, and a truck ton of people wearing camo. What does he think I'll do? There's enough folks here to reenact D-Day. I ain't gonna fight all of them. Saa might, though. I guess it makes *a little bit* of sense.

—I DON'T THINK I CAN DO THAT, SIR!

—Aster, don't make me go in there. There are a lot of antsy people here, so please, do as I say so we can all go home without anyone getting hurt.

—SIR?

—Yes, Aster?

Here we go.

—EAT MY SHORTS!

Whoa, that felt good. Saa snorted, but Bruce Willis didn't find it funny. He turned around and walked back behind the soldiers. I can't hear what he's saying. He must be giving orders or— OH CRUD! THEY'RE GONNA SHOOT!

Thunk. Thunk. Thunk. The shots make tiny mounds inside the garage door. I'd be dead already if it were any thinner. The *walls* aren't thick enough. I hear bullets zipping by everywhere. I take Saa's hand and drag her behind some steel barrels. She looks more confused than scared. How did this happen? How did they know we're here? I know how they found us. An anonymous tip. You just have to time it right. The average response time is about eight minutes in Salt Lake City. It's amazing what you can find on the Internet.

The bullets stopped. Bright light is seeping in through the holes in the walls, a thousand light beams crisscrossing in the floating dust. In all that chaos, Saa didn't feel the handcuff close around her wrist. She didn't hear it klink around the steel pole next to her. I crawl backwards towards the rear wall. She tries to follow me, but her arm stays behind. A few tugs on the pole. She knows it won't budge, but she tries anyway. She looks down at the duffel bags. Why'd I take them out of the van? Why'd I bring them in the first place? There. Two and two. She puts herself together as best she can.

She watches me back away. She ain't struggling; she's just . . . sitting there. I thought she'd be frantic, "survive at all costs." I guess they don't have that rule. She doesn't seem angry either, just hurt. I don't think it's the betrayal that stings the hardest. It's that I'm the one doing it. She likes me. I like her too; that's what makes this so hard.

She looks like she's given up. I don't know why it bugs me, but it does. She's smart, courageous. She's got that Klingon thing: "You're outmanned, you're outgunned, you're outequipped. What else have you got?" "*Guile.*" Giving up doesn't seem like her. Unless . . . Unless she's not. She knows what's happening; that I'm sure of. Maybe she's *choosing* to play her part.

I don't want to think about it. I press the button on the timer. I don't need my Kibsu instincts to know what happens next. Three minutes from now the building will explode. The acetylene in those cylinders will burn to twenty-two hundred degrees Celsius. There'll be nothing left. Nothing left of her but some charred bone fragments. They'll find smaller bones next to hers. Someone my age. No recoverable DNA, except maybe for the pint of blood that spilled under the floor gratings. That one's mine. Either way, I'm dead. Maybe not a hundred percent dead, but dead enough they'll stop looking for me.

—Goodbye, Saa.

She's shaking the handcuffs against the pole.

—Set me free, Aster.

—I wish I could.

—Aster! *Shyesecht het?*

—I want to help you, but I *can't*. It's just me, Saa. There's a whole world out there against us and I can't . . . keep running like that. I'm not strong enough.

She's smiling.

—*Set. Me. Free.*

She said it softly, like a lullaby. She wants to be free, free from all this, free from suffering, from being alone. She wants what everyone else has, but she knows she can't get it. She's asking me for the one thing I *can* give.

I see myself moving. Must be one of those telepathic brain farts. I walk back to her slowly. I take the key out of my pocket. She could kill me if she wanted to, snap my neck like she did Jean-Pierre's. I don't seem to care. I take the handcuff off her wrist. She rubs it a little while she stares at me. There's so much there I can't make it all out, too many emotions fighting for a spot at the window. I hug as much of her as I can. I think I need it more than she does. Her hand moves up my side, up to my face. I feel her giant thumb rubbing against my cheek. She kisses my forehead and smiles.

—I'm sorry, Saa.

It's time to wake up. But I don't, because all of it was real.

—You need to go.

And she's up. All those feelings, they're gone now. She's a grinning five-year-old again, itching for a fight. I better hurry. There's only two minutes left. I pull out the grid. One last look before I squeeze inside the storm drain. I'm going to miss you, Saa.

. . .

I can still hear her. I think she's laughing. That's right, Saa. You give them hell.

55

Wake Up

She's alive. Half a block was removed from the map, but there isn't a scratch on her. She's still shaken. This was not as easy as she hoped it would be. She looks . . . sad, but I am the one crying. I wanted so much to believe she was safe, that this was all a ruse, yet I could not shake the image of that column of smoke from my mind. I could not stop thinking I had lost her too.

—You planned all this, didn't you?

—Can we talk about it later? I just want to lie down for a bit.

—You scared the hell out of me, Aster. Never do that again.

—I had to.

—You staged your own death.

—Well, yeah. They'd never stop coming if they thought I was still alive.

—And Saa?

— . . .

—Forget I asked.

—I wish there'd been another way, but you saw what happened with Jean-Pierre. There was no place for her here.

—She was a link to you. Another alien for the colonel to chase after. Now she's dead. Every shred of evidence you ever existed burned down, thanks to Saa— I know now why you did not want me to kill her. Consider me awed.

—Ain't nothing to be proud of.

—On the contrary, Aster. It was a well-laid plan, brilliantly executed. Saa is dead and so are you in the eyes of the authorities. The only one left alive is m—

— . . .

I heard myself say it as if it came from someone else's mouth. I *am* the only one left. The only one they will be looking for. I am the only person who knows Aster, the only person left alive who can lead them back to her. I am the *one* thing that threatens her freedom . . . and I am dying.

—Aster.

—Yes, Samael.

—Did you do this to me?

—Do what?

—You know perfectly well what I'm asking. Do you have anything to do with my sickness?

—You ain't sick. You been eating lots of warfarin.

— . . .

—It's rat poison—I didn't know what it was either. My great-grandma killed Stalin with it. That's what she thought, anyway.

—You've been poisoning me?

—I'm sorry, sir. I just—

—Sir? Since when?

—Back in the Philippines. I put it in your coffee every morning.

—Aster, that was three years ago.

—That's . . . when I made my plan. I told you about it.

—I— . . . Why?

—You know why. Because you're the Tracker, and I'm . . . You killed my mom.

—I did not! I told y—

—Stop. You know that ain't true. Look me in the eye and tell me you had nothing to do with it. She'd still be alive if it weren't for you, right? I could be wrong, but I think that's why you took care of me, 'cause you felt guilty for murdering my mom.

Kill the little bitch!

Snap her neck!

Breathe.

I reach inside my coat pocket and quietly pull out my knife. I wait until she's midsentence before I turn and stab at her chest. She grabs my arm and stops me. She's faster than I am now, stronger. She turns the blade downward and pushes it into my thigh. Severed femoral artery. I'm dead in minutes. She holds my hand while I bleed out in front of her.

Breathe.

I reach inside my coat pocket and quietly pull out my knife. I switch hands behind my back and go for her kidney. She doesn't stop talking, but I feel her hand wrap around my wrist. I would struggle, but her other hand crushed my trachea already. I didn't see it coming. My lungs burn as I gasp for air and watch her face slowly blur into darkness.

Breathe.

I *lunge* at her, both hands reaching for her throat. She's three feet away, watching me fall face-first on the ground.

I reach inside my coat pocket. I . . .

. . .

There's nothing I can do. She knows it, or she'd have killed me by now.

It seems I have been bested by my creation. The apprentice has become the master. It is . . . fitting, in a way. I wanted to end this cycle of death, to lift the curse on my family. I suppose I have, or I *will* have when they lay me to rest. I might have a year, or a month. It doesn't matter. I feel oddly at peace, with death and with life. I will leave something of me behind, my final opus.

—Can I ask a favor of you?

—Yes.

—Will you stay with me until . . . the end?

—Yes, sir, I will. We can do whatever you want, go wherever you wanna go.

—Thank you. . . . What will you do then? After I'm gone.

—I don't know. Take them to the stars, I guess.

—By yourself? You're still young, Aster. You need help. You need me.

—I need someone *like* you. Someone older. I need a face to put on what I'm doing.

—We made a good team, you and I.

—Your cousin can do that.

—What?

—You said you have a cousin. That means he's just like you, right? He's everything you are, except he's innocent. I was innocent when you found me. Now I ain't. And you know what, sir? One of us has to be.

—I *saved* you.

—Did you? I was just a kid. I didn't have much of a life, but it was mine. My life. You took it from me. Your cousin didn't. He didn't take my mother's life, my grandmother's.

—When I met you, you were . . .

—You were gonna say "weak," weren't you? It's ironic, because the old Aster would have let you live. That Aster wouldn't hurt a fly. She was a good kid before you came into her life. She's gone now, thanks to you. All that's left is . . . what you made of me.

I wanted to change. . . . I saw what I'd become when I hurt my mother and I wanted that man gone. That's why I chose to help Aster. I didn't do it for her, I did it for me. I couldn't bear to look in the mirror and see the monster anymore. I tried to change. Perhaps I did change, but the monster never really left.

Aster saw it too. She saw what I was, and she knew she'd end up exactly like me. She needed me gone like I needed me gone, before there was nothing left of her. Aster killed me for the same reason I saved her. I was afraid to die alone, forgotten, but I feel more at peace now than I ever have, with death and with life.

I *do* leave something behind. She is the best of me.

—Aster?

—What?

—I'm proud of you.

CONCLUSION

56

Rebellion (Lies)

2005

I'm not *entirely* sure what I want to do with my life. That's normal, right? I'm seventeen. I'll be eighteen in a month, but I don't think I'm supposed to have all my ducks in a row on the first day. There's the stars thing. I'll do that, for sure, but I need to finish school first. There's time, I think. We don't know if the bad guys are coming—maybe Saa and her crew were the only ones who picked up the signal. Even if they're on their way, there's a chance they'll go chasing after the sphere.

I don't think the stars thing is a full-time job, though. Maybe it is, but I'll still need a hobby. My ancestors all had other things they cared about. Grandma was all about CO_2 levels and the ozone layer, so was her mom, but there are tons of supersmart people working on that now. I don't know how much I can help. Maybe I can save the Alabama red-bellied turtles. I did raise thirty bucks to help when I was younger, but now I can do a lot more. There still ain't that many left; I checked. All it would take is a big oil spill, and boom. All gone.

We'll see. I gotta do the stars thing, though.

Take 'em to the stars! The "them" part is hard. I spent five years trying to send a beach ball towards the stars and that ain't even launched yet. It's ironic, but Samael did more about space travel than me *or* my mom ever did. Someone won that ten million bucks he offered as a prize for flying to space. One project won, but there's a dozen more companies making rockets because of that contest. New people, new designs, new ideas. It's pretty neat. It's my money he gave away, so I guess I helped. I wanted to name the prize after Samael, 'cause, well, it was *his* idea and I felt bad for poisoning him. He said: "Let the dead lie." The only thing he wanted is for me to drop his ashes in the garbage at the Prague airport. He never said why.

It's weird not having him around. After Pa died, I needed . . . There's a part of me that's sorry he's gone. The other part, well, the other part is still figuring things out. We are the Kibsu. Sure. Except there's no "we" and there ain't going to be a "we" for a while. It's just me. And the rules.

About those rules, I think it's time for a cleanup.

Fear the Tracker. Always run, never fight.

Nope. Don't need that one anymore. There ain't a Tracker left to run from. Samael has a cousin, sure, but he doesn't know anything. He might know he's not like everyone else, but he never heard about us, or the sphere. You can't be the Tracker if you don't know there's anything to track. I have no idea how I'll get him to help me, but I'll figure it out sooner or later. I mean, it can't be harder than secretly sending something outside the solar system, can it?

Preserve the knowledge.

That's the easy rule. I can see why they put it first. I mean, I can do that. The knowledge is in a box at home. I'll try to add some after I finish school. I'm going straight to college. I never finished high school, but all my papers are fake anyway. Might as well give myself a diploma.

Survive at all costs.

That one seems a bit obvious. I get why it's there. It's supposed to make me feel better if I have to kill someone, but I don't think we're that special. Tons of people would kill to save themselves.

Anyway, I'll keep it, in case my granddaughter is superdepressed or something. You never know.

Don't draw attention to yourself.

That's a keeper, for sure. The colonel's dead and pretty much everyone thinks I am. Still, I ain't taking any chances. I don't want to live in a hospital basement again.

What's next? Oh yeah. *Don't leave a trace.*

IIIIII dunno. Maybe. It's good, but I think it's sort of implied with the drawing-attention thing. Or maybe this one implies the other? Whatever, I say it's redundant, and I don't really like rules, so bye.

There can never be three for too long.

Ewww, that one. I ain't ready for a kid, I sure ain't ready for two, but I know the math looks bad if my daughter decides to have nine babies and her kids do the same. Still, I'm not going to blow my brains out just because I have a granddaughter. What kind of person does that? We need to work on this one a little.

There can never be sisters. That sounds weird.

There can only be one child. It's clear, to the point, but it doesn't have that "ancient rule" zing. Kinda like *Don't have two children,* or the one-child Kibsu Policy . . .

There can be only one! Too bad it's taken. Maybe that's a good thing. Information gets lost, he said. I wouldn't want my descendants to start wiping each other out with swords.

One mother, one daughter . . . I think that works. It doesn't have a verb, though. Meh. It's fine. So what do we have?

Preserve the knowledge.

Survive at all costs.

Don't draw attention to yourself.

One mother, one daughter.

That's better, I think. Yep. Better. I'll teach that to my daughter. She'll think I'm supercool. The rest I'll make up as I go. I'm allowed; it's my first time being the Kibsu, even if I'm the Hundred and . . . Two. Gawd, that's a horrible number. My mom had a good one. Hundred and One, that's cool. Grandma had that nice round number. Even the Ninety-Nine ain't bad.

. . .

Hundred and Two, that's, like . . . Mr. Pink. Why do I have to be Mr. Pink?

57

No Heaven

Crud, I almost forgot. I need to add *one more* rule.

Try to have some fun.

EPILOGUE

CYCLE 9748 (APPROX. A.D. 2146)

Green. White. Green. White. A hapless man stared at the blinking light above his head, unsure if it was real or not. He hadn't seen anything, touched anything, thought anything, in centuries. It would take a few minutes for his brain to process visual stimuli and turn the blur into something concrete, hours to recognize what he was looking at, days to make sense of it all. One by one, he remembered some of the things he once knew. His name was Hah-Saak Shere-sa Tereshiin Kih Meeha. He was twenty-seven. He was an environmental engineer on the arc ship *Haas-kee II.* He had a younger sister back home.

There were still many things Shere-sa did not know: Why the ship had brought him out of stasis. *When* the ship had brought him out of stasis. The why wasn't immediately clear. He was, as far as he could tell, the only one awake. There were no alarms, no apparent failure he was meant to correct. The when, on the other hand, was displayed in bright light on every screen around him. Nine hundred cycles. Everyone he knew outside the ship was dead, obviously. His sister was dead, but so were her children, their children, and— Shere-sa rushed to navigation as fast as his recovering body would allow and punched in the only coordinates he knew. The large screen filled with murky spectacle, a nameless nebula the computer numbered automatically. Shere-sa fell to his knees. The star that warmed his face as a child had, as scientists predicted, gone supernova, leaving behind a neutron star spinning frantically inside a cloud of dust. It wasn't his sister who died, not the people he knew, their children, or their children. Everyone had died. His entire race, what was left of it, now slept on a handful of arc ships roaming the galaxy in search of a new home.

Shere-sa wished he were still asleep. He wished he'd died with his sister. He wished for a million different things, and when he was done wishing, only one truth remained: He was awake, and there had to be a reason for it. Shere-sa combed through the ship's systems looking for purpose. He found what he was looking for in the communication logs. A faint signal thirty-eight light-years away. Shere-sa recognized it immediately. They were still sending out scout ships when he joined the academy, the government hailing the pilots as heroes. He himself had volunteered, but he lacked the physical skills to become a citizen. Science, he thought, was the next best thing, his chance to help. Shere-sa's despair made way for something new. Perhaps it was hope, or a nascent belief in destiny. He had, after all, spent years training for this very moment. When a scout ship found a suitable planet for relocation, the pilot would activate a beacon to guide the arc ships. It was Shere-sa's job, his main purpose, to set a course and restart the environmental and farming systems before they could wake up everyone.

His newfound enthusiasm faded when he brought the signal's location on-screen. During his training, Shere-sa had taken part in thousands of simulations. In each of them, he woke up on a ship exactly like this one, heard a beacon exactly like this one, and steered the ship towards it. Unlike all the beacons he'd seen, however, this one was moving away from the nearest star instead of orbiting it. This one seemed to lack a planet.

Shere-sa started making a list of possible explanations: the beacon was on a ship and accidentally turned on, the beacon was on a ship that was destroyed and now floating in space, someone found a suitable planet but was unable to land, someone found a suitable planet, but the beacon was removed, by natural forces, by an enemy, by—Shere-sa realized the list would keep growing indefinitely. In the end, there were only two possibilities. There was a planet nearby they could settle on, or there wasn't. He was only beginning to grasp the magnitude of the decision he had to make. If his was the only remaining arc ship, the survival of an entire species was at stake. On the one hand, ignoring the signal meant giving up what could be their only chance. On the other, waking up everyone on the ship meant they had, at best, a few decades to find a home. There were a hundred thousand people lying in the cargo holds, half of them impregnated before launch. In fourteen months, there would be one hundred and fifty thousand mouths to feed. The hydroponic bays could only produce so much, and with every system back online their core reactor would run out of fuel a thousand times faster.

☼

Shere-sa thought he might have a panic attack but still laughed at the irony. On a ship filled to the brim with people, he was utterly and totally alone. He went back to the cargo hold where he'd awoken and, as he stared at the endless sea of stasis pods before him, he was filled with a sudden sense of calm. He did not know these people. Aside from the maintenance crew, they were all citizens, mindless brutes who saw him as a lesser being and never missed a chance to remind him of it. They were his people, the best of them at that, but Shere-sa didn't sign up to save *a* people; he joined this mission to save his sister, his best friend, the girl at the market he never got the courage to talk to. They were all gone now, and all the people like them, because better people, the very ones he was looking at, didn't think they were worth saving.

*

Shere-sa took one last look around, crawled back into his stasis pod, and hummed himself to sleep with a song his sister liked to sing. Perhaps he'd wake up again in another thousand years. Perhaps not. As the world around him began to fade, Shere-sa etched a smile. He just didn't care.

FURTHER READING

("Miami," by Ariane Moffatt.
I'm adding music to everything now.)

This is it. The end of the end. I'm a bit emotional about writing this, but it feels wrong to cry about having too much fun for a few years. You already know how this works, so without further ado, let's learn some stuff.

There were all kinds of great scientific missions in Aster's lifetime. The Hubble telescope launched in 1990—it's been doing its thing for over thirty years!—and for a while I was tempted to center this story on it. The Cassini probe—its real name is Cassini–Huygens—visited Saturn again, entering its orbit for the first time, and the Huygens lander touched down on the planet's largest moon, Titan. It's supercool, plus it's a joint venture between *three* space agencies. The *Sojourner* rover was part of the Mars Pathfinder mission and launched in 1996. Seven years later, the Mars Exploration Rover mission gave us two more: *Spirit* and *Opportunity*.

In the end, I chose *New Horizons* because it's awesome and I like the continuity after exploring every other planet with the *Voyagers* in the last book.

Lots of people wanted to send something to Pluto because, well, we'd never been. In 1992, a scientist at JPL made a phone call to Clyde Tombaugh, the guy who discovered Pluto in 1930, and asked for permission to visit "his" planet. There were, in fact, a whole *series* of proposed missions to Pluto that fit into the New

Frontiers program at NASA, a new program for medium-sized missions (things that cost more than a buttload of money but less than a boatload of money). In the end, five projects were submitted to the New Frontiers competition and they narrowed it down to two: New Horizons, from the Johns Hopkins University Applied Physics Laboratory, and another similar Pluto mission from the University of Colorado that was backed by JPL among others. I'd love to make this suspenseful, but you already know who won. The celebrations didn't last long, however, because the NASA administrator George W. Bush appointed didn't like the idea and wouldn't include it in the budget for the following year. That was . . . bad, and they didn't have aliens willing to sign big checks for them. Their best bet, as well as Aster's once Samael was caught at a meeting with the New Horizons team, was for the mission to be included in the Planetary Science Decadal Survey. That's very much like a shopping list for the following decade of space stuff prepared by the National Research Council. That particular decadal survey put a mission to Pluto at the top of the list. It also gave us a bunch of Mars rovers.

New Horizons launched on January 19, 2006, on top of an Atlas V rocket. Once it reached Earth orbit, the Centaur second stage—the same Centaur used to launch the Voyager probes—fired for nine long minutes. That gave the probe a ton of speed, enough to enter a gigantic orbit around the sun, but not enough to escape its pull. That's when the third stage comes in. They used a Star 48B rocket, slightly bigger than the regular Star 48 like Aster wanted. When it fired, the probe reached a speed of 58,536 kilometers per hour. That's the fastest launch velocity *ever. Apollo 11* took seventy-six hours to reach the moon's orbit. *New Horizons* did it in nine.

On June 13 of the same year, a couple months past the orbit of Mars, *New Horizons* flew by a small asteroid with the cute name

132524 APL in the asteroid belt. The people of Earth thought that was cool and decided to test the probe's instruments on this tiny rock. It worked fine. Then something terrible struck: a chunk of irony of cosmic proportions—in the Alanis Morissette sense of the word.

New Horizons launched in January of 2006 towards Pluto, the only planet of the solar system we'd never visited. On August 24 of that same year, the International Astronomical Union *deplanetized* Pluto! For real! *While* they were on their way there!

New Horizons was about halfway to Jupiter, but it was now going to explore a "dwarf planet." The last *real* planet, as it retroactively happened, had already been explored by *Voyager* 2 fifteen years earlier. Don't get me wrong, going to Pluto is awesome no matter what you call it, but CAN. YOU. IMAGINE? I bet at least one member of the International Astronomical Union got his car keyed that day.

The probe reached Jupiter in February 2007 for a gravity assist maneuver and stole fourteen thousand kph of speed from the biggest planet in the process. We think of gravity assist as a rather quick thing, something that fits in one scene on a TV show, but *New Horizons* observed Jupiter's atmosphere and its rings for about four months. It also took some really nice pictures of Europa and Ganymede along the way.

After Jupiter, the probe spent most of the voyage in hibernation, except for periodic system checks. That must have been stressful. It helped preserve the probe's power and systems, but every time you turn something off there's a real chance you won't be able to turn it back on.

Absolutely nothing happened on February 25, 2010, but the probe had traveled half the distance to Pluto, or 2.38 *billion* kilometers.

In December 2014, they turned *New Horizons* back on for

the last time and someone's ulcers probably started to clear up. By April 2015, the probe was taking reasonably good pictures of Pluto. The closest it got to the planetary has-been was about eight thousand kilometers, in July of the same year.

PLUTO

Planet or not, Pluto is awesome, but we knew that already. For starters, its orbit isn't on the same plane as the other planets. Imagine all the planets spinning on a flat surface, like your kitchen table. Pluto's orbit would go through your foot and the ceiling fan. It would probably give you the finger too. It's such a rebel, its orbit is superoval compared to everything else. Sometimes it's even closer to the sun than it is to Neptune.

There were, of course, plenty of things we *didn't* know about the dwarf planet, but you wouldn't think its size was one of them. Well, its size was one of them. Pluto, *New Horizons* determined, is roughly 2,370 kilometers in diameter, a little bigger than we thought. That's still 30 percent smaller than our moon, so maybe that dwarf planet thing isn't so crazy. Our moon doesn't have moons, though. Pluto has five: Charon—that's the big one, about half the size of Pluto—Hydra, Kerberos, Nix, and Styx. ♩♫ Suite Madame Bluuuuue . . . ♪ ♬

The probe found all sorts of atmospheric activity on Pluto. There are clues that suggest it might even have an internal ocean of water and ice. *New Horizons* took pictures of a gigantic one-thousand-kilometer nitrogen glacier on the surface. If you're *really* into glaciers, that's, by far, the biggest one we've ever seen. It's called Sputnik Planitia.

All in all, *New Horizons* collected 6.25 gigabytes of pictures and data during its flyby of Pluto and Charon, which it then had to transmit back to Earth. Six gigabytes is roughly what your Internet provider will charge you for if you've used up your data plan and streamed *Pacific Rim* in HD. It took *New Horizons* fifteen months to send it all. In its defense, Netflix would be a lot slower if it streamed from four and a half light-hours away at one or two kilobits per second.

So to recap, Pluto was a planet, then it wasn't, but it was, at the very least, the farthest thing we'd ever looked at up close. Well . . . I feel for you, Pluto lovers. I really do.

A couple months after the Pluto encounter, mission planners implemented a course correction towards 2014 MU69, better known under its stage name, Ultima Thule, and now officially called 486958 Arrokoth. You've probably seen pictures of it. It's like a poorly made two-ball snowman. The big ball was called Ultima and the smaller one Thule. It was, at that time, 6.4 billion kilometers from Earth, about one and a half times the distance to Pluto.

New Horizons should have power until the mid-2030s, so it will keep transmitting for a while. Though it will never overtake the *Voyagers*, it's still traveling pretty fast on a path that will take it out of the solar system.

That's all I have to say about the probe, but Aster didn't put the sphere *on* the probe, now did she? That's right; she put it on top of the slightly larger Star 48B third stage. You'll be happy to know the third stage reached Jupiter faster than the actual probe did. There's no one at the wheel, so it's going where it's going, but it passed Pluto's orbit in 2015, just four months after *New Horizons*. It's on an escape trajectory out of the solar system, so there is hope for our survival after all.

One more thing: when Samael meets the folks at Johns Hopkins University, he tells them this cockamamie story about sending his dead father's ashes on the space probe. I made that up, obviously. I mean, it *is* obvious that I made this up, right? Well . . .

Clyde Tombaugh—the one who discovered Pluto—died between that 1992 phone call and the 2006 launch of *New Horizons,* and they legit put some of his ashes inside the probe to honor him. Here's the best part. I *really* made it up. I had no idea this happened when I wrote Sam's story.

VENETIA BURNEY PHAIR

As you heard from Aster, Venetia Phair, then Venetia Burney, got to name Pluto when she was eleven years old. It's a good story, but it gets much better when you start digging a little, and, as most good stories do, it involves little green men. The first thing to know is that Venetia's entire family was in the business of naming things. Venetia is the daughter of Charles, a reverend who taught at Oxford, and his wife, Ethel. Her granddad, the one who passed on her suggestion to the astronomers, was named Falconer Madan. Now *that's* a superhero name if I've ever heard one. Other than having a badass monicker, Falconer was a librarian at Oxford—yay, libraries!—and had a brother named Henry who named not one but both moons of Mars. They're called Phobos and Deimos. Look them up if you have a minute. My bet is Mars was out sick the day they picked moons.

Clyde Tombaugh, who discovered Pluto, liked the name Venetia suggested, in part because it started with *pl.* Now *pl* doesn't sound that great to most of us, but it happens to be the initials of Percival Lowell, who predicted the existence of a mysterious "Planet X" beyond Neptune. Percival also spent over a decade studying Mars, enough to write three books about it. Since there were no rockets, or space telescopes, studying Mars meant staring at it through the lens of a ground-based telescope and taking notes. Percival did that, a lot, and he meticulously sketched the planet's features on paper, as he saw them. Some of the markings on the surface looked to him like canals. He also saw dark spots at the intersection of these canals, which he termed "oases." These, he believed, were signs of an advanced alien civilization irrigating their drying planet by tapping the polar ice caps. I know, that's a lot to conclude from pencil sketches. As you'd expect, the rest of the scientific world was, let's say, skeptical—most astronomers couldn't even see the things he saw—but while Percival wasn't the most popular guy at scientific conventions, the idea was exciting enough to earn him some very avid followers.

I think Aster was right and they should have named the probe after Venetia Burney Phair, but they did the next best thing. They named a crater on Pluto after her, and *part* of the probe. Starting in 2002, a bunch of students at the University of Colorado built a gizmo that can detect space dust, and in 2006 they renamed it the Venetia Burney Student Dust Counter. It's a really cool project. Students designed the thing, of course, but they also ran their part of the mission until 2010.

In January of 2006, just as *New Horizons* was launching, eighty-seven-year-old Venetia was interviewed by NASA to talk about her planet-naming experience. It's online[3] on the NASA website and well worth a listen. Venetia Burney Phair died in 2009.

SPACE PLANES

In the last book, Lola had settled in Gulfport, Mississippi, mostly because I liked the place when I visited thirty years ago. It also happens to be real close to NASA's Stennis Space Center, where they test rocket engines. It's not as well-known as other NASA sites, but you've probably seen pictures of them testing the really big rockets. They worked on the *Saturn V* in the sixties, the Space Shuttle main engine, and more recently the ridiculously big Space Launch System (SLS) NASA plans to use for

3. https://www.nasa.gov/topics/history/features/Venetia_phair.html.

the Artemis program, which will send the next generation of astronauts to the moon. I checked their annual report to see what they were working on in 1999 and, lo and behold, half of it was space planes. Space planes are cool. They're what a kid imagines when you talk about spaceships: a thing with wings you can fly around in, like an X-wing, or *Galactica*'s Viper, not a giant tube with a tiny cone on top.

The Space Shuttle was *sort of* a space plane. It had wings, looked spaceshippy enough, but it couldn't fly to space. It still needed the big tubes. It could fly *back* from space, if gliding counts. Its wings weren't shaped like that of an airplane, so it couldn't get lift. I never quite understood the concept. The rockets that sent it to space were extremely powerful, but the shuttle itself was huge and absurdly heavy (*Challenger* weighed 165,000 pounds, empty). Fully loaded, the whole thing was 70 percent the weight of the big *Saturn V* (4.4 million pounds), for about 20 percent the payload. We could have built the International Space Station in a fraction of the trips with a heavy-lift rocket, reduced risk, and saved a ton of money. Though it was "reusable," launching the shuttle cost about ten times more than launching a Russian Proton rocket with the same payload.

Lola had just lost her mother when *Challenger* exploded soon after lift-off in 1986, and Aster saw *Columbia* disintegrate during reentry in 2003. Both incidents could have been avoided, and in both cases engineers had sounded the alarm but were ignored or even sanctioned. The O-ring problem that resulted in the *Challenger* disaster was well-known. In *Columbia*'s case, they knew a piece of foam from the external tank had hit the wing during lift-off. Engineers requested they take images of the shuttle in orbit to see if there was significant damage. They asked three times. They were turned down three times. Part of the reasoning at NASA was that if the shuttle was damaged, there was nothing they could do about it, so they were better off not knowing. The shuttle program killed fourteen astronauts, two full crews, in 135 missions. For comparison, there were four cosmonaut fatalities in the Soyuz program's *seventeen hundred plus* missions, zero in the last fifty years.

The other space planes they were working on at Stennis Space Center were the X-33, X-34, and X-37. The first was an uncrewed suborbital vehicle used to demonstrate technology for the VentureStar vehicle, a *big* space plane that was supposed to replace the space shuttle. Neither the X-33 nor the VentureStar project went very far. The X-34 was also a technology demonstrator, also uncrewed, and also abandoned very quickly.

The X-37, however, is a thing. It's another robotic space plane that uses a rocket as a launch vehicle. It's pretty small, about thirty feet long, half as wide. The project began in 1999 at NASA but was transferred to the Department of Defense in 2004. It first launched in 2006 and is now operated by the United States Space Force. No one knows what they're doing with it. There's been plenty of speculation: spying, of course, testing some secret electromagnetic drive technology, et cetera, et cetera. If you're into conspiracy theories, this is the space plane for you.

THE PRIZE

Samael gets involved with the New Horizons program at Aster's request, but he also makes his "own" contribution to space travel. He offers $10 million—of Lola's money, but it's the thought that counts—for the first private venture to send someone to space. He probably got the idea from New York hotel owner Raymond Orteig, who, in 1919, offered $25,000 to the first pilot to fly across the Atlantic. The prize was won in 1927, by a fellow named Charles Lindbergh aboard his *Spirit of St. Louis.* I said "probably" because I don't want to put words in Samael's mouth.

I *do* know that's where real-life entrepreneur and major space nerd Peter Diamandis got the idea for the XPRIZE he created in 1996. The prize was, well, what Samael did: 10 million bucks to the first project to send a pilot one hundred kilometers aboveground and do it a second time within two weeks. Contestants weren't allowed to get government money, the goal being to stimulate innovation and create low-cost solutions that could make space travel affordable to the masses.

In total, twenty-six teams participated. Some had big corporate funding, others were basically me turning my garage into one big fire hazard. The XPRIZE, renamed Ansari X Prize, because money, was won only eight years after its creation, on the forty-seventh anniversary of the Sputnik launch.

The winning vessel was *SpaceShipOne*, whose folding rear end allows it to increase drag during reentry while maintaining control. That project was started by aircraft designer Burt Rutan, and a mysterious angel investor who turned out to be Paul Allen, cofounder of Microsoft. Rutan then partnered with British magnate Richard Branson to create Virgin Galactic.

Many of the nonwinners weren't so lucky. Texas-based Armadillo Aerospace went into "hibernation mode" in 2013 following setbacks, but former employees started a new company and have projects in the works. XCOR Aerospace filed for bankruptcy in 2017. Rocketplane Limited also went belly-up but was reborn and may still have something coming. The Canadian Arrow project gave birth to PlanetSpace Corporation but died fairly quickly. The UK's Starchaser project looked promising but never really went anywhere.

There are several space travel companies in business today that did not enter the contest, but I'd venture to say the X Prize is largely responsible for their existence. I don't think it's a coincidence that the years in which twenty-six projects were competing in a new space race also saw the birth of the larger private aerospace manufacturers we know today. Elon Musk's SpaceX was founded in 2002 and is already ferrying people to the ISS; Amazon's Jeff Bezos started Blue Origin in 2000 and is aiming for both suborbital and orbital space flights in the very near future.

It probably won't come as a surprise when I tell you the team that won the X Prize had the most money, but their budget was still chump change compared to what NASA spends. We don't know exactly how much money went into *SpaceShipOne*, but we can guesstimate it at somewhere between \$20 and \$30 million. That's for the space plane, AND the big *White Knight* cargo aircraft used to launch it. NASA's program for the experimental X-15 cost a hundred times that, and they didn't have to pay for the B-52 bomber they used as a drop ship. To give you another example, when Elon Musk founded SpaceX, he figured that if his company built most of the hardware in-house it could cut the price of launching a rocket by a factor of ten and still make a 70 percent profit.

It's safe to say that the X Prize achieved its goal of lowering the cost of space travel. It also spawned tons of innovative concepts and designs. I honestly think it was one of the most significant events in the history of space travel and exploration. Did it bring space travel to the masses? Okay, we're not there yet, unless "the masses" are stupidly rich people. It certainly helped create the space tourism industry.

As I'm writing this, Virgin Galactic's first commercial flight has been delayed until 2023. Early buyers—they have hundreds of reservations—got a "deal" at \$250,000 a ticket, but the price has nearly doubled since then.

Blue Horizons launched a few people already but isn't selling to the "average" person yet. When they begin to offer commercial flights on a regular basis, they will likely be in the same price range as their competitors.

These are all suborbital space flights: fly a hundred kilometers or so into the air and experience weightlessness for a while on the way down.

Going into orbit and beyond will cost you a *little* more.[4]

Axiom Space really wants its own space station, but they already have a deal to send passengers for a short vacation on the ISS. Their first flight—on a SpaceX Crew Dragon capsule—was originally scheduled for 2021. The three paying customers each shelled out in the neighborhood of $55 million for their seat. Axiom is planning three trips each year in the near future. If you're wondering what real astronauts think of having space tourists on an already crowded station, they won't have to deal with them much. NASA approved the construction of a separate viewing module just for Axiom, and plans are under way for adding several more commercial modules to the ISS. Boeing has been rather quiet about it, but they also plan on taking passengers to the ISS at some point, so there'll be lots of tourists spinning above our heads pretty soon. NASA said it would charge $35,000 a night for a stay, which is pretty cheap compared to the price it will cost to get there.

You can even plan a moon trip if you want. SpaceX isn't going there yet, but they already sold a trip around it on their big Starship rocket to Japanese billionaire Yusaku Maezawa.

On the cheap end, if all you're looking for is to experience weightlessness, you can fly right now on Space Adventures's commercial equivalent of the "Vomit Comet" astronauts train on. It's a big plane that flies up and down over and over again, giving you twenty to thirty seconds of weightlessness each time. It's "real"

4. https://www.discovermagazine.com/the-sciences/six-ways-to-buy-a-ticket-to-space-in-2021.

weightlessness, as in the same you'd experience on the ISS—astronauts only float because the station is constantly falling. That trip will only set you back about eight thousand dollars.

Yes, it still costs a fortune for a "regular" person to go to space, but we can, which is cool, and the industry is still in its infancy. I think there's a good chance I'll be able to travel to space for the price of a high-end cruise before I die. If the prices don't change, then each book of mine you buy gets me about the thickness of the book higher off the ground. I write short books, so it could take a while, but if I *do* achieve that dream at some point, it will be in large part because someone started a contest a couple decades ago.

WALTER REED

Walter Reed, the man, was a U.S. Army physician. He helped confirm the theory by Cuban doctor Carlos Finlay that yellow fever was transmitted by a type of mosquito, a key moment in the history of epidemiology. They named a bunch of things after him and, for whatever reason, many are connected to government conspiracies, secret weapons, and, of course, aliens. There's the Walter Reed Army Institute of Research in Maryland, just north of D.C. It's the largest biomedical research facility run by the U.S. Department of Defense, so it's easy to imagine how many secret things they're involved in. It's basically an all-you-can-eat buffet of conspiracies. If you want to fall down the rabbit hole, look up Joseph C. Sharp—he worked there in the sixties and seventies—and invisible weapons. I wrote about them before in *Sleeping Giants*. Walter Reed is part of the U.S. Army Medical Research and Development Command, who supplied the experimental immunosuppressive agent to stop Vincent's body from rejecting his new legs.

Then there's the Walter Reed Army Medical Center in D.C., where Aster was kept in a pink room. From 1909 until it closed in

2011, it was the U.S. Army's most important hospital. Dwight Eisenhower died there; so did Leslie R. Groves, who led the Manhattan Project, and General Douglas MacArthur. According to most versions of the conspiracy, the pathologists who performed the autopsy on the alien whose ship crashed near Roswell, New Mexico, were from Walter Reed. In 2007, the *Washington Post* published a series of articles about the neglect several patients allegedly endured and the horrible living conditions in some of the facilities (mold, mice, cockroaches in rooms with open-wound patients, et cetera), particularly in Building 18, a former hotel just outside the hospital gates. A whole bunch of people were fired or resigned as a result of the scandal, and the hospital was closed in 2011 and replaced with the Walter Reed National Military Medical Center in nearby Maryland. The cockroaches stayed behind, but the conspiracies followed. This new hospital is where Donald Trump was admitted when he was diagnosed with COVID. You can google the plethora of nonsense theories that ensued, but I would suggest you don't. As far as I know, there was never a windowless pink room with Backstreet Boys posters in the basement of any of the buildings, but as I've said many times, I've been wrong before.

THE ENTR'ACTES

There aren't any real people in the Entr'actes this time around. I couldn't find shrunk-down beings from another planet in historical records. I couldn't even find legends from the era with the right kind of characters either. Bummer. That said, the settings in which each of these chapters take place are very much real.

In the introduction, Sereh spends eighteen of her years on a small spaceship getting from her dying world to ours. While she travels, she's transformed to resemble us. Organs disappear; her entire DNA is rewritten. That's why her children won't be eight feet tall or have two hearts. It's never been done, of course. We've modified DNA to affect an organism's development, but we've never taken a grown living thing and made it into a different thing. I needed help for this—see the acknowledgments section of this book—but we managed to do pretty much all of it using biological processes that already go on in the human body. An adult's skeleton, for example, regenerates itself completely—we call it remodeling—over ten years or so. Sereh's updated DNA just has to tell her body to rebuild smaller. It's a massive morphological change, though, so I did my best to cover the unintended consequences of rapidly shrinking people, like the huge amount of loose calcium it would generate. I don't mind when people write to tell me I made a mistake, but in this case, I'd be thrilled to hear from a biologist with a better plan for this than mine.

The first Tracker, Hah-Waari Kaas-ma Tereshiin Kih Traahen, goes through the same process in his own little ship. He almost drowns in the great "Salt Lake" after crashing, before making his way to Ḥalpa. In modern terms, he was learning to swim in Sabkhat al-Jabbūl, a saltine lake near the city of Aleppo (Ḥalab) in Syria. Back then, this is the eastern edge of a rapidly shrinking Hittite empire. The first people he meets call him Tereshiin, part of his rank (like the "sub" in "subcommander"), I suspect because his last name sounds like *awari*, a border guard in Hittite, and his first name is similar to *kāsma*, meaning something like "voilà!" They probably thought he was really proud of his job. Imagine asking, "Hey, what's your name?" and getting: "Behold the accountant Steven!" as an answer. The Hittites called their language *Nešili*, "the language of Neša," Neša being a place, and not a person as the Tracker surmised.

The Tracker was found because people spotted a streak of light in the night sky and came to collect "fire from the heavens." What they were looking for was iron from a meteorite. By the time the aliens landed, the Hittites would have already developed a better oven, called a *plumery*, and been producing wrought iron for about two hundred years, but the mines and technology were rare or nonexistent elsewhere until the fall of their empire.[5] We also found iron objects in Egypt and Mesopotamia that are much older than the invention of the *plumery*. The metal in these is more malleable than mined iron and contains high concentrations of nickel, making it very likely that it came from fallen meteorites. Meteoric iron is well-known, but does it necessarily follow that the people who used it knew where it came from? I think it does. The Sumerian name for iron, *an-bar*, and its Hittite equivalent, *ku-an*, both mean "fire from heaven."[6] The meaning of the Egyptian word for iron, *bia*, has been the object of much debate, but a new word for iron emerges at the beginning of the thirteenth century B.C., *Bia-n-pt*, meaning, literally, "iron from the sky."[7]

After seeing a trail of light on the horizon, the Tracker crosses the Euphrates into Assyria. The river was called Mala in Hittite, and Purattu on the other side. He'll search for the missing ship for a few years, before finding its pilot, along with four-year-old Kish.

Sereh, aka Nidintu, walks into the city of Arbailu (Erbil in today's Iraq) pretty banged up and is saved from a life of slavery by a local merchant. Indentured servitude, or debt slavery, isn't that much better than the type of slavery we're more familiar with,

5. Diana R. Haidar, "Assyrian Iron Working Technology and Civilization," 2011, https://minds.wisconsin.edu/bitstream/handle/1793/53126/Diana%20Haidar.pdf?sequence=1&isAllowed=y.
6. T. A. Rickard, "The Use of Meteoric Iron," *Journal of the Royal Anthropological Institute of Great Britain and Ireland* 71, no. 1/2 (1941): 55–66, www.jstor.org/stable/2844401, accessed March 14, 2021.
7. "Iron from the sky: Meteors, Meteorites and Ancient Culture," https://www.open.edu/openlearn/science-maths-technology/science/geology/iron-the-sky-meteors-meteorites-and-ancient-culture.

but the former was a matter of contract law, not property, and those contracts generally included a way out, typically through payment. The convoluted scheme the merchant comes up with to make Nidintu a free woman is taken from an actual case in the Middle Assyrian Empire.[8] The interesting part about it is that the male slave who manumitted the woman before marrying her had no legal standing to do any of that, so all the parties involved, including the "owners," had to agree on the whole thing. They probably gave the groom credit as a courtesy, or to keep their own names out of the paperwork.

Kish and the Tracker fight each other when he goes on a rampage in a small village near the "upper sea" in Nairi. That's Lake Van in today's Turkey. What counts as "upper" changes based on one's point of view. It also changes whenever an empire expands or contracts. Lake Van was called "upper sea" under one Assyrian king, but the same name was used for the Mediterranean under the next.[9] The final Entr'acte ends with Kish heading east, towards the sunrise. She's actually heading to the "great sea of the sunrise," aka the Caspian Sea.

The Entr'actes take place at the onset of what's called the Late Bronze Age collapse. It's a period of, well, really bad things. It's hyperviolent, and it leads to the fall or decline of just about every empire in the area: the Hittites, the Kassites in Babylonia, the Mycenaean kingdoms, the Mitanni, even the New Kingdom of Egypt had it rough. Governments crumbled, resulting in a bunch of small, isolated communities. Trade routes were blocked. Education slowed to a crawl or stopped completely in places. American historian Robert Drews states that "[W]ithin a period of forty to fifty years [. . .] almost every significant city in

8. https://scholarship.kentlaw.iit.edu/cgi/viewcontent.cgi?article=3004&context=cklawreview&httpsredir=1&referer=.
9. https://www.jstage.jst.go.jp/article/orient/40/0/40_31/_pdf.

the eastern Mediterranean world was destroyed, many of them never to be occupied again."[10] That bad. It's hard to point to the main cause of that catastrophe, but we know several factors likely contributed: the spread of ironworking (an iron sword will slice through a bronze sword like butter) and the new military tactics that ensued; climate change was involved—it always is—so were frequent invasions by the so-called Sea People. It's a good name, but we don't know much about them other than the fact that they came by boat. Whoever they were, they were extremely badass, and they raided just about everyone: Anatolia, Syria, Phoenicia, Canaan, Cyprus, and Egypt.

Anyway, this is how the history of the Kibsu began. Sereh, aka Nidintu, was the first one to land on Earth after being transformed, but she lost the memory of her past and settled into some kind of normal life. Her daughter, Kish, was the first to call herself "the path." *Kish* is the One, and she learned everything she knew from the first Tracker. I suppose you can call her mother the Zero, but I don't think she'd like that.

Thank you so much for reading. I wrote a little something else for you before we say goodbye. There have been 102 Kibsu since the beginning. During the course of this series, we've met or heard about a quarter of them. That's a lot of Kibsu to keep track of, so I thought it'd be nice to have them all in one place and in chronological order.

10. Robert Drews, *The End of the Bronze Age: Changes in Warfare and the Catastrophe ca. 1200 B.C.* (Princeton: Princeton University Press, 1993).

KIBSU BY THE NUMBERS

Here are their names, approximate dates for their turn at being the Kibsu, and a bit of what we know about them. Remember that their turn comes when their mother dies, not at birth. The Ninety-Six, for example, lasts from 1854 to 1879, even though she was born in 1826. From 1826 to 1854, she was part of the Ninety-Five.

#0

Sereh/Nidintu and Kish
Approx. 1220 B.C.

Sereh was the first to land on Earth, also the first to look human, but she (most likely) had completely lost her mind. Her daughter, Kish, was the first "clone" born on Earth and the first to be called Kibsu (the path).

#1

Kish (daughter unknown)
Approx. 1200 B.C.

The One learns who and what she is from the Tracker, but she chooses humanity. She has the sphere, but no real plan other than to run from the man who raised her.

. . .

#7

Varkida and several daughters
Approx. 890 B.C.

The Seven becomes a Scythian warrior and founds the *hamazan* (hell yeah!). She sets the goal, Take them to the stars, and she writes the rules. The One chose humanity, but the Seven will guide the lives of everyone who follows. If there's ever a vote for Kibsu MVP, she's on the ballot for sure.

#8

Name unknown
Approx. 870 B.C.

Varkida's eldest twin is the first to live by the rules. She's the one who carved the bow and hid the sphere in today's Kazakhstan before Lola unearthed it.

#9

Name unknown and her daughter, Nourah
Date unknown

Nourah's mother is killed by the Tracker on their way to the Kingdom of Quwê.

#10

Nourah and Ishtar
Approx. 850 B.C.

Nourah and her daughter, Ishtar (born 830 B.C.), live in Quwê. Nourah sells horses before giving up her daughter and killing herself. The knowledge the Tracker gave the One is lost when Nourah dies.

#11

Ishtar (daughter unknown)

Approx. 825 B.C.

Ishtar is the first Kibsu to start from scratch, having lost all knowledge of who and what she is.

. . .

#20

Mer-Neith-it-es and Hemut-Taui

Approx. 552 B.C.

Mer-Neith-it-es is an Egyptian EN-priestess in Thebes. She wasn't afraid of the Tracker. She's the one who sent them on a wild-goose chase across the planet.

#21

Hemut-Taui/Mer-Neith-it-es (daughter unknown)

Mer-Neith-it-es's daughter assumes her mother's identity and moves to Persepolis.

#22

Mer-Neith-it-es (daughter unknown)

The third generation to live under the same name. The Twenty-Two dies in today's Pakistan after teaching at the ancient University of Taxila.

. . .

#32

Aglaonike of Thessaly (daughter unknown)

Approx. 187 B.C.

The Thirty-Two forms a ragtag team of astronomers in Thessaly before being accused of witchcraft. She was superbadass and could predict eclipses.

. . .

#61

Name unknown
Date unknown

We only know she spoke Coptic. Mia and Lola read about the Kibsu symbols in her journals.

. . .

#65

Eurybia (born Nabia) and Zosime
Approx. A.D. 921

Born in the Abbasid Caliphate, the Sixty-Five is sold to Vikings. She moves to Athens with her only surviving child.

#66

Zosime (daughter unknown)

I suppose she lived in Athens.

. . .

#70

Name unknown and Agnes
Approx. A.D. 1030

The mother was killed by the Tracker when Agnes was eleven.

#71

Agnes and Eila
Approx. A.D. 1043

Illuminator, gave birth at twelve. Spent her life transcribing and illustrating books at a monastery in Dalheim, Germany.

#72

Eila (daughter unknown)
Approx. A.D. 1060

Agnes's daughter left Europe to go where science was still alive. She likely went to Al-Andalus, a Muslim-ruled chunk of the Iberian Peninsula where great work was being done in astronomy and mathematics. My bet is she went to Córdoba.

. . .

#86

Name unknown and Sura
Approx. A.D. 1590

We don't know anything about the Eighty-Six, other than the fact that Sura saw her being lapidated.

#87

Sura and Ariani (born in 1598)
Approx. A.D. 1608

Sura is a trader in Amsterdam and works with the VOC, aka the Dutch East India Company. The Eighty-Seven is the reason the Kibsu are rich like Batman.

#88

Ariani (daughter unknown)

I have no idea what happens to her, but she was the Eighty-Eight.

. . .

#92

Name unknown
Date unknown

The Ninety-Two "found her mother's bones boiled clean in a wooden box. He had left a note: 'I'll see you soon.'"

#95

Name unknown and Emily (born in 1826)
Approx. A.D. 1844

The only thing we learn about the Ninety-Five is that she told her daughter: "Knowledge is like spring. It will surely arrive, but it will do so in its own time." We know every Kibsu who comes after that.

#96

Emily and Annie (born in 1858)
1854–1879

Emily married John Couch Adams and *almost* discovered the planet Neptune (Lola really liked hearing that story). She died in 1879 at the age of sixty-one while visiting her daughter in London. She was stabbed thirty-nine times, most likely by a serial killer.

#97

Annie (daughter unknown, born in 1890)
1879–1915

Annie studied the sun, and she hunted serial killers at night. She may or may not have killed Jack the Ripper. "She hanged herself after breakfast on a crisp April morning in 1915." We don't know her daughter's name, but we do know who she is. It's Sarah's mom!

#98

Name unknown and Sarah (born in 1905)
1915–1932

Sarah's mother moved to Berlin in 1920 posing as an Armenian coffee trader. She married Ahmet. They had to leave Germany earlier than expected in 1932 after Mia killed two little girls at summer camp. She died that same year. She jumped off the boat with a bag of silverware tied to her ankle. She was looking at global warming, in part because she was looking for an excuse to live a normal life.

#99

Sarah and Mia (born in 1925)
1932–1960

Sarah worked for the OSS and sent her daughter to Germany to exfiltrate Wernher von Braun before they moved to Moscow. She probably killed Stalin. She continued her mother's work on $C0_2$ levels. Sarah died in 1960 when she dropped a ballistic missile on herself and the Tracker (Leonard, Samael's uncle).

#100

Mia and Lola (born in 1962)
1960–1981

Mia fell in love with Billie in Moscow. She also married Sergei Korolev but lost both of them and her unborn child when the Tracker kicked her off a launch platform for the R-7 rocket. Her daughter, Lola, was born on the island of Mallorca.

#101

Lola and Catherine (born in 1987)
1981–1989

Lola and her mom found a bow that belonged to the Eight and went on a treasure hunt together looking for knowledge about their past. Lola's mother died along the way, but Lola found the sphere. The Hundred and One didn't last long. Lola gave up her child and faced the Tracker (Samael and his brother Uriel). She died at Grand Central Station in New York at the age of twenty-seven.

#102

Aster, aka Catherine (no daughter yet)
1989–

Aster won the Kibsu's three-thousand-year-old fight against the Tracker. I don't know what the future holds for her, but I have a feeling she'll be just fine.

THE PLAYLIST

Chapter	Song
1.	"Just a Girl," No Doubt (1995)
2.	"Why Does My Heart Feel So Bad?," Moby (1999)
3.	"Run," Collective Soul (1998)
4.	"Bitter Sweet Symphony," The Verve (1997)
5.	"Criminal," Fiona Apple (1996)
6.	"Interstate Love Song," Stone Temple Pilots (1994)
7.	"Stupid Girl," Garbage (1995)
8.	"Common People," Pulp (1995)
9.	"Karma Police," Radiohead (1997)
10.	"Exactly like Me," Bran Van 3000 (1997)
11.	"Army of Me," Björk (1995)
12.	"Dry the Rain," The Beta Band (1997)
13.	"Into the Void," Nine Inch Nails (1999)
14.	"You Learn," Alanis Morissette (1995)
15.	"Down by the Water," PJ Harvey (1995)
16.	"It Girl," The Brian Jonestown Massacre (1996)
17.	"Miss Misery," Elliott Smith (1997)
18.	"The Facts of Life," Black Box Recorder (2000)
19.	"The Mess We're In," PJ Harvey (2000)
20.	"Daughter," Pearl Jam (1993)
21.	"Trouble," Coldplay (2000)

22. "Girl, You'll Be a Woman Soon," Urge Overkill (1994)
23. "Spybreak!," Propellerheads (1997)
    (Author's cut: replace "Spybreak!" with "Running 2" from the *Lola rennt* (*Run Lola Run*) soundtrack if it's available in your area)
24. "Porcelain," Moby (1999)
25. "Godless," The Dandy Warhols (2000)
26. "Flower," Moby (1999)
27. "Hard to Explain," The Strokes (2001)
28. "Come On Let's Go," Broadcast (2000)
29. "Make It Happen," Playgroup (2001)
30. "La Valse d'Amélie," Yann Tiersen (2001)
31. "Blue Monday," Orgy (1998)
32. "Bang," Yeah Yeah Yeahs (2001)
33. "High and Dry," Radiohead (1995)
34. "Dead Leaves and the Dirty Ground," The White Stripes (2001)
35. "Dissolved Girl," Massive Attack (1998)
36. "Big Time Sensuality," Björk (1993)
37. "Eighties Fan," Camera Obscura (2001)
38. "Du Hast," Rammstein (1997)
    (Author's cut: replace "Du Hast" with "Wish (Komm zu mir)" from the *Lola rennt* (*Run Lola Run*) soundtrack if it's available in your area)
39. "Evil Angel," Rufus Wainwright (2001)
40. "The Shining," Badly Drawn Boy (2000)
41. "We're Going to Be Friends," The White Stripes (2002)
42. "A Perfect Day Elise," PJ Harvey (1998)
43. "Let Forever Be," The Chemical Brothers (1999)
44. "2 Rights Make 1 Wrong," Mogwai (2001)

45. “There Goes the Fear,” Doves (2002)
46. “Lose Yourself,” Eminem (2002)
47. “Time for Heroes,” The Libertines (2002)
48. “Quelqu’un m’a dit,” Carla Bruni (2002)
49. “Heartbeats,” The Knife (2002)
50. “The Scientist,” Coldplay (2002)
51. “Mr. Brightside,” The Killers (2004)
52. “Neighborhood #1 (Tunnels),” Arcade Fire (2004)
53. “Butterflies and Hurricanes,” Muse (2003)
54. “This Fire,” Franz Ferdinand (2004)
55. “Wake Up,” Arcade Fire (2004)
56. “Rebellion (Lies),” Arcade Fire (2004)
57. “No Heaven,” Champion (2004)

Further Reading.

“Miami,” Ariane Moffatt (2015)

Acknowledgments.

“Midnight Radio,” Stephen Trask (performed by John Cameron Mitchell) (2001)

Epilogue II.

“Good People,” Jack Johnson (2005)

ACKNOWLEDGMENTS

(Midnight Radio)

This is my sixth novel. When I sold my debut, I signed for two more books. When that was over, I got a deal for another three books. Three plus three equals six. I shouldn't be surprised, but I am. It's hard to explain. Every time I signed a book deal, it felt like I got a job for a few years, but never, not once, did I envision a point in time where I'd have written six novels, and a novella to boot. This still feels just as new, and weird, and exciting, and I still have absolutely no idea what I'm doing. I'm beginning to suspect that will never change. The other thing that will never change is how grateful I am for all of it.

Let me first thank my rock, Barbara, and my son, Theo. You've been there through it all and I couldn't have done any of this without your support. Thanks to my agent, Seth Fishman, and everyone at the Gernert Company. Thanks to my editor, Lee Harris, and the billion people at Tordotcom who make this possible. Thank you, Jillian Taylor and the Michael Joseph crew, for all the hard work on the other side of the pond. While I'm at it, I want to thank all the editors and publicists and copy editors and translators and everyone else who worked on the foreign editions of my books.

Some special thanks for this one in particular. Thank you, Jen Albert and Derek Künsken, for Frankenstein-level help with shrinking Sereh during her voyage here. She blames both of you for the pain. Also to Dave Kaiser, and Sage Bramhal Ouchark for much-needed help with Aster's southern speech. Y'all were superhelpful.

Most of all, thank you for reading all the weird things that come out of my mind.

✲

EPILOGUE II

Good People

AUGUST 6, 2005

[*Hi there! Can I take your order?*]

—I'll have the basil noodles, with an iced tea, please.

—No she won't. Will you give us a second, ma'am? What did I just say, Aster?

—I ain't a child, sir. I can order my own food.

—I know! You're a bright and incredibly resourceful . . . —How old are you?

—I'm eighteen!

—You're an incredibly resourceful eighteen-year-old woman. And you have to try the Kung Pao chicken.

—Okay, fine! I'll have the Kung Pao chicken, with iced tea.

—She means green tea. I'll have the same.

—No! I want regular iced tea, in a can if you have.

[*Two Kung Pao chicken, one iced tea, in a can, one green tea.*]

—Thank you.

—Now, are you gonna tell me why I'm here?

—We're having a nice meal, Aster!

—I don't mean here here. I mean how did you find me? And why did we have to meet in Washington?

—Because I live here? What's the matter, you don't like Washington?

—Not really, no. I been here once, and it didn't go so well.

—Well, I hope you leave my city with good memories this time around. The chicken will help; I promise.

—Have we met before? I think I'd remember, but—

—No! That's why I called you!

—Okay, but where'd you get my number? How do you even know I exist?

—Can I tell you a story, Aster? I think you'll like it.

—Uh. Can't you just—you know—answer my question instead?

—Once upon a time—

—I guess not.

—Near an isolated, idyllic little pond, a mother duck sat on her nest, keeping six precious eggs warm until they were ready to hatch.

—That's "The Ugly Duckling," sir. I know that story.

—No it's not. On a crisp March morning, Mother Duck felt something moving under her butt. One by one, the eggs began to crack. One yellow duckling broke out of his shell, then another, and another, and another. Mother Duck gasped as the fifth egg broke open. You see, that duckling wasn't yellow like the others; he was—

—Black, or gray, whatever. And he wasn't a duck at all. He was a swan.

—Yes! How did you know?

—Because he's the ugly duckling? He was bigger and the other ducklings called him ugly and—

—They did not! And he wasn't bigger at all. He was much smaller than other swans, just about duck size for that matter. Mother Duck was kind but strict and the swan's four yellow siblings never dared make fun of him, not even once.

—Did he grow up, see his reflection in a lake, and figure out he was a swan?

—He did indeed. He even met a few swans who strayed from the flock.

—That's the ugly duckling, sir! Except for not calling him ugly, but still.

—Would you please stop interrupting? There was one thing this unusually small swan didn't know but would soon find out after spending some time with his own kind.

— . . .

—You're not going to ask what it is?

—You said not to interrupt.

—I did, but you're supposed to at this particular point in the story.

—You want me to ask what it was?

— . . .

—What was it?

—Swans are jerks.

—What?

—They are! They're bullies. They steal food and eat duck eggs, even ducklings! Because they're so big, there's really nothing the ducks can do about it. The unusually small swan realized that if the other swans ever learned of the idyllic duck pond, they would kill every duck or push them away and claim it for themselves. So the small swan devised a plan to lure the other swans away and save the duck pond.

—You're talking about me, aren't you?

—Why would you say that?

—It ain't that subtle, sir. How do you know all that?

—It's just a story. Do you mind if I keep telling it? Thank you. Can you tell me what's missing from this story so far?

—I don't understand.

—I want to know if you were paying attention or not.

—I was! I was listening the whole time!

—So what's missing?

—I . . .

—An egg, Aster! An egg! Mother Duck sat on six eggs. Four yellow ducklings hatched, then the swan. We're missing an egg.

—What was in it?

—I'm glad you asked. It was an owl. Well, half owl, but for our purposes, let's just say it's an owl. Not just any owl, though, a great horned owl. Sometimes it's called tiger owl, or hoot owl. You'll find them pretty much anywhere in America. My point is it's a very big owl.

—I know what a great horned owl is, sir. I been trying to save some turtle from extinction in the South and those owls eat them sometimes. That ain't why the turtles are going extinct, though, the owls eating them. It's just one more thing they have to deal with.

—Fascinating. Did you know swans and owls are mortal enemies?

—They are?

—They are. Owls and swans have been at war for ages. In fact, the owls exiled the swans from their lands. That's why the swans are a threat to the ducks.

—Is that part of the story, sir? 'Cause I don't think that's true.

—Did I say: "the end"?

—No, you didn't.

—Then of course it's part of the story.

—Sorry.

—And just like the swan, the owl also worried other owls would come and kill all the ducks. . . .

—What did he do?

—I don't know. I haven't figured that part yet. I guess I should say: "the end."

—What? That's not an end, sir.

—Why not?

—I wanna know what happens!

—You do? Does that mean you liked it?

—I— Well, yes, but I feel like there should be a moral to it or something?

—Thank you, Aster. That's kind of you to say. And I suppose the moral is . . . that ducks have a lot to worry about.

—I'm confused, now. If I'm a swan . . . and everyone else is a duck, then— Wait! Are you the owl?

—If I were, what would that make us?

—Hmmm. I don't know. Two people who worry about ducks?

—Not enemies?

—I never seen you before in my life, sir. But you seem nice, and you said you're paying for lunch, so . . . Can I ask a question?

—But of course! Ask away.

—Are there more owls?

—Oh yes. But you can stop with the bird names now.

—This whole time, I thought it was just us, being . . . different. My whole family did.

—Not your whole family. Our people met once. In fact, I would not be alive today were it not for an encounter between our ancestors.

—For real?

—Yes! For real!

—Wow. You never answered my first question.

—How do we know about you? We—my associates and I—

—You mean owls.

—What did I just say about birds? We make it a point to know these things. We've been keeping track of your family for a while now.

—By "a while," you don't mean like three months, do you?

—Not exactly.

—Whoa.

—Whoa indeed. I must say, Aster, I was impressed with the probe idea. Sending that . . . thing to outer space is an ingenious solution.

—Well, we don't know if it'll work. The probe ain't even launched yet.

—It will! Launch, I mean. I don't know if it'll work any more than you do, but I think there's a good chance it will.

—You're just being nice now.

—Yes, that too. My point is there's less reason to worry about your people now. Mine, on the other hand—

—What? Are they coming?

—I don't know that they will, but if they do, I'd rather be prepared. That's . . . why I asked you here, because I need your help.

—Oh, sir, I'm sorry. I been through a lot lately, like you wouldn't believe. I don't think I'm ready to risk my life again and—

—I want you to go to college.

—What?

—In Chicago. There's someone there I'd like you to meet. She's your age and she just left home to go to college.

—Is that a bad thing?

—No, that's really good. In fact, it's important that she does. Only she misses home and now her father's ill, so I'm worried she'll want to come home.

—What's that got to do with me?

—I'd like you to help her deal with all this, make sure she sticks with it. I don't think she has anyone to talk to.

—You want me to be her friend?

—Yes! I think you two would make great friends!

—Is she—you know—like me?

—She's a nerd like you.

—You know what I mean!

—She's not. She's a duck, through and through.

— . . . I'm sorry, sir, but I can't.

—Because there's things you have to do.

—Exactly.

—You want to take people to space.

—How— Yes, I do. That's . . . kind of our thing.

—You'll need a degree for that, won't you? Chicago's a good school.

—I'm sure it is, but, like, wouldn't I need to apply first? School starts in a couple weeks.

—Well . . .

—You already got me in.

—You'll probably want to think about it. I understand. It's a big decision.

—You already know what I'm gonna say, don't you?

— . . .

—Crud.

—It's frustrating, I know. For what it's worth, it's still your decision, even if I know you're going to make it.

—Fine. What's her name, that girl you want me to meet?

—Rose. Her name is Rose.